PUBLICATIONS PRESENTS...

WWW.COM

MADISON
AUTHOR OF THE SCATTERED LIES SERIES

LONGWOOD PUBLIC LIBRARY

5 Star Publications
PO BOX 471570
Forestville, MD 20753

WWW.COM
Copyright 2012 by Madison Taylor

All Rights Reserved. No part of this book may be reproduced, stored in a retrieved system, or transmitted in any form or by any means without prior written authorization from the Publisher.

ISBN -13: 978-0983247371
ISBN-10: 0983247374
Library of Congress Control Number: 2011938654
First Printing: August 2012

Printed in the United States

All stories are a work of fiction from the authors and are not meant to depict, portray, or represent any particular real person. Names, characters, places, and incidents are either the product of the author's imagination or are used fictitiously, and any resemblance to an actual person living or dead is entirely coincidental.

www.5starpublications.net
www.tljestore.com
www.iammadisontaylor.com

Acknowledgments

As always, I would like to thank **GOD** for His blessings. Without him, there would be no me. To my family and friends, thank you for always being there for me.

To 5 Star Publications, **(Shawn, LaQ'uita), thank you for believing in me** *and my ugly book covers. (LOL)*

I also give thanks to my team: **Publicist Makeda Smith, Editor Carla M. Dean, Tonya Patterson, Kayon Cox, Anna Draper, and Melody Vernor-Bartel.** We did it again!

To my muse, the best is yet to come! Thank you for supporting and believing in me all these years.

PROLOGUE

Dressed in black Armani suits and black Prada sneakers, Chance, Justice, Patience, and Seven pulled up in front of World Financial Bank, the largest currency distributor in the world. According to Justice, World Financial held a minimum of five hundred million dollars in their vault.

"Bottoms up," Seven said as she hopped out the SUV, with the other ladies following suit.

Justice flashed her badge to the security guard at the entrance. "Hello, sir. We're with the FBI, and we need to see the bank manager."

"Right this way," the guard replied, then led them to a private area located in the rear of the bank.

Knock! Knock!

"Mr. Jude, the FBI is here?" he announced, entering the office.

Mr. Jude stood up from his desk. "FBI?" he repeated, confused.

"Yes," the guard responded.

"Mr. Jude, I'm Special Agent Kennedy. We're here to inspect the room," Chance lied.

"Are you sure? I thought it was no longer needed. In fact, I'm almost certain," Mr. Jude affirmed.

"Actually, Mr. Jude, next week is the last week. We just have to make sure the equipment is up and running so they can stream it back to headquarters," Chance answered, thinking quickly.

"Oh, okay, even though I think this is a bit much. No one is thinking about robbing this bank."

"And why do you say that?" Justice asked.

"Because they would never get past the high-tech security system," he answered confidently.

"Well, you never know. They said September 11th would never happen, but look. One can never be too careful," Patience stated.

"True," he replied before leading them to a secure area.

He turned around to glance at the ladies once more, flashing a fake smile while thinking, *Something looks strange about these women.*

"Here we go, ladies," he said, opening the door.

Since 9/11, banks had installed command centers. Ammunition, SWAT uniforms, and high technology equipment were stored in these rooms that only top government officials knew about. The security system could shut down the entire bank, preventing anything from working, even cell phones.

Only a handful knew that on the first Friday of every month, the government took the system offline for thirty minutes to back it up. This was more than enough time for Seven to hack into the system and change the images.

"Done," Seven announced as she signaled for the ladies to pull out their weapons.

Mr. Jude gasped and damn near shitted on himself, while raising his hands in the air. "What's going on?"

"We're here to make a cash withdrawal," Chance informed him, exercising her sense of humor.

Scared to death, Mr. Jude tried to press the pendant on his jacket, but Justice noticed and swiftly busted him in the head with her gun, knocking him to the floor.

"Next time, mi gonna put a bullet in your fucking head," she warned him in her Bajan accent. "Now take the bumbaclot blazer off."

Chance giggled. "We know about the alarm pendant on the blazer," she said, kicking him in the ribs.

"Please, I have a family!" he cried.

"So, don't do anything stupid, or I promise Mayor Bloomberg will be visiting them this evening," Chance whispered in his ear after snatching him up from the floor.

Seven, who was typing something in on the computer, yelled out, "Guys, we have less than twenty minutes before the system reboots! Let's move it!"

The ladies looked up at the clock and then quickly changed into the Swat uniforms that were hanging on hooks in the room.

Chance ordered Mr. Jude into the private vault. "You know what to do," she told him, pushing her pistol into his back.

Bleeding from his head, Mr. Jude did exactly what he was told. Once inside the vault, the ladies started loading the money into large duffel bags. By now, Seven had joined them and noticed Mr. Jude looking up at the camera.

"You're not gonna get away with this," he lashed out with the little courage he had left in him. "Do you know whose money this is?"

Not amused, Chance replied, "No. Enlighten us."

Mr. Jude laughed. "I'd rather not, but I tell you one thing, you guys will never get away with this. They're gonna kill you and your families," he warned. "They have eyes and ears everywhere. They can see you right now."

Trying to scare them, Mr. Jude looked up at the camera.

The ladies paused for a second and then looked at each other, thinking, *If only Mr. Jude knew.*

Growing annoyed, Patience shouted, "Shut the fuck up," and then grabbed a duffel bag from Seven.

Chance looked down at her watch again. "Alright, Seven, let's go outside. Here, Justice, tie Mr. Jude up," she ordered, handing her some tie wraps.

In a final attempt to scare them, Mr. Jude blurted out, "Trust me, they're gonna hunt you down and kill you."

Patience looked over at Justice, who was now putting stacks of money in the duffel bag after having secured Mr. Jude's hands behind his back. Then Patience reached into her pocket and handed Mr. Jude a piece of gum. At first, he refused, pressing his lips tightly together until she placed her gun to his head.

"Open your mouth," she ordered.

After Mr. Jude slowly opened his mouth, Patience shoved the stick of gum inside and forced him to chew. Suddenly, his windpipe closed up, making it difficult for him to breathe. He dropped to his knees in a coughing fit and then began going into convulsions. Within minutes, Mr. Jude was dead from the gum that had been laced with cyanide.

Seven entered the tellers' area and fired shots in the air, causing pure pandemonium, while Chance forced all the back office employees into the tellers' area.

"Everyone move to the center of the building. If anyone tries something stupid, I will not hesitate to put a bullet in you," Chance announced with her semi-automatic handgun in the air.

Frightened, the people did as they were told. One person, who was clearly confused by it all, blurted out, "Aren't they suppose to be police? Is this some kind of joke?"

Justice ran out from the vault with two heavy duffel bags. "Here," she said, handing them off to Chance before running back inside.

Seven laughed to herself as she noticed the puzzled look on several people's faces when they tried to use their phone but didn't have service. *Stupid motherfuckers. I should kill all of them just for being stupid,* she thought.

Again, Justice came out and handed Seven two more duffel bags.

"Ten minutes!" Chance yelled, looking at the clock.

As Seven turned her back to walk towards Chance, one of the security guards tried to reach for his weapon. Bad move. Chance sprayed his body with bullets, making everyone scream in horror. To avoid any other interruptions, Chance and Seven killed the other two guards.

Justice and Patience joined Chance and Seven.

"We're done!" Chance announced.

Just then, a muffled voice from outside the bank shouted through a megaphone, "This is the police! Come out with your hands up."

With a smirk on their faces, the ladies cocked their semi-automatic handguns.

Seven smiled and said, "Right on time!"

"You have thirty seconds or we're coming in there after you!" the voice yelled.

"What you think, Seven? You think thirty seconds is enough?" Patience smiled.

"Thirty seconds? Shit, I can destroy a country in thirty seconds," Seven joked.

Seven pulled out her BlackBerry and typed in a code. "Alright, ten seconds," she uttered to herself.

Ten seconds later, a barrage of bullets came flying through the window and lasted for what seemed like five minutes. Everyone screamed. The police on the outside ran for cover, some trying to return fire.

"Where the fuck are the bullets coming from? Get down! Everyone get down!" the officers could be heard yelling.

Boom! The SUV the ladies had arrived in exploded.

When it was all over, not a single civilian in the bank had been seriously hurt. They only suffered minor injuries from the shattering glass. However, the police officers weren't so lucky. Ten were seriously hurt from the exploding truck.

Laughing, the ladies escaped to their secret hiding spot to lay low until things calmed down.

"What the fuck happened here?" one of the detectives asked.

"We're still trying to figure it out. According to the people inside the bank, the robbers were women posing as police."

One of the head detective's phone rang, and he immediately answered. Once the caller spoke, the detective instantly recognized the voice.

After excusing himself, he whispered into the phone, "I'm already on it. The entire fucking police force is looking into it."

v

"There's no way in the world anyone could've pulled this off without the help of the government. I want that person and their family dead five seconds ago," the voice on the other end said.

Click!

The detective sighed. Whoever was behind this had just validated their death certificate. He joined the other law enforcement agents who were inside the vault trying to figure out how in the hell someone had robbed World Financial Bank.

"Whoever did this knew the system would be down for thirty minutes," one agent said.

"How? Only a few people know this," the detective whispered.

Watching from their secret location, the ladies were in tears from laughter as they listened to the scenarios the agents created.

"Let's help them out a bit, Seven," Chance said.

Seven nodded, and then pulled out her laptop. "Technology...isn't it a motherfucker?" she teased, while rapidly typing.

The computer in the vault went black, and then one white letter at a time slowly appeared on the screen welcoming them to **WWW.COM**.

FIVE YEARS EARLIER

CHAPTER 1
CHANCE COHEN
"TO PROTECT AND SERVE"

Chance arrived back in the office as Linda was gathering her things to leave.

"What time are you getting out of here?" Linda asked.

"In a couple of minutes. I just have to finish up this report before Burgos has my ass," Chance said with her usual touch of humor.

"Where were you?" Linda inquired.

"I had a few errands to run," Chance answered nonchalantly.

A co-worker came by their desk, preventing Linda from continuing with her questioning.

"Cohen, I have a message for you," she said, handing her a piece of paper.

"Is something wrong?" Linda asked, noticing Chance's facial expression.

"No," Chance replied, snapping back to reality.

Just as Linda was about to say something, Chance's husband and daughter walked in.

"Mommy!" Zoe yelled, running towards Chance.

Chance's face lit up. "Hi, Zoe," she said, hugging her tightly and planting a big kiss on her cheek. "How was school?"

"Difficult. Mommy, can you help me with my homework?" Zoe frowned, causing everyone to laugh.

"Hi, honey," Chance said, kissing her husband Sean.

"Hey, that's your child," he teased.

Chance giggled and replied, "I know."

"Hi, Aunt Linda," Zoe said with a big smile.

"Hi, Zoe. Hey, Sean." Linda greeted them with a hug and kiss.

"Are you ready?" Sean asked, turning towards Chance.

Chance hesitated for a second. She had some paperwork to catch up on, and she also wanted to return Ave's call. But, all that would have to wait until the next morning. She decided she would go home to spend some quality time with her family.

"Yep. Let me grab my bag, and we're out of here. I'll just come in early and finish up what I have to do. No biggie."

"If you want, I can finish it up for you, Chance," Linda offered.

"Nah, Linda, it can wait. Thanks anyway."

Linda shot Chance a suspicious look, wondering why she was being so secretive all of sudden. "Alright, don't say I didn't offer. But, hey, my car is in the shop. So, can you drop me off?"

"Sure," Chance replied, then turned toward Sean and asked, "Baby, is that alright?"

"Of course. We just need to stop by the store and pick up a hero sandwich for Zoe," Sean said.

They pulled into the parking lot of the strip mall, and just as Sean was about to get out, Chance stopped him, stating she would go inside because she needed to pick up a few other things for the house. Linda declined to go with her, and Zoe stayed in the car playing with her Nintendo DS.

Chance was in line when she heard a storm of gunfire. Reacting quickly, she ducked for cover and drew her weapon.

"Everyone get down! Somebody call the police!" she shouted as she ran to the door.

Upon exiting, she saw two men standing in front of her car firing shots. *Oh my God,* she thought. *My family.*

Immediately, she returned fired, hitting one of the men in the shoulder. *Tah! Tah! Tah!* They returned fire. Bullets smashed through everything, while customers scurried and screamed for dear life. Unharmed, Chance crawled behind the counter. However, hearing the sound of someone's footsteps on the broken glass, she knew it was only a matter of seconds before they walked up on her.

She could hear customers crying and moaning from their inflicted gunshot wounds. *Kat! Kat! Kat!* With that succession of shots fired, the moans suddenly stopped, and the footsteps got closer. Chance cocked her gun; it was either her or them.

She picked up a large piece of glass from off the floor and used it to see over the counter. She could see the back of one of the gunmen's head. Quickly, she jumped up. *Bang! Bang!* Her shots made his body drop like a fly. Again, she ducked back behind the counter.

"I'm gonna kill you," the injured man screamed and then sprayed the counter with bullets, hitting Chance several times.

Before passing out, she heard the sound of sirens and a loud explosion.

*****

Three months later, Chance woke from a coma. Sadly, when she opened her eyes, there was no one by her bedside. Still vague about what happened, Chance called out for her husband.

"Sean," she said in a weak voice.

One of the nurses came to her aide. "You're awake."

Weak, she struggled to speak. "Where am I? Where's my husband?"

"Cedars-Sinai Medical Center and Rehabilitation Home. You were shot. You have been in a coma for three months."

Chance's eyes widened. "I was shot?" she asked, confused and seeking confirmation.

"Yes. Maybe the doctor should tell you what happened," the nurse told her, afraid she had already said too much.

It was Lieutenant Burgos who had to break the news that practically killed Chance. According to the medical examiner, Sean and Zoe died from a gunshot wound to the head. Linda had been hit in the stomach and arm, but as she was being transported to the hospital, the ambulance lost control and crashed, killing everyone including Linda.

Chance took the death of her family hard; she couldn't believe they were gone. She was sitting in the hospital room trying to come to terms with everything, when she heard a knock at the door. It was her confidential informant, Ave.

"Sorry about your family," he said, while standing in the doorway.

"Thank you. What are you doing here?" Chance replied.

Ave looked around nervously before stepping inside the room and shutting the door.

"I needed to talk to you. I know who killed your family."

Chance sat up straight in her bed and asked, "Who?"

"Ramon and Daniel," he said, while taking a seat in a chair near her bedside.

"Who?" she repeated, the names not ringing a bell.

"Word on the street is your partner Linda use to work for them years ago. One of their workers remembered her from back in the day. They went back and told Ramon and Daniel, who ordered the hit. You and your family just got caught up. That's how they do, nah mean?" Ave said, flexing.

"I never heard of Ramon and Daniel. Who are they?"

"Straight nightmares. Nothing moves without these niggas' say-so. Anything you need or want, they got. They have mayors, governors, and senators on their payroll," Ave informed her.

"How do I find these people?" Chance asked, ignoring Ave's warning.

Ave sucked his teeth. "That's what I'm tryna tell you, ma. You can't. These niggas are like ghosts, for real. Have you ever heard of Shark Enterprise?"

"No," she replied and then waited for him to go on.

"Well, Ramon and Daniel are the CEO's."

"What's it called again?" she asked.

"Shark Enterprise. It's the most powerful company in the world."

"What do they do?" Chance inquired, wanting to learn more about those who had taken the lives of her loved ones.

"Everything."

"So how do you know them?" Chance asked, raising an eyebrow.

"Because I'm Ave, and my ear stays to the street. From what I heard, they run their operation via the internet."

"The internet?"

"Yes, the internet. You know you can buy mad shit on the internet nowadays."

Is Ave bullshitting me? Chance thought. "So let me get this straight. Ramon and Daniel put the hit out on Linda and my family."

"No, not your family. They put the hit out on Linda and *her* family."

"What! Linda's family is dead?" Chance asked, surprised.

"Yes, they killed everything in the house, including the dog and fish, yo," Ave said, humoring Chance.

She couldn't help but to laugh. Even with the subject being death, Ave still managed to make jokes.

"Damn! Have you ever seen these guys? How do they look?" she inquired.

"I used to fuck with this girl name Patra Stevens. She was a bad bitch. You know how I like them. Well, she was fucking with Daniel."

Chance shrugged her shoulders and shot him a look to let him know she was waiting for him to finish.

"Oh...well, Daniel had feelings for the hoe on the low. One night, I was over there getting my dick sucked...you know how I do...and the nigga knocked on the door. Patra looked through the peephole, and when she saw it was Daniel, she almost passed out. Me? I was ready for war. I had my shit cocked back and everything," Ave explained, fronting. "But, Patra didn't want any problems, so I hid under the bed. Yo, shit got crazy!" Ave continued, getting louder. "I'm under the bed the whole time this nigga was pounding her out while confessing his love to her. Saying shit like if he catches her fucking someone else he's gonna kill her and the nigga, too. Yo, I can't front. The pussy and head was bananas, but it wasn't worth dying for, feel me?" Ave said, talking like he was on the corner with his dudes.

Chance couldn't help laughing her ass off. Ave was funny, always fronting and lying whenever he told a story.

"So where can I find this Patra?" she asked him.

"In the grave. They killed her." Ave nonchalantly said, then popped a Jolly Rancher candy in his mouth.

"She's dead?" Chance asked, wanting to make sure she heard him correctly.

"Yep! According to the streets, she had some powerful information on them and was gonna blackmail Daniel. That shit almost cost Daniel his life, because when Ramon found out, he wanted to kill him. Instead, he made Daniel kill Patra's ass, which is crazy because she was Daniel's bottom bitch for real. Still, they killed her, cutting the bitch's feet and hands off."

Chance turned her face away in disgust, but she still didn't believe Ave's story. "If these people are who you say they are, why haven't they popped up on the FBI list? How was this girl Patra able to get information?"

After all they had been through, Ave started getting pissed off with Chance doubting him.

"Come on, have I ever lied to you? If your ass would've called me back, I would've told you about the hit on Linda. I left several messages for you that night. Once I got word, I called you. Damn, man!" he shouted.

This wasn't the first time Ave had information for Chance, but she had to be sure. Within three months, she had lost her family and partner. So, this news was a little upsetting.

"Don't take it personal, Ave," Chance said, attempting to calm him. "I really appreciate you coming down here. I just don't understand, you know?"

Ave waved his hand at Chance. "It's cool. I know you're going through a lot. For real, I don't know how I would be if I lost my family. You're strong, that's for sure. Again, you or your family had nothing to do with it. Y'all were just collateral damage, another case of being in the wrong place at the wrong time. Now Linda? She should've known once they found out that she was dead. As for Patra, you know how niggas be with good pussy," he said, giving Chance a funny look. "If I know Patra, she winded that pussy on him to the point of making the nigga's eyes roll in the back of his head, because she did it to me," he added, causing them both to laugh.

"Ave, you're a fool," she said between her laughter.

"All jokes aside, though, Daniel is a weak nigga. It's Ramon you have to be careful with, but like I said, both of them are like ghosts. You know how people say they saw Elvis, even though he's dead? Well, that's them."

Chance sighed. *There's gotta be a way to get to them*, she thought to herself before asking, "So who runs their operation?"

What the fuck...is Chance hard of hearing? he wondered, then rolled his eyes and in a frustrated tone, replied, "Their operation is run via the net. Are you not listening?"

"I heard you, motherfucker, but how does the product get to the streets, ass?" Chance asked, annoyed.

"Oh, my bad! They have five lieutenants: Khalidi, Jeremiah, Cowell, Seth, and Zhang. They oversee most of the operations."

"What do they sell?"

"You won't believe it, but these niggas just don't push drugs. They sell humans, guns, whatever. They're like Burger King; 'Have it your way'. Yo, real talk, these cats are nothing to fuck with. They're killing government officials and their families," Ave stressed.

Chance nodded. "I see. Any hits out on me?" she inquired, anticipating the answer.

"Nah, you're good."

Trying to hide her relief, she then asked, "So how did you find me?"

Ave put another piece of candy in his mouth. "Like I said, I'm Ave," he replied with a wink.

Chance smirked. "Well, *Ave*, this better not be a set up, or you're gonna be dead on the ave."

He stood from the chair and went closer to Chance. Staring deeply into her eyes, he said, "I would never set you up, but anybody else, yes. You've always kept it one hundred with me,

and I feel fucked up that I wasn't able to help you and your family."

Chance rose up in the bed, outstretched her arms, and hugged him. "Awww, thank you."

Ave sat down next to Chance and there was brief moment of silence.

"So what are you gonna do?" he finally asked.

"First, I'm gonna get better and then kill every last one of them. Anyone who was involved; anybody who profited from it; anybody who opens their eyes at me," Chance affirmed.

Ave nodded. He loved hearing gangster shit like that.

"You kill 'em all, ma, but I don't think you can do it alone. These niggas make the *Mexican Cartel* look like choirboys. They operate on a totally different level. You can't even get in their circle without them doing a background check. They're like the CIA," he proclaimed.

Chance let out a small giggle. "CIA?"

"Okay, play with them if you want. But, my advice is to get some help, but not from anyone with the FBI. I hear they're helping them out on the low. Get someone who they fucked over and has a grudge, but got the heart of a lion. Most of all, you're gonna need someone who's crazy skilled with computers. I'm telling you, everything runs via the internet."

Taking it all in, Chance nodded in agreement at Ave's advice. He was right. She couldn't tell anyone in the Bureau.

"I'm not good with computers, and I don't know any hackers," she told him.

"Neither do I, but hold up. Didn't someone hack into the CIA secured system?" he asked.

"Yeah, a few years ago, but they never found out who."

"Damn, that person would be perfect."

Ave glanced at his watch. It was time for him to go. "Ma, I'm about to bounce. Have to pick up my kids from school; you know, do the father thing," he said, standing up.

Chance smiled. Ave had come a long way since the time when she busted him a few years ago coming across the state line with two bags filled with guns. He cried hard and promised if she helped him out, he would become her secret informant. Not even Linda knew about him. She had to admit all Ave's tips were good and led to big arrests. She was actually surprised he showed up at the hospital. She remembered the night she got the message from him for her to call him because it was important. She now knew he was trying to warn her about Linda. Maybe if she had returned his call, her husband and daughter would still be alive.

"You and the kid's mother are working things out?" she asked, trying to keep her mind from reliving that night.

"Hell naw! Man, I'm ready to O.J. that bitch," he snapped.

Chance laughed. "Please don't."

"Nah, I'm not, but that's one nut I regret," Ave responded, shaking his head in disgust. "Anyway, I'm out. Get better and be careful out there. If you need anything, let me know," he said, then kissed her on the cheek.

"You do the same. Wait…how can I find you?" Chance asked as he headed toward the door.

He turned around. "Where else? On the ave," he replied with a wink. Just as he was about to exit the room, he thought of something. "Yo, there is a person who might be able to help you. She's a doctor. Her name is Dr. Green. My man Byron use to mess with her."

"Does Byron have a last name, or how about a first name for this doctor?" Chance asked.

"Byron Adamson. As for the girl…" Ave paused, thinking hard. "I can't recall her first name. Just know it starts with a 'P'. Byron worked for Ramon and Daniel, but some shit jumped off and Ramon terminated him."

"Huh?" Chance said, not totally sure she understood what he meant.

"Some shit went down, and Ramon put the hit out. If I hear anything else, I'll call you. Later."

Sadly, that was the last time Chance saw Ave alive. Some dudes ran up in his apartment and put a bullet in his head. His baby's mother found him three days later.

*****

Revenge is gonna be sweet, Chance kept reminding herself as she dealt with the political bullshit at the Bureau. Chance found out she had been transferred to an office outside of Los Angeles before she returned to duty, something they did when an agent suffered a great loss. Her first day on the job, Internal Affairs Bureau (IAB) was there waiting for her.

Instead of getting upset with the politics of the job, Chance decided to use them to her advantage. She went from being a field agent to special foreign intelligence operations and espionage agent, specializing in cyber-based attacks and focusing on high-technology crimes committed in the last two years.

Perfect! They picked the wrong agent to fuck with, and now I'm gonna beat them at their own game. I guess Ave was right, Chance thought. Someone at the top was definitely helping Ramon and Daniel. It had been two years since the death of Linda and her family, and the FBI didn't have any leads. Not to mention, word at the Bureau was that Linda was a dirty agent, and that's what resulted in her being killed.

Chance simply smiled at the fake-ass co-workers who offered their condolences. Silence was golden. She had learned two things from Linda. One, the FBI was great at covering shit up, and two, believe half of what you see and hear.

In her spare time, Chance investigated Shark Enterprise, but came up empty every time. On paper, they appeared to be a great company. They worked, were educated, and had never been arrested. It got her thinking maybe Ave had the names mixed up. Then she remembered the lieutenants that Ave told her about, but they came up clean, also.

Some days, Chance wanted to give up on her search. But how could she give up on trying to find those who had killed her family? She glanced at the family portrait on her desk. There was not a day that went by that she didn't miss them.

Chance Smith met Sean Cohen while she was in the academy. While most men were intimated by her career choice, Sean embraced it, encouraging her to become the best agent. She wasn't sure they would work out because Sean was Irish, but

after a couple of dates, Chance knew he was the right man for her. A year later, they were married. She had a great career, a loving husband, and then Zoe came along, making life perfect.

Growing up in South Central Los Angeles wasn't easy, especially when surrounded by nothing but drugs and gangs. But, it was her dreams of a better life that kept her motivated.

Being a single parent, Valerie did the best she could while raising Chance and Chauncey. As for their father, Leroy, he was never around, always in and out of rehab or prison. Valerie loved Leroy so much that she would always take him back. In fact, she loved him so much she gave her life for him. Leroy had given Valerie HIV, but that wasn't the worst of it. Leroy would take Valerie's medication and sell it for drugs. Faced with the painful ordeal of watching her mother die, Chance wanted to kill her father. At the same time, she was angry with her mother for allowing him to do that to her. Even on Valerie's deathbed, she made Chance and Chauncey promise to forgive their father and to look after him after she was gone.

Six months after Valerie died, Leroy passed. Chance and Chauncey attended his funeral only out of the love and respect of their mother.

Chance had two consolations, though. One being her mother lived long enough to watch her two children graduate from high school, and two, she wasn't alive when her son was murdered. It was Thanksgiving and Chauncey was home visiting from college. When returning from playing football with his buddies, a group of teenagers robbed him for his jacket and sneakers. One of them fired a single shot into his chest, killing him instantly. His killers were never found.

After losing her mother and brother, Chance vowed never to let anyone get close to her again. That's why she knew it was a blessing from God when she found Sean, who became her family.

It was getting late, so Chance cleaned off her desk before heading home. She was about to get into her car, when Lieutenant Burgos pulled up.

"Agent Cohen, got a second?"

"Sure, Lieutenant Burgos."

"Follow me," he told her.

Driving to an isolated area, Burgos parked and then got out. Chance did the same.

"Why did we come out here?" she asked, looking around at the deserted area.

"This is where those punks assaulted my daughter," he explained. "She caught a flat tire and was waiting for help. They drove by, noticed she was alone, and then they offered to help. Those bastards took turns raping my daughter. Then they beat her and left her here to die. She hasn't been the same since," Burgos said, breaking down.

Chance lowered her head as her eyes filled with tears. "I'm sorry. I didn't know."

Composing himself, Burgos continued. "I was a field agent at the time, and Linda was my partner." He smirked. "Just like you, the Bureau told me it was being handled by a special task force. Linda got a tip that the suspects were in Iowa. We flew out there, and the rest is history."

"Do you regret it?" Chance asked.

Burgos faced her. "Not one day. That's why I think you should have this," he said, then walked over to his car, opened the rear door, and pulled some files from the backseat. "Linda kept two set of files."

"Two sets?" she repeated.

"Yes. In this world you have to since things have a tendency to disappear," he said, handing them over to her.

Chance stood there with a look of confusion. "I thought the Bureau said her files were destroyed."

"Like I said, we keep two sets of case files."

"How did you get these files?" she inquired.

"When Linda's cover was blown years ago, she gave me the files in case something happened to her."

Chance looked down at the files in her hand. "You know who killed her?"

"I have an idea," he replied.

"Is it true what they say about Linda? Was she dirty?"

"Aren't we all?" Burgos joked.

Chance nodded.

"Linda would kill me if she found out I gave you these files."

"Why?"

"You were like a daughter to her. She was so proud of you. That's why I'm giving them to you. I know if anybody can get the killers, it would be you."

Chance smiled at the compliment. "Sir, do you remember a few years ago when someone hacked into the CIA database?"

"Yeah, why?" Burgos asked.

"Did they ever find out who did it?"

"Umm...well, they traced it back to an IP address belonging to some dumb immigrant named Abel Danek aka Abel Day, but they didn't think it was him."

"Oh."

"Why you ask?" Burgos said.

"I was just thinking how the hell someone could hack into the government's database."

Burgos nodded. "Yeah, I said the same thing," he responded while starting to walk back to his car. "You be careful with these people. They are nobody to play with."

"Neither am I."

"I'm serious, Cohen," Burgos said, getting into his car.

"So am I. How are we writing this up?" Chance asked, leaning over into his driver's side window.

"You are officially undercover," he replied, then winked and drove off.

Chance drove straight home and went through Linda's files a thousand times, but came up empty. Shaking her head, she remembered Linda had never been good at keeping notes. She started to get frustrated, but then thought about what Ave had said about Daniel messing with a girl named Patra and his friend Byron Adamson.

It took some digging, but Chance found a young lady by the name of Justice Evans, who had filed a missing report on Patra. It wasn't the best lead, but right now, it was the only lead.

According to her driver's license, Ms. Evans now lived in Atlanta.

As for the doctor who Ave had mentioned, after searching the state's medical license database there was only one whose name started with a 'P'. Her name was Patience Green. In regards to Byron Adamson, he was found shot to death in his car.

The leads were small, but they were the only two Chance had to go on. First stop, Atlanta.

CHAPTER 2
JUSTICE EVANS
"JUSTICE WILL PREVAIL"

America is not so friendly after all, the beautiful Bajan thought.

At twenty-eight years old, Justice Evans thought she would be further in life. Instead, she was a struggling single woman who worked two jobs while attending school at night. Some days, she wished she hadn't left London. As a teenager, Justice heard so many wonderful things about *America, the home of the free and land of the brave.* So, when her cousin Patra sent for her, she jumped at the opportunity.

Back home in Barbados, it was so hard to survive. The only way to make money was to work on the resorts where Patra worked with her mother. There were always a lot of tourists, some wanting more than just seeing the sights. That's where Patra met a Jewish man who showered her with money and gifts. Then, one day, Patra was gone. After several years went by, Patra's mother finally gave up looking for her, assuming her daughter was dead.

Then, one day out of the blue, Justice received a letter with a plane ticket in it from Patra. She was alive and living in Las Vegas. Ecstatic, Justice hopped on a plane to Vegas. When she arrived at the airport, Justice almost walked past Patra. She didn't recognize Patra with her long, blonde, Beyoncé-looking weave. Her skin was blemished, and by the look of her clothing, she was dressed like a hoe. *What happened to my beautiful, innocent cousin?* Justice thought.

Once Justice got settled, Patra filled her in on the last ten years of her life. She had met a man named Earl on the resort who promised to give her the world if she left with him. Young, broke, and naïve, Patra left. It wasn't long before her dream turned into a nightmare. Their first night together he raped her. After that, she became his sex slave. That was only the beginning, though. When Earl wasn't raping her, he pimped her out to his friends. Some nights, he made her sleep with ten guys. This went on for years, until one day, Earl came home, gave Patra five hundred dollars, and kicked her out.

With no place to go and too ashamed to return home, she stayed at a shelter where she met Diamond, who introduced her to prostitution and drugs. Patra worked the streets until she saved up enough money to move to Las Vegas for a fresh start. At first, she was on the right track, working as a dancer for LAVO Nightclub and going to school for her GED during the day. However, that all changed when she met Arty.

During the ride to Patra's place, Justice kept looking at her out the corner of her eye. She could not believe how she looked. *What happened to my Bajan-beauty cousin?*

Patra lived in a small two-bedroom apartment in a rundown neighborhood right outside of Vegas. Justice giggled when she entered Patra's apartment. *Nothing about Patra has really changed. She's still sloppy, but at least she attempted to clean up,* Justice thought.

The first couple of weeks, Patra hid her lifestyle from Justice. However, when Arty called threatening her, she had no choice but to go back to work.

Things were great at first, but that's before Justice witnessed the *new* Patra. One evening, Patra went to work, returning pissy-drunk, high, and with some guy who she claimed was her boyfriend, but Justice knew better. They made so much noise behind the closed door of Patra's bedroom that the downstairs neighbor banged on the ceiling. From that night, things went downhill. When Patra was home, she slept all day. When awake, she was moody and short-tempered. As she continued to bring home a different man every night, it became obvious to Justice that her cousin was a hooker.

One evening, Patra and Justice were coming from the supermarket, when a black car pulled up alongside them, and the passenger's side window rolled down. Patra must've known who was in the car, because she walked right over and leaned inside.

"Hey," she said with slight nervousness in her voice and a forced smile.

"The boss says your ass better be ready. He's flying in for a quick fix," Arty warned.

"Sure," Patra replied while silently praying they didn't see Justice, but it was too late.

"Who's that?" Arty asked in admiration.

"Mi cousin Justice. Her from London," Patra said in her Bajan accent.

Arty tapped his man. "Yo, look at shawty. Gotdamn she's beautiful. Yo, bring her over here," he said.

"Is that your cousin for real? She's fucking sexy as hell. Yo, look at honey," Lamar, the driver, remarked.

"Yes, she's mi cousin, but she's not into this lifestyle," Patra told them.

"Did we fucking ask you?" he snapped, grabbing her by the hair through the window. "You weren't either, remember?" He threw Patra's head back. "All she needs is a little convincing," he added, licking his lips.

Patra had to think quickly. "Not out here. You don't want everyone in your business. Mi bring she by the club in a couple of day once my aunt leaves."

"Yeah, I wanna taste that pussy," Arty said, licking his lips. "Make sure you have your ass to work on time," he warned, then released a little chuckle. "You used to look like that," he commented before signaling his driver to pull off.

There was no way in hell Patra was going to bring Justice into the lifestyle of prostitution.

"Who was that?" Justice asked in her Bajan accent.

"Nobody," Patra answered.

"Patra, what's going on?" Justice demanded with her hands folded.

"We need to get you a job so you can find you an apartment real fast," Patra stated, walking away.

*****

That night after dinner, Justice was in her room getting ready for bed, when all of a sudden she felt woozy. Finding it difficult to keep her eyes open, she stumbled to the bed. The last thing she remembered before passing out was a knock at the door.

"Sorry, Justice," Patra mumbled, while coming into the room and putting her in the closet.

"Patra…" Justice called out groggily.

"Just, please trust me. It's for your own good. Mi promise to tell you everything later," Patra said, her voice cracking.

Patra had slipped an Ambien in Justice's drink during dinner, and the drug was quickly working.

A hard knock at the front door made Patra jump. After throwing some clothes on top of Justice, she closed the bedroom door and went to answer it.

"What took you so fucking long to open the door?" Daniel asked, grabbing Patra by the neck. "You better not be in here fucking no other guy."

Struggling to breathe, Patra managed to get enough air to respond, "No, me was sleeping."

Glaring, Daniel started squeezing her neck tighter. He didn't know why he was open off of her. Before she became a drug-addicted whore, Patra was bad, with beautiful skin, sandy blonde hair, bedroom eyes, and a nice slim body. It didn't help that Daniel had a thing for island women. Now she was washed up.

Daniel's two henchmen did a quick check of the house to make sure everything was clear. Then they went to stand outside the front door to do their job of keeping an eye out for any danger that may be lurking in the area.

"I heard your cousin is in town," Daniel said.

Scared, Patra replied, "Yes."

While removing his jacket, Daniel looked at Patra and asked, "So where is she?"

"She's not here."

Growing impatient with Patra, he took a deep breath, and in a composed tone, he again asked, "Where is she?"

Just by the sound of Daniel's voice, she knew it was only a matter of seconds before he knocked the piss out of her. "She's at the hotel with mi family," she quickly lied.

"Why isn't she staying with you?" he inquired.

"Because mi have to work and make your money," Patra said, touching his face gently while hoping to distract him from the subject.

Yearning for her touch, Daniel submitted to Patra's kisses. Seconds later, she was on her knees in front of him, pleasuring him the way he liked. Although aware of Patra's lifestyle, Daniel couldn't help getting weak for Patra. She made him feel so good.

"You like that, daddy? You like the way me suck this huge cock?" she moaned.

"Ahhh, yes, baby! Damn..."

Patra stood up so they could go into the bedroom to finish, but feeling freaky, Daniel feeling freaky wanted to stay in the living room.

"I wanna fuck right here," he told her.

Flashing a fake smile, Patra dropped back down to her knees and continued giving him head. Daniel was in his glory.

"You know what would make daddy happy?" he said.

"What? What would make me daddy happy?"

"Call your cousin."

Patra stopped. "I told you she's not…"

Before she could finish her sentence, he slapped her ass to the floor.

"You told me what, you stupid cokehead whore? Are you disobeying me?" Standing over her, he kicked her in the side and then dragged her by her weave into the bathroom, where he took off his belt and wrapped it around her wrists and the shower curtain rod. "I told you to call her over here. I didn't ask you what the fuck she was into," he said, while knocking the piss out of her.

MADISON

Accustomed to the beatings, Patra cried, "I'm sorry, daddy! Please," as blood gushed from her mouth.

"You stupid bitch!" he yelled, delivering punches not only to her face, but her body, as well.

Although still in a groggy state, Justice could hear Patra's cries from afar. She fumbled her way from underneath the clothing and out of the closet. She peeked out the door, and from where she stood she could see Patra tied to the shower rod with blood dripping from her mouth, nose, and eyes.

Smack!

"Bitch, when I tell you to do something, you do it."

"Yes," Patra responded in a weak voice.

Justice wanted to rescue Patra, but the effects of the Ambien prevented her from doing so. Instead, she stumbled to the bed and fell into a deep sleep.

Daniel smiled at the sight of Patra's bloody face before untying her. "See, that's what I like. I like when you listen."

Bleeding and in pain, Patra cleaned her face and then followed him into the bedroom where he laid across the bed.

"Now where were we?" he asked, while massaging his dick.

As Patra proceeded to pleasure him orally, Daniel degraded her in the worst way, calling her everything from a bitch to a crackhead whore.

After they were done, he said, " Here's a couple hundred dollars," and tossed it at her in disgust. "Let me fuck your cousin, and I'll double that. Don't go and smoke all of it up in a pipe either, you crackhead whore. Now go wash that pussy and clean up this house," he snidely said before exiting.

*****

The next morning, Justice woke up and went into Patra's room, but with Patra lying on her side, she thought her cousin was still sleeping. Right when she turned to exit the room, she heard Patra mumble, "Justice." That's when she walked around to the side of the bed and damn near fainted. Patra's face showed

the signs from being badly beaten. She had a swollen lip, a black eye, and bruises all over her completely naked body.

"Patra! What happened?" Justice asked.

"Nothing. Help mi up," Patra said, struggling to sit upright.

"Pat, please tell me what happened."

"Nothing," Patra repeated, grumbling in pain. "We have to get you outta of here," she said with no explanation as to why. Then she stood up from the bed and limped over to her dresser.

"Patra, what's going on?"

"Justice, mi have no time to run down details," Patra responded, while opening the top dresser drawer and pulling out some money. "Mi fuck up mi life, you hear? But, mi won't fuck up yours. I want you to take this money and get the fuck outta here."

Justice slapped the money out of Patra's hand. "I'm not leaving without you."

Patra stared at her cousin, remembering when she used to look just as beautiful as Justice. Now, after years of abusing her body, she looked fifty years old. Patra plopped down on the bed and started crying. She knew if she didn't get Justice out of there, she would end up like her.

"Just, mi can't go with you right now."

"Why?" Justice asked.

"Look at me. I can't go back home. Not like this," Patra explained.

"Why? Remember what Momma said when we were little? If things don't work out, we can always come back home," Justice reminded her.

Patra wiped away her tears. "Okay, but in the meantime, you take this money and get yourself a place while I go into rehab."

Justice's face lit up. "Honest?"

"Honest," Patra responded, then busted out laughing.

"Honest" is what they used to say when they were younger. It was their way of making a promise.

*****

As planned, Justice found an apartment and job on the other side of town. Patra, on the other hand, did not go into rehab. She relocated to another apartment building and was not only drinking and doing drugs, but she started selling drugs out of her apartment.

Justice was at work when she got a call from the local hospital. Death was only a heartbeat away for Patra, as someone had beaten her to within an inch of her life. Feeling she had truly hit rock bottom, Patra promised Justice that she would go into rehab, stating she was tired of being tired.

Believing her, Justice invited Patra to live with her until a bed became available, and for the next couple of weeks, Patra stayed in the house watching movies and reading her bible.

It was the night before Patra was scheduled to go into a two-year rehab program, and Justice could tell her cousin was nervous.

"What you thinking about?" she asked, walking up behind Patra who was staring up at the stars through the window.

Patra laughed. "Remember when we wanted to come to America? We was gonna become famous."

Justice nodded. "Yeah."

"What happened to that dream? I would give anything to go back to that day," Patra stated.

"Me, too. Are you nervous?" Justice asked.

"Scared to death, but I'm gonna do it this time. But, this time, I'm gonna do it for me," Patra said, turning to face her cousin.

"You don't have to do it alone, though. I'll be there with you every step of the way."

Patra hugged Justice tightly as if it would be the last time they would ever see each other. Then Justice finished helping Patra pack her things.

"What about this stuff? Should I put that by the door?" Justice asked, pointing to a box.

"Oh no, that's just some papers and stuff. They won't allow that in there."

"Alright. Well, do you want me to keep it?"

"Yes, please. It's my trump card," Patra said with a sense of humor.

*****

Patra was still sleeping when Justice left for work the next day. Justice had stood over Patra and said a silent prayer, praying that whatever demons Patra were fighting, God would remove them from her life.

Unfortunately, Patra never made it to rehab. She stole Justice's rent money and skipped town. Justice was so upset that she washed her hands of her cousin. However, a couple of months went by, and Patra still hadn't surface. This wasn't like her. So, Justice went to Patra's old neighborhood to ask around about her, but no one had heard from or seen Patra in months. Becoming more concerned, Justice decided to file a missing person report.

After Patra up and vanished, Justice decided it was time for a fresh start. Therefore, she relocated to Atlanta. While unpacking one of the boxes, she came across a copy of the missing person report on Patra. After reviewing it, Justice realized she didn't leave any forward information. *What if they found Patra?* Justice thought. She decided to give them a call and received the unthinkable news. Patra had been found dead in a wooded area outside of Las Vegas.

Devastated, she caught the first flight to Vegas. According to the medical examiner, Patra was stabbed twenty times. The killer also cut off her hands and feet so she couldn't be identified. However, the description Justice provided in the missing person report was enough for them to identify the body.

Justice signed the release papers for Patra's body to be sent back home and then hopped on the next plane back to Atlanta. *At least Patra is at peace now,* she thought as the aircraft ascended into the air.

*****

MADISON

With the economy doing bad and companies downsizing, Justice worked at TD Bank as a part-time accountant during the day and part-time as a maid at the downtown Marriot Hotel at night while trying to finish getting her Bachelor's degree in Finance and Accounting at Emory University. When time permitted, she also worked side gigs for a catering company. Tonight, she was working as a server, although it was suppose to be her day off. She needed all the money she could get, though.

The party was being held at a secret location. A car picked up the servers and transported them to the location. All cell phones had to be left at the door. You were searched before entering the mansion. Before the servers started, they were given a list of rules. It was then that Justice wondered what the hell she had gotten herself into.

For most of the evening, Justice remained in the kitchen plating the food, until one of the servers needed help carrying some trays into a private VIP area. They approached the door and knocked to gain entry. The two beefy men who answered directed them over to where they placed the food on a table in the room. Already warned that they were not to attempt to scan the room, Justice and the other servant stared straight ahead.

At the end of the night as Justice was on her way out, one of the guys walked up to her and asked, "Don't I know you from somewhere?"

"I'm sorry, but I don't think so," she responded.

"I don't forget a face that beautiful," he flirted.

Justice simply smiled and left.

*****

One more hour to go, Justice thought as she cleaned the bathroom. "Oh my God!" she shouted, holding her chest as she looked up. "I didn't hear you come in. You scared me." She then giggled with relief.

"I'm sorry. I didn't mean to. Is this room 806?" the intruder asked.

"Yes. They wanted to make sure you had everything you needed. They were short staffed on the day shift," Justice explained before exiting.

The next day as Justice was getting ready for work, the doorbell rang. Wondering who it could be, she peeked through the curtain and saw a lady standing outside.

"Yes?" Justice asked upon opening the door.

Chance stood there stumped for a second. It was the maid from last night. "I'm sorry," she finally said. "I was looking for Justice Evans."

"Aren't you the guest at the Marriot?" Justice asked, recognizing her.

"Yes, and you're the maid, correct?"

"That's right. I'm Justice."

Chance extended her arm to show her badge. "My name is Agent Chance Cohen. I'm from the FBI."

"FBI?" Justice repeated in a high-pitched voice.

"Yes. I need to talk to you about Patra Stevens. May I come inside?"

Justice stood in a daze for a second before saying, "Patra? Yes, come inside, please."

"Thanks," Chance said as she entered the apartment.

After Justice led her to the living room, she asked, "Patra? What about her?"

"Has Patra ever mentioned someone by the name of Daniel or a company called Shark Enterprise?"

Justice tried hard to recall, but came up with nothing. "Not that I can remember. When Patra was drunk, she rambled on about lots things, though. Why?"

"I think someone she was involved with killed her," Chance said.

Justice's eyes filled with tears, and starting to feel weak, she took a seat on the couch. "Patra was into a lot of stuff. She was with a different man every night."

Chance took a seat next to her and nodded, but remained quiet.

"She made sure I never saw their face," Justice continued. "I just heard the way they degraded her."

Chance looked up at a picture hanging on the wall. "That's Patra?"

"Yes," Justice replied as she looked up at the photo, as well.

"She was beautiful."

"Yes, she was. That picture was taken a year before she disappeared," Justice said.

"Disappeared?" Chance repeated.

"Yes. Patra was kidnapped from Barbados and brought here as a sex slave. When the man got tired of her, he threw Patra out," Justice explained.

"Damn! I didn't know that."

"Yeah, a lot of people don't know. Patra didn't want this lifestyle; she was forced into it and didn't know how to get out."

"So sad. Million of kids are kidnapped every day. Human trafficking is a huge business," Chance informed her.

"Tell me about it."

Chance sighed. She had run into a dead-end.

"Well, I won't keep you. If you think of anything that could possibly help us find your cousin's killer, please give me a call."

Justice took the card out of her hand. "I will. Sorry I couldn't help more," she said while walking her to the door.

She was happy the FBI was investigating Patra's death. Hopefully, her killer would be brought to justice soon.

*****

It was a week after Chance's visit, and Justice was cleaning out her other room, when she came across a box.

This doesn't look familiar, she thought. After opening it, she saw it was Patra's box of things.

Remembering what Patra had said about it being her "trump card", Justice started to rummage through the contents. She became horrified at what she saw. There were pictures of children naked and chained like animals. In addition to the

pictures, there were bank statements. But, when Justice saw a small finger, she damn near threw up.

She tossed everything back in the box and ran downstairs to look for Chance's card.

"Where the hell is it?" she screamed, tearing up the place.

Finally, she found it on one of the end tables. Her hands shook as she dialed the number, but her call went straight to voicemail.

"Damn!" Not wanting to leave a message stating what she had found, she simply said, "Hi, Agent Cohen. This is Justice. Can you please call me back?"

After leaving her number, she disconnected the call.

"What the hell was Patra into?" Justice mumbled to herself.

CHAPTER 3
SEVEN DAY
"SEVEN DEADLY SINS"

"Today is your lucky day, Seven," the C.O. announced.

"Just like last night was yours," Seven whispered, licking her lips and causing the C.O. to blush.

"Well, I kept my promise. In your personal belongings, there are keys to an apartment in New York. The rent is paid up for six months. The utilities are turned on, the fridge is stocked with your favorites, and a debit card loaded with three thousand dollars is waiting for you on the dresser. I promise to put more on it once I get my income tax return," the C.O. explained.

Seven nodded, but remained quiet.

"So when can I fly out there to see you?" he asked.

"In a few weeks. You know they're gonna put me in a halfway house for the first couple of weeks until I find a job," Seven told him.

The C.O. checked his pocket. "Oh, I almost forgot," he said, handing her a business card. "My sister-in-law works at a temp agency. She already has a job set up for you."

"My, my, my, we have everything covered, don't we?" Seven said, brushing her body up against his.

The C.O. swallowed hard. Although they had just fucked into the wee hours of the morning, he couldn't get enough of her.

Seven Day was thirty years old and the kind of woman that men left their wives to be with. She was the forbidden fruit the bible was talking about. Not only was she sexy as hell, but she was smart and savvy, as well. Life had made her that way. In

Seven's mind, there were only two things a woman needed to make it in this world: sex appeal and brains.

Her mother, Shaunice, named her Seven because she was lucky to be alive. While waiting for the bus one day, a drunk driver jumped the curb, hitting a seven-month pregnant Shaunice. The doctor could only save one, so Shaunice made the decision for her unborn child to be given a chance at life. Shaunice was an African American who married Abel, an Ukraine immigrant. Shaunice married Abel so he could get his green card. Initially, it was supposed to be a business arrangement, but somehow the two fell in love.

Abel did the best he could, but he couldn't raise Seven. Here he was an uneducated immigrant, who barely spoke English, trying to raise a beautiful daughter in America. To keep a roof over their heads and food on the table, Abel traveled from state to state for work. Sadly, Seven didn't make things any better; she was always getting into something. A smart girl with too much time on her hands, she gave truth to the saying, "Idle time is a devil's playground." She was way beyond her years, with the beauty of Amber Rose, attitude of Mary J. Blige, and educated like Condoleezza Rice. Some said she was too smart for her own good and deceitfully wicked. For instance, she was twelve when she hacked into her math teacher's personal computer and discovered he liked kiddie porn. While most would've been disgusted, Seven was somewhat aroused. The thought of a young girl having power over an older man turned her on.

One afternoon, Seven stayed after class to speak with her math teacher. She wanted to know how far he would go to keep his fetish a secret. When they were alone, she pulled out some pictures she had printed from his computer. Shocked, he offered to pay her, but Seven didn't want his money...yet. She wanted him to live out his fantasy. So, she removed her clothes and offered herself to him. As he popped her cherry, she whispered in his ear, "This is one of the *seven* deadly sins."

Most teenaged girls wanted their first time to be special. For Seven, it was special because she learned the power of the pussy.

Her math teacher was the first of Seven's victims. When she was fifteen years old, Seven was arrested for disorderly conduct. In the police car ride to the station house, one of the officers made a comment about how she was too beautiful to be in trouble. Seven flashed her wicked smile in response. Next thing she knew, her and the two officers were having a threesome in the backseat on a dead-end block.

It took some time, but Abel and Seven finally got their act together. They moved back to New York where Abel got a job as a truck driver. Seven graduated from college and was offered a position with Goldman and Sachs as a computer analyst. To celebrate her graduation, Abel took Seven to Atlantic City for the weekend.

While on the way back to New York, Abel started getting tired and decided to pull over on the side of the road. A tap on the window by a state trooper awakened Seven, who was already in the backseat sleeping.

"Excuse me, is everything okay?" the officer asked.

Still sleepy, Seven raised up. "Uh...yes," she replied, then looked up front for her father.

"Is there a problem?" the officer inquired when he noticed Seven looking around.

"Yeah, my father. He's missing."

That night remained one big blur for Seven. All she remembered was the officer popping the hood of the trunk and then asking several questions about her dad. Next thing she knew, two DEA agents showed up and took her into custody under charges of drug trafficking.

Seven thought it was a prank her father was playing on her to teach her a lesson for all the bullshit she had put him through when she was a kid. It wasn't until she was sentenced to five years in prison that she realized it wasn't a prank. Till this day, she still doesn't understand how it happened or why.

Sadly, two months after she was sentenced, her father was found dead in Michigan. Seven didn't even attend his funeral. After what he did to her, she was happy he was dead.

In prison, Seven lived like a queen. Instead of messing with other inmates, she fooled around with six correctional officers, two from each tour. But, it was Deputy Young, the warden of the facility, who was her ace in the hole. Last night was the best; Deputy Young ate Seven's pussy like her life depended on it. Seven reached an orgasm just watching her perform.

Deputy Young was a stuck-up white woman from Key West, Florida. Seven knew by the way she carried herself that she wasn't getting fucked right at home. Seven could also tell she was bi-curious just by the way she gawked at her, especially after she watched Seven in action with one of the correctional officers.

Seven was riding one of the C.O.'s into heaven, when Deputy Young caught them. Their eyes met briefly, and Deputy Young's nipples got hard. Seven licked her lips and continued, putting on a show for her audience until Deputy Young walked away, quietly closing the door behind her. Since no disciplinary charges were filed against her, Seven figured Deputy Young liked what she saw. So, Seven presented the opportunity.

Seven had just come back from taking a shower, when Deputy Young wanted to see her. Seven deliberately didn't wear any bra or panties. At first, Young played hard to get, which was cool because Seven loved the challenge. But, Seven finally cornered her, and from the way Young was breathing, Seven could tell she was hot and wet down below.

Seven slid her hand up the tweed skirt of Young's suit and ripped her thong off. Young released a soft moan. With her middle and index fingers, Seven explored Young's pussy, making her moan louder. She stared deeply into Young's eyes as she finger-fucked her.

"You like this, don't you?" Seven whispered in her ear. "I've seen the way you look at me," she added right before passionately kissing her.

Deputy Young thought her body would burst into flames. She'd never felt this way before. She didn't know what to do with herself. Seven giggled to herself at the thought of turning Young out. Seven lifted Young and plopped her down on the desk, pulled up her skirt, then kneeled down and proceeded to tease her with the tip of her tongue.

In paradise, saliva rolled from the side of Young's mouth, but Seven wasn't done yet. Her intention was to make Young her sex slave. She looked around the room, and her eyes landed on an eight-inch metal baton resting on the conference table, which she quickly walked over and grabbed. Upon seeing the metal object, Young's look of pleasure turned to one of fear. Seven kissed her, assuring her nothing was going to happen. Seven opened Young's blouse, lifted her bra, and began sucking on her rock-hard pink nipples before making her way down to her stomach and then back to her pussy. All Young could do was moan.

As Seven continued eating her, she took the baton and slowly slid it inside Young. The coldness of the object caused Young to jump, but Seven twirled and slowly moved it in and out of her, fucking her fast than slowly. When she was on the verge of cumming, Seven shoved it so deep inside her that it caused Young to scream in pleasure. Then Seven removed the baton with Young's juices all over it and placed it her mouth. She wanted Young to taste her own juices. Young sucked on it, while Seven went back down until she released in her face.

After they were done, Seven leaned over and with confidence said, "Your husband can't fuck you like that," before exiting.

Seven got a kick out of controlling people's minds with her deviate sexual ways. Some of the male correctional officers had even thought about leaving their wives just to be with her. But, today, she was leaving that all behind. She wanted a fresh start.

As she exited the federal detention center in Miami, Seven knew the people she had encountered while there would remember her for the rest of their lives.

Six hours later, Seven Day was in New York City. She inhaled a long, deep breath. *Ah, the smell of stinkin' air. There's no place like home,* she thought. Sadly, home for her was in a rundown halfway house in Brooklyn.

On her first day of freedom, Seven had to check in with her parole officer. While she waited her turn, all eyes were on her.

"Seven Day!" a woman yelled.

Seven sighed and stood up. "Yes."

A fat Puerto Rican lady glared at Seven. Even with her criminal record, she would trade places with Seven in a second.

"Right this way," she said, leading her to the back.

"I'm Angela Lopez. I will be your PO for the next couple of months. As a condition of your release, you are required to stay in a halfway house for thirty days or until you find work. Then you can move out, but you must notify me first. And the residence cannot be in a drug-infested area. At random, I can check your piss, and if it comes back dirty, you will either be sent back to prison or to a drug program," PO Lopez said, then paused to try to catch her breath. "Any questions?"

"Not at the moment."

"It says you were just released from Miami's federal prison for drug trafficking," she stated, looking up at Seven for confirmation.

With a sarcastic expression on her face, Seven replied, "That's what it says."

"It also says you finished college. I find that hard to believe," she snidely remarked.

Seven smirked. *If she's trying to piss me off, she better try harder.*

Lopez reached in a drawer and pulled out a drug test kit. "Put this in your mouth. Make sure it gets nice and wet," she ordered.

"Oh, it will get nice and wet alright," Seven replied with another smirk.

They were just about done, when PO Lopez handed Seven a paper. "Here's a list of jobs you can check out."

Seven looked at the paper and then handed it back to her. "No, thanks. I already have a job lined up. I'm starting tomorrow."

"Really? Is it legal?"

Seven smiled. "Of course."

"That's great. I wish all my clients were like you," Lopez joked.

Seven flashed her deviant grin. "Trust me, no you don't," she replied while undressing Lopez with her eyes.

Lopez dazed into Seven's seductive chestnut eyes for a brief moment. "Well, Ms. Day, I guess that's it," she finally said, trying to focus.

"Until we meet again." Seven smiled, then switched out of the office while everyone watched.

*****

The temp agency assigned Seven to Human Resources Administration (HRA), better known as the welfare building. The last thing Seven wanted was to deal with a bunch of ghetto-ass bitches milking the system. It'd been only a week, and Seven already wanted to transfer. Her coworkers were just as ghetto as the clients. Many of the clients were ex-drug users. From day one when Seven started working there, she received dirty looks from women, while the men just gawked at her and tried to get her number. Seven, however, brushed the bitches and niggas off; she wasn't about to waste a good nut on them.

Seven had to admit it wasn't easy adjusting to her new life. Just five years ago, she was set to work at Goldman and Sachs as a computer analyst making seventy thousand a year. Now she was an ex-con making ten dollars an hour.

On the train ride home, Seven thought about all the sneaky shit she had gotten away with as a teenager and how she had swindled people out of their most valuable things. She wondered if karma had caught up with her. After two weeks on the job, Seven moved into her furnished apartment courtesy of her pussy-whipped C.O. It wasn't the Four Seasons, but he laced it up really nice.

On her way in her building, Seven bumped into a young lady who was getting out a cab. Their eyes met briefly. *Damn, she's pretty and her body is bangin',* Seven thought while trying not to stare.

"Excuse me, is this 1515 Gibbons Place?" the lady asked.

"Yes," Seven replied, then walked inside with Chance following her.

"What apartment are you looking for?" Seven asked when she noticed Chance looking at the intercom buttons.

"3F," Chance replied.

"That's my apartment."

Chance looked up. "You cut your hair. That's why I didn't recognize you."

"Sorry, do I know you?" Seven asked in a suspicious tone.

"My name is Agent Chance Cohen."

"Agent Cohen from what division?" Seven said in a standoffish manner.

Chance smiled. "You know your government?"

There was a brief moment of silence as both ladies waited for the other to make their move.

"May I come in?" Chance finally asked.

"Do you have a warrant?" Seven snidely replied.

"Do I need one?" Chance shot back in an annoyed tone.

Seven giggled. "Not this time." She winked. "No disrespect, but you don't look white," she said as she opened the door and tossed her keys on the counter.

Chance ignored the remark. "Nice place for someone who just got released from prison."

"Let's just say I earned it." Seven winked again. "I'll hook you up, if you like."

"No, thanks," she said, while still looking around.

"Let's cut to the chase. You're not here to talk about my apartment, Agent Cohen."

Chance glared at her for a second before replying, "No, I'm not."

"So why are you here?" Seven asked.

"A couple of years ago, someone hacked into the CIA's database," Chance stated, looking at Seven for a reaction.

With a poker face, Seven nodded and replied, "And?"

Chance pulled out a piece of paper. "They traced the IP address to an immigrant named Abel Danek aka Abel Day." She smirked while handing it to Seven.

If Chance thought Seven was going to confess, she was sadly mistaken. Seven reviewed the document and shook her head.

"My father he was into a lot of things," Seven retorted, handing the piece of paper back to Chance.

Chance pulled out some more papers. "Seven Day, before you were arrested, you were suppose to work as a computer analyst at Goldman and Sachs."

Not amused by the little history rundown, Seven just glared at Chance, who had to think quickly since things weren't going nowhere fast.

"Computer analyst, not a hacker." Seven smiled.

Chance took a long, deep breath, readying herself for the bullshit. "Really? Because I heard you were the best."

"I've been labeled as being the best at many things, but sorry, computer hacking isn't one of them," Seven responded, not giving in. Sensing Chance checking her out, she smiled and asked, "You like what you see?"

Chance looked her up and down. "Don't kid yourself, sweetie. I'm strictly dickly. So, unless you were born with it, don't even come at me with it," she said, stooping down to her level. "Now back to what I was saying. I know you hacked into the CIA database. So, either you tell me how willingly or I'm gonna beat it out of you forcefully."

Chance didn't realize who she was talking to, though. Seven had just come home from doing a state bid; fighting had been a part of her daily regimen.

Seven jumped into Chance's face. "Then we'll be two fighting bitches," she said with her hands wide open, calling Chance's bluff.

This isn't working, Chance thought, then sighed and said, "Your father was murdered."

Seven turned to walk away. "You're about five years late. Tell me something I don't know," she responded, plopping down on the sofa.

Chance glared at Seven for a few seconds. She was starting to piss her off. In two seconds, she was going to smack the shit out of her.

After taking another long, deep breath, she asked, "Do you know who murdered him?"

Seven rolled her eyes. "Maybe it was the CIA who killed him," she responded sarcastically. "My father pissed off a lot of people. So, it doesn't surprise me that someone put him out of his misery."

"You don't care who murdered your father?" Chance asked, trying to defuse the conversation.

Seven jumped up and charged in the direction of Chance. "It's because of my father that I did five years in prison! That motherfucker set me up. If he was alive, I would kill him myself, but somebody beat me to it."

Finally, Chance had touched a nerve. Seven pretended to be hard, but she was hurting inside. The one person she trusted in life had set her up.

"So you don't care?" Chance asked again.

"What is this, the *Dr. Phil Show*?" Seven snidely responded.

Chance shot Seven a disgusted look. *This bitch isn't even worth the paperwork,* she thought as she turned around to leave.

Curious and impressed, Seven blurted out, "Why don't you leave your number and what your looking for? If I run into any hackers, I'll pass your number to them."

Smirking inside and without bothering to turn around, Chance went into her pocket, took out a business card, and placed it on the table. "I need to know everything about Shark Enterprise."

"Who is that?" Seven asked.

Chance paused. With her back still toward Seven, she said, "You tell me," and then exited.

Seven sat there for a second, not sure if it was a set up. The last thing she wanted to do was help the FEDS. However, she was curious to find out who The Secret Society was and why the FEDS were investigating them.

Seven waited a couple of days in case Chance was watching her. Laughing to herself, she couldn't believe it had taken the FEDS this long to find out it was her who hacked into their site. *Cocksuckers,* she thought.

It took some time, but Seven managed to find out a lot about Shark Enterprise. She used to hear myths about an undercover world, but this shit was crazy. While snooping around on their site, she came across an image of a man. You would've thought he was sleeping if it weren't for the big hole in his head. She looked closer; it was her father.

"What the fuck?" she muttered, making the images bigger. *Is this some kind of sick joke?* she thought.

While printing out the picture, she called Chance, but her call went straight to voicemail. She was going to leave a message, but still wasn't sure if it was a set up. Angry and confused, Seven sat back down at the computer.

"Alright, Agent Cohen, what's really going on?"

CHAPTER 4
PATIENCE GREEN
"PATIENCE IS A VIRTUE"

You are a disgrace to the medical field and should've never been allowed to practice medicine. Your lack of good judgment cost someone their life. Dr. Green, I sincerely hope you use this time to reflect on what you did. Patients are supposed to feel safe with you.

Patience thought back to when one of the board members had chastised her. It'd been two years since Patience lost her license, but she could still hear those scolding words.

Eight years down the drain because of one stupid mistake. Some days Patience wished she would've listened to Byron and just dumped the body. Maybe she would still be practicing medicine if she had done it. The sad part about the whole situation was she didn't even make any money from her involvement. Once the police got involved, Byron skipped town, leaving her broke and homeless.

Ugh, this can't be my life, Patience thought, as she applied make-up to one of the models on the set. Patience Green was thirty-five years old and had the potential to become one of the top surgeons in the country. Instead, she was a freelance makeup artist.

Patience had been an attending physician at John Hopkins Hospital when she met Byron at a health care seminar in Minnesota. Byron was tall, dark, and handsome, resembling Delroy Lindo. He had Patience's heart at hello. Byron was charismatic, sweet, and smart. More importantly, he was the first guy who admired Patience for her brains and not her beauty. Although half Irish and half black, many thought Patience was white.

Like Seven, life was already planned for Patience before she even entered this world. Her mother Kelly worked as a nurse in a correctional facility in South Carolina, when she found out she was pregnant. Though Kelly wanted to keep her baby, her parents made her give it up for adoption once they found out the father was black. They also made her accuse an inmate named Alvin Green of rape in order to keep their affair a secret. For a reduced sentence, Alvin agreed to give up all parental rights as long as he could name his daughter. Subsequently, he was sentenced to an additional ten years in prison.

Sadly, for the next eighteen years, Patience was shuffled in and out of foster homes. At the age of five, one of the aides in the group home molested her, and by the time she turned ten, Patience had been raped by one of her foster parents' two older sons.

Abused so much in life, it started to become a normal way of living for Patience. A lot of her decisions were a reflection of her childhood, especially when it came to her choice in men. Yearning for love made her so gullible. It wasn't until she witnessed her friend commit suicide that Patience realized she wanted more out of life.

Focused and now eighteen years old, Patience had received a full scholarship to attend Columbia University for their pre-med program. When she wasn't studying, Patience volunteered at a group home; she thought of it as her way of giving back.

Her most memorable moment in life was when she met her biological father for the first time. Patience was on her way back to the dorm, when her roommate informed her a man was in the lobby waiting for her. Once she saw his face, Patience immediately knew he was her father who had come looking for her after all these years. Although pissed, Patience needed answers to some questions. Such as, why did he leave her?

So, he sat Patience down and told her the truth. Alvin and Kelly were secretly seeing each other, they fell in love, and she got pregnant. When her parents found out, she lied and said she had been raped. Patience was disturbed by the news but relieved to finally know the truth.

Alvin told Patience there was not a day that went by that he didn't think about her. That's why he had to find her; he didn't want her thinking her father was a rapist. Ever since that day, the two were inseparable.

Patience's life started to gain some normalcy. With her father in her life, she went on to graduate from John Hopkins School of Medicine and became an attending surgeon for the hospital. All she needed now was a strong man by her side. Just like her name, she decided to have patience and wait for the right man to come along since she had her share of unhealthy relationships. That's when she met Byron Adamson, her Prince Charming, who was sweet, gentle, and attentive to all her needs.

Byron even relocated to Maryland so they could be closer. A realtor, he purchased a couple of properties in Richmond, Virginia, one being an office building located in a busy part of town. That's when he convinced Patience to open her own practice. At first, Patience frowned at the idea since she had just started in the medical field and knew it took years for doctors to establish their private practices. However, Byron would not let up, claiming to be drowning in debt and needing the money, which turned out to be a lie.

Patience loved him so much that she finally gave in. Most of the patients that Byron referred to her needed gynecological care, which wasn't her specialty. Still, she provided them with care. Money was rolling in and things were going great, until a young girl from West Africa came in with severe abdominal pain. It turned out she was a drug mule and in her stomach were five kilos of pure heroin. One of the bags busted and got into her system, killing her instantly. Her death led to a full investigation, which ended up costing Patience her license. As for Byron, he skipped town, and Patience hadn't heard from him since.

After finishing the make-up on set, Patience headed out to see her father, who was in a nursing home.

"There's my babygirl." Alvin smiled.

"Hi, Daddy. How are you doing?"

"Better now that you're here," he chimed.

Patience giggled. "You're such a sweet talker."

"The nurses love it," he jokingly replied.

"Yeah, I bet. Are they treating you good?"

"Of course," Alvin responded.

"Alright now. Just because I can't practice medicine doesn't mean I don't know it."

"I know, and don't worry, you will one day. Did you hear back from the appeals board?"

"Yes, and they said it's still under review," Patience informed him, taking a deep breath.

Alvin stared at his daughter. Medicine was her life, and in the blink of an eye, everything she had worked hard to achieve was gone. He wished there was something he could do to help her.

"You know, Patience, in order for us to appreciate the joy we gotta go through the pain. When I was in prison, I cried every night. Not because I was incarcerated, but because I left you out there. Just before I gave up my parental rights, I asked your mother to name you Patience."

"Why Patience?" she asked.

"Because patience is a virtue. You need it in order to survive in the world. Those ten years were the most painful in my life, but it was all worth it," Alvin said, taking her hand. "It helped me appreciate times like this."

Patience smiled, then leaned her head into her father's chest. He always knew how to make her feel better. "I love you, Daddy."

"I love you, too," he replied, squeezing her tight.

A month later, Alvin died of cancer. Patience was sad but cherished the little time they were blessed to spend together. Every time she got depressed, she thought about how hard it was for her father to spend most of his life in prison, when all he thought about doing was finding his daughter so he could build a bond with her.

*****

Today was her first day back to work since her father's death. Patience had just arrived on Rihanna's video set, and as always, it was already chaotic. While working on one of the model's faces, one of the security guards pointed a lady in her direction.

"Patience Green?" the lady asked.

"Yes," Patience replied.

Chance looked around and then pulled out her badge. "My name is Agent Cohen. Do you have someplace where we can talk?"

"Agent Cohen?" Patience repeated, while finishing up the girl's makeup.

"Yes. I'm with the FBI, and this is about Byron Adamson."

Patience froze for a moment before telling the model to excuse her for a quick second.

"What about him?" she asked after leading Chance over to a private area, then anxiously waited for a response.

Chance looked around again before responding. "He's dead."

Patience twisted her face up. "And?"

Not another one, Chance thought. "Look, I see you're working, and this is gonna take a little more time." She pulled out a card. "I'm staying at this hotel until tomorrow morning. If you would come talk to me, I would really appreciate it."

Patience stared at the card, wondering if she should take it. Sighing, she looked at Chance, grabbed the card, and walked away without saying a word. Chance had fucked up Patience's day, because after hearing that news, she couldn't concentrate for the rest of the day.

On her way home, Patience thought about Byron. She couldn't believe he was dead. Even though he was the reason why she lost her license, she never wished death on him. She should have been happy, but a part of her still loved him.

"Ugh." She sighed, busted a U-turn, and headed over to see Chance.

*****

"Why the hell am I here?" she kept asking herself as she walked down the hallway of the hotel.

Chance was getting out the shower when Patience arrived.

Knock! Knock!

"So Byron's dead?" Patience asked, brushing past Chance when she opened the door.

Surprised by her visit, Chance said, "Well come in."

With her arms folded, Patience turned around and asked, "How did he die?"

"He was shot to death in his car," Chance replied, taking a seat on the bed while Patience continued standing.

"Interesting. I guess that was his karma for ruining the wrong person's career?" Patience snidely replied.

"Excuse me. I don't follow," Chance said, confused by her statement.

Patience took a deep breath. "Because of Byron, I lost my medical license."

"Lost it?" Chance repeated.

Patience took a seat in a nearby chair and told Chance everything. It was the first time she had talked about it to anyone, and it actually felt good.

"So what does Byron's death have to do with me?"

"Have you ever heard of Shark Enterprise?" Chance asked.

"No. What's that?"

"Well, Byron worked for them, and the girls you provided care for…they were prostitutes for Shark Enterprise."

"Oh my God! Are you serious?" Patience stared at Chance in disbelief. "They were little girls, just babies. Some weren't even teenagers."

Hearing this brought back many painful memories of her being raped. *How could I have been so stupid?* she thought. *I should've known something was wrong when so many of the girls he referred to me tested positive for STDs.*

Judging by Patience's reaction, Chance believed she had no idea what Byron was doing.

"You're lucky, because there were many doctors before you that didn't make it," Chance told her.

"There were others?"

Chance rose from the bed, went over to the desk, and handed Patience some papers. "That was Byron's job. He would romance female doctors and get them to take care of the girls. The ones who refused were killed," she explained, causing Patience's eyes to widen.

She gasped. "Killed?"

"Yes," Chance said, handing her pictures of a few bodies.

Patience thought she would be sick from reviewing the photos. "Why me? Why did he spare my life?" Patience started to cry once she realized how lucky she was to be alive.

Chance sighed before sitting back down. "I don't know. That's why I was hoping you could help me."

Nodding, Patience replied, "Yes. Anything I can do to help, I'll do." Then she wiped the tears from her face.

Just as Chance started to say something there was a knock at the door.

"Excuse me," she said.

Chance looked through the peephole. It was Justice. *What the hell is she doing here?* Chance thought.

"Ms. Evans, how did you find me?" Chance asked upon opening the door.

Standing there with a box in hand, Justice said, "Your credit card."

"My credit card?" Chance asked in surprise.

"Yes...but I have something I need you to see," she said, brushing past her.

"Come in," Chance grumbled sarcastically since Justice had already entered the room.

"Hi," Justice said to Patience, then after putting the box on the bed, she asked Chance, "Can we speak in private?"

"It's okay. Patience, this is Justice. Justice, this is Patience," Chance said, introducing the ladies.

Excited, Justice got right to the purpose of her visit. "Remember you asked me about Shark Enterprise and a guy named Daniel?"

"Yes," Chance replied, wanting Justice to get on with it.

Justice opened the box. "Look at this." She handed Chance pictures and bank statements. "I think this was the reason Patra was killed. These are children."

Chance remained silent while viewing the disturbing pictures.

"I checked these accounts, and they have over a hundred million dollars in them," Justice stressed.

Just then, there was another knock at the door.

"It's like Grand Central Station in here," Chance mumbled.

This time it was Seven. Chance flung open the door.

"What the hell? How did you find me?"

"Why didn't you tell me that your partner, husband, and daughter were murdered?" Seven stormed in, glaring at Chance and waiting for an answer. "You have a lot of explaining to do, Agent Cohen."

Chance looked around at the women before telling Seven to have a seat so she could explain.

"A couple of years ago, I was on my way home with my family. We stopped at the local convenience store. I went inside to get Zoë, my daughter, a sandwich for school the next day," Chance said, reliving the nightmarish event. "I was in line when I heard the shots." Her voice cracked as she took a seat on the bed. "At first, I thought they were firecrackers, but I heard them again. I looked out and saw two gunmen firing shots into the car." Chance broke down.

Saddened, Seven replied, "I didn't know. All the article said was that your family and partner were killed and you were in a coma."

Chance nodded while wiping away her tears. "Yeah, for about three months. I didn't even get to attend my family's funeral."

"These people…they put a hit out on your family?" Patience asked, wiping tears from her eyes after being moved by Chance's emotional story.

"No. They put the hit out on my partner Linda and her family. My baby and husband were just innocent bystanders."

"So how did you find us?" Justice asked.

Chance giggled. "The night my family was murdered, one of my informants left me a message to call him. He was trying to warn me about the hit. When I was in the hospital, he came to see me. He was the one who told me about Patra and Byron."

"Where's your informant now?" Seven inquired.

"Dead. Someone put a bullet in his head."

"You think these people did it?" Patience asked.

"It wouldn't surprise me."

"Well, *these* people," Seven began, "are Ramon Ramirez and Daniel Munger. They run an organization called The Secret Society."

"Who are they?" Patience asked.

"The most powerful and feared men in America," Seven responded. "They run their operation from the internet."

"Internet?" Justice said.

"Yes," Chance said, joining in. "Seven is right. Everything is run via the net. That's why no one has been able to catch them. It's like they don't exist. They have five lieutenants who run their operation, keeping their hands clean."

Silence filled the room; everyone was in deep thought.

"Chance, you said no one was able to get close to them, right?" Justice asked.

Chance nodded. "Yes."

Justice then looked at Seven and Patience. "That's because they were going about it all wrong."

Seven nodded in agreement. "Yeah. They're going after Ramon and Daniel when they should be going after their lieutenants first."

"Exactly!" Justice said.

Still lost in thought, Patience just looked back and forth between the ladies while listening.

"You might have a point, but no one is crazy enough to go up against them," Chance stated.

"I'm not!" Seven exclaimed.

"Me either," Justice said.

Chance sighed and thought to herself, *These girls have no idea who these people are.*

Humored, Chance replied, "Ladies, these aren't your average drug dealers. These people are fucking dangerous. They have killed federal agents."

Seven screwed up her face. "Oh please! These niggas put their pants on one leg at a time just like the rest of us. I hate when people say someone's a killer. Chance, no one is born a killer. Shit just happens."

"I agree with her," Patience joined in. "They want everyone to believe they are killers, but anyone can be a killer. Shit, a ten-year-old can kill someone."

"You may be right, but these people are still ruthless," Chance explained.

"So!" Justice said.

"You guys think this shit is a game, huh? Like this is some audition for a TV show. These people will kill you and your family," Chance snapped.

Seven pulled out a photo. "It's because of these people that I lost my family. You see this picture? That's my father. You know where I found it? On their fucking website along with other pictures of people they have murdered. These people killed your family. You should want them dead more than anything," Seven said, directing her comment at Chance.

Shocked, Chance replied, "I do, but it's not that simple."

"I'm with the other girls, Chance. If you plan on seeking revenge, you're gonna need some help. We're willing to help, so let us," Patience told her.

Chance looked each of them in the face. While their hearts were in the right place, there was no way she was going to allow them to put their lives on the line.

Seven sensed Chance's vibe, so she blurted out, "How about this? We dig up whatever we can on these dudes and exchange information. If it's more than what we can handle, we walk away. But, if it's something we can help with, then let's do it."

Patience and Justice agreed. Chance, on the other hand, was still apprehensive.

"Alright, but don't go out there asking questions."

Smiling, Seven responded, "Good. Now so we don't step on anyone's toes, let's decide who's gonna do what."

"Well, I work in the banking business and was also a server at one of their parties. I can find out where the money is coming from and where it's going."

Patience sighed. "I used to be a doctor. So, I can check around and find out what doctors they have on their payroll."

Chance was surprised at how willing these ladies were to help her. "What about you, Seven?"

"Internet is my thing. I'll find out everything."

Although still hesitant about the idea, Chance smiled. "And I'll take care of everything else. Please, please be careful, though. If anyone gets wind of this, we're all dead."

Nodding their heads, the ladies replied in unison, "Okay."

It was getting late and the ladies had much work ahead of them. So, they decided to call it a night.

"Hold up. When and where do we meet up?" Patience asked.

Chance was so nervous that she had forgotten about that important detail. "Alright, we're gonna meet up at an old warehouse right outside of Burlington, New Jersey. You can't miss it." She looked each of them in the eyes before continuing. "This shit is about to get serious. That means we don't talk about this over the phone, Facebook, Twitter, or any other social networks. If you're in a relationship, no pillow talks with your mate. This stays between the four of us."

"Oh, and do not Google Shark Enterprise," Seven told them.

"Yes," Chance said in agreement. "Nothing should be done from your computer or phone. We meet up in two weeks at the warehouse. Bring everything you've learned about the organization or anything else you think is important. Is there anything else?"

"No," all three women replied.

"Well, I guess I'll see y'all in two weeks. Let's meet up around eight o'clock in the evening."

MADISON

After letting the ladies out, Chance put the double lock on the door and went to pour herself a drink before plopping down on the bed. *What the fuck have I started?*

CHAPTER 5
WWW.BOOTCAMP.COM

For the past two weeks, Chance had been on pins and needles. What the fuck was she thinking letting civilians put their lives on the line? Was she that desperate to catch her family's killers? *What if one of them gets caught and leads the killer back to me?* Chance thought. She sighed deeply as she waited for the others to arrive.

"You didn't think we were gonna show up, huh?" Seven said, scaring the hell out of Chance.

"No, I didn't," Chance replied.

Seven smirked. "That makes two of us," she said, laughing as she placed her stuff on the table.

Moments later, Justice and Patience arrived.

"Talk about low-key. I thought you were trying to set us up," Patience commented while looking around at the creepy surroundings.

Anxious, Chance blurted out, "Let's get down to business," and then led them into another room where there were three desks with chairs, a large flat-screen monitor, a laptop, and a podium with a microphone attached to it.

The ladies looked at each other and then at Chance.

"This use to be one of the FBI's training houses," Chance explained. "Justice, why don't you start? Tell us what you found."

Feeling like she was in school giving a presentation, Justice stood up and started speaking. "Without sending a red flag, I was able to trace some of their finances with the account numbers Patra left behind. They have over fifty thousand employees across the United States and hundreds of accounts divided up into five businesses—pharmacy, firearm, sports and entertainment, and charity work. All of these companies fall under one umbrella, but every month, they transfer large sums of money to one account at World Financial Bank."

"I heard of that bank," Patience interrupted.

"It's the largest bank in the world," Justice continued. "This is the bank the federal government uses to supply city, state, and federal employees with their payroll checks."

"Why would a prestigious bank like that be doing business with these guys?" Seven questioned.

"Because money is money no matter whose hands it comes from," Chance said, annoyed.

"Exactly. The government doesn't care as long as you pay your taxes," Justice informed them. "They're pulling in money from all over the world. Just last year alone, they grossed over two hundred million dollars."

"Alright, so we know where the money is going, but how are they getting it?" Chance asked.

Patience stood up. "I can answer that," she said, then plugged in her flash drive and started the slideshow. "These are pictures of doctors, and pharmacists who mysteriously died over the past five years. Chance, you're right; these people are no joke. Not only did they kill these people, they killed their families, too. Doctors and pharmacists are scared to say anything about them. However, I do know they are using pharmacies to hide the drugs."

"Hide drugs?" Seven said.

"Yes, prescription drugs and some illegal drugs," Patience responded, then walked over to her bag and pulled out what appeared to be a medicine bottle. "These are how they're selling some of their drugs." She handed the bottle to the ladies to view. "A doctor writes a prescription, and the patient goes to the pharmacy to have it filled. Looking at it, you would think it was pills inside, but it's cocaine."

The three ladies shook their heads in disbelief.

"They're using prescriptions to sell illegal drugs?" Chance asked, amazed. "Fucking genius!"

"They have street hustlers, too, but they're cleaning up their money by using pharmacies. They also use children to smuggle in the drugs. Three hundred children have died in the last two years as a result," Patience stated.

"You gotta admit these motherfuckers are good," Seven said. "But, it all makes sense."

"What are you talking about?" Patience asked.

"I did some research, and Shark Enterprise has been around since the early eighteen hundreds. It was formerly called The Brotherhood. But, Shark Enterprise has been up and running on the internet for the past six years trafficking everything from humans to drugs. With a simple click, your wish is their command. They do so by using "hidden services" sites on the Internet. These types of sites allow users to surf the Internet and communicate anonymously without leaving digital footprints. Four of the websites were housed on two servers based in the United States."

"How? I thought the web is monitored by IP addresses?" Justice asked.

"It is, but Shark Enterprise uses Yahoo and Google search engines," Seven explained, only further confusing the hell out of them, leading her to clarify. "When you log on to the Internet, which is the most useful tool in the world, your IP address automatically registers with Google or Yahoo. A guy named Seth, who used to work for Google, developed this application. This is how they get their clients. Seth monitors people's activity to see what they're interested in by the keywords and phrases they search. So, if a person types in the words sex shop, guns, and oxycodone, Shark Enterprise catches these phrases, hack into their computer, and starts sending them emails on the subject."

"I see. So, people don't even know their computer is being hacked into," Chance said.

"Exactly, and they create it so you can't block them and their messages don't go into your spam mailbox. With a simple click, these people are able to get your entire life history!" Seven exclaimed.

"And I thought the Internet was the best thing that ever happened?" Justice laughed.

"Me too," Patience said, and then asked, "How did you find out all of this?"

"I hacked into *their* network," Seven told them.

"Impossible! If you hacked into their system, you would've been dead five minutes later," Chance stated.

"You're right! Most hackers hack into the IP address. I just hacked into the host's IP address. Every site must use a host, so I hacked into their site and copied their entire network."

"Are you crazy? They're gonna find out!" Justice said, panicking.

"No, they will not. They don't even know I was in there," Seven explained.

"Shark Enterprise aka The Secret Society is run by two individuals—Ramon Ramirez and Daniel Munger," Seven stated. "They are responsible for fifteen hundred deaths. Two hundred of those killed were law officials. If they believe one of their own is slipping, they kill them and their families. They have a site showcasing the pictures of the victims' dead bodies in case any of their employees even think about trying something stupid," she told them, changing the slide.

"These men are not your average criminals. They have five lieutenants who handle everything. There is no head to cut; it's a conglomerate. If one betrays the money and power, the others betray him. Jeremiah Samuels handles all their drug trade, from the fields in Colombia to the streets of Harlem. When one of his workers came up short, Jeremiah tied him to the back of his car and dragged him fifty blocks, skinning him alive."

Justice put her hands over her mouth, shocked at the sight of the body on the laptop screen. Seven proceeded to the next slide.

"Then you have Khalidi Phillips, who handles their human trafficking. They say he's the worst pedophile in the world. He travels to poor countries to buy children, some as young as three weeks old. He then sells them to the highest bidder. Last year, he made a girl have sex with a dog before putting a bullet in her head. If the kids are not bought, he puts them on the street, the youngest being five years old. He keeps them doped up on crystal meth and crack."

"Wait! I know him," Justice said.

Seven stopped in the middle of her presentation. "You do? From where?"

"Not Khalidi, but the one in the picture with him. He was at one of the parties I worked. He made a pass at me."

"You were in the room with him?" Chance asked in a stunned tone.

"Yeah, a friend of mine caters their parties. She was short on servers and asked me to help out," Justice explained.

As Seven continued, Chance made a mental note to investigate that further.

"Up next is Nigel Cowell; he's German. He handles the gun trades and explosives. A former Navy Seal, he shot his wife and her parents in the head because she filed for divorce. Then there's Zhang Lee; she handles all the financial business. She graduated from The University of Texas at Austin. She's a powerful woman. She caught her boyfriend with a hooker and buried both of them alive. Rumor is she's sleeping with Ramon now. Seth Brin is in charge of their technology infrastructure. He used to work for Google and Apple; no one has ever been able to crack their code. Ladies, these are the people who run The Secret Society."

"What about Ramon Ramirez and Daniel Munger?" Patience asked. "Are they in any of those photos?"

Chance stood up. "It was hard, but I saved the best for last," she said, uploading some images "It took some digging, but here's the infamous Ramon Ramirez and Daniel Munger."

When the photos of the men appeared on the screen, the women's eyes widened. They were fine as hell, the true definition of *Bad Boys*. Not only were they nice looking, but you would think they were at a photo shoot.

"Eye candy. All lieutenants are required to dress and talk like a businessman. Ramon even sends them to etiquette school," Seven said with a wink.

"Etiquette school?" Patience repeated. "Damn."

"It makes sense since they are dealing with business people," Chance said.

"Business people? These motherfuckers are rubbing elbows with people like Bill Gates, Warren Buffet, and Mike Bloomberg. That's who's at their dinner table," Seven said.

"Can't lie; they are fine as hell," Justice voiced.

"Are you sure it's them?" Seven asked. "The picture was taken at Bush's inauguration."

"Yes. They usually keep a low profile," Chance explained.

"Damn, they got invited to Bush's inauguration," Justice said in a tone of disbelief.

Patience sucked her teeth. "I'm not surprised. Everyone in the Bush administration were crooked," she stated, causing the ladies to laugh and nod their heads in agreement.

After Chance finished laughing at Patience's remark, she said, "There are not a lot of photos of them, but these dudes travel in plain sight."

"Plain sight?" Seven repeated.

"Yes. Ramon and Daniel run the organization, but you rarely see them. Many believe they travel with an army, but they don't," Chance affirmed. "When Ramon is in New York City, he takes the subway or bus. He's not an easy target, though. His bodyguards are always only a foot away. Before he takes the train, they scope out the area, and if anyone looks suspicious, they kill with no questions asked," Chance pointed out, changing the slide.

"On the other hand, Daniel loves Miami, just like the late great Gianni Versace. Daniel eats breakfast at the same restaurant and then walks back to his mansion. The difference between him and Gianni is that there are snipers on every rooftop in a twenty-block radius whenever he goes outdoors. A few tried to get close to him, but they were hit before they even knew what happened. Even the waiters in the restaurant carry guns."

Learning this information left the ladies speechless. *Damn*, they thought while staring at the screen. This was way more than they had anticipated.

Chance looked at their expressions and smirked. "Is anyone having second thoughts?"

Everyone remained quiet for a second before Seven blurted out, "So what's next?"

"Seven, this isn't some movie, and we're not Charlie's Angels. These men have no regard for human life or any remorse for taking one," Chance snapped.

Seven snapped, "I thought we've been through this already. After learning this today, I know we can bring these dudes down."

Patience stood up. "I'm with Seven on this one, Chance. These people affected our lives, too. We have to at least try. It's time to give them a dose of their own medicine."

"How? How when no one has ever gotten close to them?" Chance asked, getting frustrated.

"Like I said, they were going about it wrong," Justice restated, studying the evidence. "The agents' covers are always blown because they're focusing on Ramon and Daniel. They can spot an agent a mile away. What they need to be focusing on are the lieutenants. For instance, Khalidi's weakness is women. With the right woman, he will spill his guts."

Seven nodded. "I see what you're saying. Attack their empire from inside by using their lieutenants and working our way up to the big dogs."

Justice smiled. "Exactly."

Shaking her head, Chance replied, "It won't work."

"Yes, it will, Chance. All you need is the right women," Patience said.

Chance looked at them. "NO!"

"Why not?" Seven asked.

"Because you guys aren't trained for this stuff. You're law abiding citizens."

"Trained for what? To fuck and lie to a man? We're women. We got all the training we need!" Seven exclaimed.

Chance hated to admit it, but these ladies were right. Without them, there was no way she would've gotten this information. With her hands folded under her chin, she gave in.

"Alright, it's a go, but I'm in charge," she stated with them nodding in agreement. "The only problem now is which of us is woman enough?"

"Leave that to me. I can ask my friend to let me be a server at one of their parties," Justice told her.

"A server ," Seven stated flatly.

"Yes. They will think I'm a pretty server and try to buy me," Justice explained.

"And put your ass on the strip," Seven warned. "Ain't nobody gonna take you seriously."

Chance and Patience giggled at Seven's remark, but Justice, not seeing the humor in it, rolled her eyes.

"Actually, it's perfect. They will call themselves trying to rescue you by offering you a green card or some shit like that. Make sure you use that Bajan accent," Chance said.

"Okay," Justice replied.

"Yeah, it's turning me on," Seven half jokingly answered, playfully tapping Justice.

"Seven…what about you?" Chance asked.

"I'm gonna clone their sites; get the listing information for their customers, transactions, anything that comes through their site."

Chance nodded. "Good, 'cause we gonna need that."

"I'll see what new drugs they have on the market," Patience offered. "I met Byron at a seminar, so I'll attend some and hopefully meet one of them."

"So you know one of them?" Seven asked.

"I unknowingly used to work for them," Patience explained.

"What?" Justice yelled.

"It's a long story. Basically, my fiancé got me caught up in some bullshit, which ended up costing me my medical license," Patience told them.

"Where is he now?" Seven asked.

Patience grinned. "Dead."

"Byron worked for The Secret Society. His job was to find doctors who would perform abortions on underage girls and treat their STDs," Chance stated.

Seven sucked her teeth. "And you was gonna marry a creep like that?"

"I didn't know until it was too late," Patience further explained.

"Damn," Seven simply said.

"Fuck him! That bastard deserved to die," Patience shot back.

"So you were one of the doctors?" Justice asked, shaking her head in disgust.

"Look, I didn't know," Patience answered in a defensive tone.

"Calm down, everyone!" Chance yelled. "Justice, Patience is not the one to blame here."

"Yeah, she's right," Seven agreed.

"Let's stick to the topic, alright? We need a plan and quick," Chance stated. "If we're gonna go up against these people, we better be ready. For now, we go back to our daily lives. We pretend like we know nothing. We have to remain low-key. What about y'all jobs?" Chance wondered.

"I'm freelancing, so I make my own schedule," Patience responded.

"My temping assignment is almost over, so I'm fine," Seven said.

"What about your PO?" Chance asked.

"I'll be done with that in a couple of weeks. As long as I'm looking, she won't violate me."

"Justice?" Chance said.

"I don't know. I work two jobs, and I'm in school." She sighed and then said, "I'll figure something out."

"Alright, just let us know," Chance said.

After Justice and Patience left, Seven stuck around to brainstorm some ideas.

"You still nervous?" Seven asked.

"More like concerned, and you?"

"A little, but I know we can do this if everyone plays their part."

"So they killed your father?" Chance inquired.

Seven lowered her head. "Yeah, my father did a lot of side jobs to make ends meet. It's funny because I was so upset with him that I was happy someone actually murdered him."

"Why?" Chance asked.

"My father took me to Atlantic City for the weekend to celebrate me graduating from college and my new job. I was in the backseat of the car sleeping and woke up to state troopers' flashing lights in my face. They found a kilo in the trunk. Before I knew it, I was being handcuffed and charged with drug trafficking."

"Did it ever occur to you that it was the only way he could save your life?"

"Not at that time."

Chance shook her head. "Damn. What about your mother?"

"She died when I was a baby," Seven replied, then grew silent.

"Well, it's getting late, and it's time for me to get going," Chance finally said.

"I'll keep digging and think of a plan. See ya in two weeks," Seven told her before heading toward the exit.

"You never did answer my question. Was it you who hacked into the CIA database?"

Seven stopped and turned around. "At this point, does it matter?"

"No, but I would like to know if I can trust you," Chance said.

Is she fucking serious? Seven thought, and then took a deep breath, walked up to Chance, and stared directly in her eyes. "Now that's funny, considering you came to me for help."

"Just need to know what side you're on, that's all."

Seven turned away to leave, but paused once more and sarcastically said, "Can you imagine how dangerous I could be if I wasn't on your side? Now that's something you should be worried about."

*****

So these ladies wanna be agents? Well, I'm about to give them the training of their lives. Chance was pretty sure by the time she finished with them, they would be begging for her to stop. She had transformed the old abandoned warehouse once used as the FBI's training headquarters into a boot camp. In one room there were photos, maps, and other documents, while the other rooms were used for interrogations, just one tactic the FBI used on their agents for counterterrorism training.

The ladies were on time, with Seven arriving first. Chance greeted them from the top of the stairs.

"Welcome to boot camp, ladies."

"What the fuck?" Seven said, looking around.

"This is what you wanted," Chance said, coming down the stairs. "You didn't think I was gonna send you to a gunfight with a knife, did you?"

The ladies dropped their bags in disbelief.

"Let's get down to business," Chance ordered, leading them into another room. After turning on the monitor, she began. "Shark Enterprise aka The Secret Society is our main priority, our only priority. They are strong, powerful, and the most feared organization in the world. Therefore, we must be careful. A simple slipup could cost you your life. We must be a step ahead of them at all times. In order to do that, their lives must become ours. But, we have to be invisible doing it. Every other week they are running background checks on their employees. If anything appears out of order, they kill first, no questions asked. Friends and family do not exist in this organization. They have eyes everywhere. Let's start with Khalidi. As Seven stated, Khalidi is a smooth-talking, sexy motherfucker. Although he's the scum of the earth, this man has been linked to the most beautiful women in the world. When he's not romancing them, he's selling them. He's famous for saying he has never met a woman he couldn't fuck." Chance paused before asking, "Are you up for this, Justice?"

Justice strutted up to the screen to get a closer look at Khalidi. He was sexy as hell, reminding her of Idris Elba. "When mi done with him, he gonna wish him was a nut in his father's penis," she said, making the other girls laugh. "Mi meet men like him before. You have to let them think they are in control. It feeds their ego."

The ladies cheered in agreement.

"While Justice is working Khalidi, I want you to work on Jeremiah, Patience. He loves your kind of women?" Chance said.

"And what type is that?" Patience asked.

"Those Kim Kardashian motherfuckers. You know, the fake type," Seven answered for Chance in a joking matter, making the women laugh again.

"Fuck you, with your fake Amber Rose-looking ass. Black and yellow, black and yellow," Patience started singing.

Seven cracked up. "It's cool. At least I know how to fuck, unlike you with that whack-ass sex tape you made. You're supposed to hold the dick and suck it."

By this point, Justice and Chance were laughing their asses off. Even Patience laughed at that one.

"I don't know what y'all laughing at. Chance looks like a knock-off Kenya Moore," Patience snapped.

Seven fell out. "Oh shit, I was wondering who you looked like. What the fuck is she known for anyway?"

"Shut up! No, I don't. And she was in a lot of beauty pageants," Chance said.

"From the projects," Seven humored.

"Who does Justice look like?" Patience asked, continuing the joke.

"Well, her forehead is too little to look like Rihanna, so I don't know," Seven said, staring at her.

After a few more laughs, the ladies went back to work.

"Patience will work on Jeremiah," Chance instructed. "He attends health care seminars in an attempt to recruit doctors."

★ ★ ★ ★ ★

"I'm on it," Patience replied.

"Seven, I need you to get us inside of their website."

Seven stood up. "Already did it." Walking over to the computer, Seven plugged in a wireless card and then logged onto the computer. "Welcome to The Secret Society website."

"How are we gonna monitor their activity, though?" Chance asked.

"I'm glad you asked. I fixed it to when they log on, they will be logging on to our website."

"I'm fucking confused. English, please!" Justice yelled.

Seven changed the computer screen. "Ladies, welcome to WWW.COM. When they type in www and then dot-com at the end, it routes them to us."

"You hacked into www.com's hosting?" Patience asked in disbelief.

Seven winked and smiled.

"You're fucking crazy. How would you know when it's them logging in?" Patience inquired.

"That's why I put a filter on the system. It flushes out any unwanted traffic."

"How long before they know you hacked into their system?" Chance questioned.

"They won't!"

Chance had to admit these ladies had hidden talents.

"Seven, you work on that, along with Zhang Lee and Seth. I'll handle Cowell," Chance said, then led them into another room.

The women looked around the room. There was enough firepower for Armageddon. Chance had everything from handguns to hand grenades, cameras, and other espionage devices, some as small as diamond earrings. Chance noticed their looks of admiration.

"Scary, right?"

"I guess it's true when they say big brother is always watching," Seven said.

"Indeed," Chance responded.

"Which makes me wonder who's watching them?" Patience said while checking out all the devices.

After the ladies played with the toys for a few minutes, Chance explained the next step.

"What we're about to do requires a particular state of mind. Revenge is an emotion that can get you killed. So, with that being said, I'm gonna train you not to be seen or heard. We're going up against the most ruthless organization since the Gotti Family. For the next couple of months, I'm gonna work the shit out of you."

Together, the ladies turned the old warehouse into a top security command center. They went through different kinds of scenarios. In one drill, Chance locked them in the rooms with different temperatures to see how they would react. Amazingly, the ladies handled it like pros. They went through everything from planting bombs to target practice.

When they weren't training, the ladies returned to their everyday lives. Although the training was rough on their bodies, the ladies looked forward to it every weekend, and during the next couple of months, they formed a tight bond.

It was the final night of training, and Justice was up first. Her friend who owned the catering company called and asked her if she could fill in. Wanting a moment to speak with Justice alone, Chance suggested they take a walk in the woods.

"Are you up for this?" Chance asked.

"Ready as I'll ever be," Justice responded.

"You can always change your mind."

Justice nodded. "Back home, you hear only in America you can be free and get justice, but how can you when men like Khalidi are alive?"

"True, but you don't have to be a hero, either."

"I'm not trying to be, but Patra deserves some justice."

Chance nodded but remained quiet.

Minutes later, Seven and Patience joined the ladies with bottles of beer in their hands.

"Hey, is everything okay?" Patience asked.

Chance and Justice looked at each other before Chance responded, "Now it is."

★ ★ ★ ★ ★

"Alright then! Let's bring these bastards down!" Seven cheered, handing them a bottle each.

"After tonight, our lives will change forever. No matter what happens, I just wanna say thank you," Chance expressed.

"You're welcome," the ladies responded.

Chance raised her bottle. "A toast to WWW.COM, where you enter at your own risk."

CHAPTER 6
WWW.KHALIDI.COM

The big party was being held in a mansion on Fire Island in Miami. Though they went over the plan a thousand times, Justice was still nervous as hell. All she kept thinking about was slipping up and getting caught.

Chance hid two microphones in Justice's earrings, and the buttons on her uniforms served as cameras. Chance also gave her an earpiece to put inside her ear.

Before leaving for the party, Justice took one last look in the mirror and muttered, "Here goes nothing."

Just as they expected, everyone had their phone confiscated before walking through a metal detector. Justice literally almost pissed on herself when the alarm went off as she walked through. She knew for sure she was caught. However, it turned out the two bobby pins in her head had set it off.

Whew, she thought while making her way to the bathroom to splash some water on her face.

"Justice, you need to calm down," Chance uttered through her earpiece.

"Okay," she softly mumbled as she tried to calm her breathing.

The party was packed, drinks were flowing, and people were dancing. Justice was placing some trays on the table, when she felt someone staring at her from across the room.

There he was—the notorious Khalidi Phillips—standing there in a black tailor-made suit, white shirt, and no tie. He was thirty-eight years old from North Carolina and raised by his grandparents. With that southern hospitality, Khalidi charmed the pants off of women.

Damn, he's fine, Justine thought.

She turned around so the cameras could get a close up of him. When he looked in her direction, Justice quickly turned the other way, but it was too late. He had already caught her eye.

Oh God, he saw me, she thought as she finished placing the trays down.

Khalidi walked over to her. "Hello."

"Hi," she shyly responded.

"Someone as beautiful as you should not be setting tables," he stated with a smile.

"Damn, he's fine as fuck," Seven whispered through her earpiece, causing Justice to laugh.

Khalidi looked at her as if she were crazy. "Did I say something funny?"

"Talk…talk," Chance and the girls coached.

"No, I'm sorry."

"Then it's my face," he joked, hoping to break the ice.

Justice laughed again. "No."

"What's your name?" he asked.

"Tell him your real name. If he finds out you lied about your name, he's gonna kill you," Chance instructed.

"Justice…Justice Evans," she replied using her Bajan accent, and then cleared her throat.

"I love your accent. Where are you from?" he inquired.

"From London," Justice answered, trying hard not to stare or be swayed by the 'I AM KING' cologne scent by Sean John. "I have to get back to the kitchen," she quickly said before attempting to walk away, but Khalidi gently grabbed her hand.

"I'm not done."

Justice looked down at his hand before gently removing it from her. "Yes, you are," she told him, while staring deeply into his eyes.

MADISON

"What the fuck are you doing? She's gonna blow it," she heard one of her cohorts say through the earpiece.

"Chill out, guys. Mi got this," Justice mumbled, praying no one was watching her.

Obviously, her plan worked, because throughout the night, Khalidi couldn't take his eyes off of her. *She's stunning,* he thought, *and playing hard to get.*

But, Khalidi was not the only man who noticed Justice. Every man in the room watched her. The other ladies had a blast watching them drool over Justice.

While Justice was in the kitchen, Khalidi entered and signaled everyone to leave. When she tried to walk out, he grabbed her hand again, but this time with a little force.

"Do you know who I am?"

Again, Justice looked down at his hand. "I thought we already had this conversation."

Khalidi chuckled at her smart remark. "Do you know who I am?" he repeated.

Justice rolled her eyes in a seductive way. "Enlighten me."

"Powerful, rich…"

Justice nodded. "And obviously full of yourself," she said, cutting him off.

Khalidi grabbed her by the waist and stared deeply into her eyes. "A man who gets anything he wants."

Gently removing his hands from her waist, Justice replied, "Some things are priceless."

He pulled her back, pinning her against the counter. "Everything has a price."

"You think so?" Justice said, playing along. "Well, I can't be bought," she added before gently pushing him away and walking off.

Annoyed, Khalidi grabbed her by the arm, forcing Justice to look back at him.

"Sir, I was hired to serve food, not be your personal servant. So, if you don't mind, I would like to get back to doing that."

Khalidi reluctantly released her arm. As he stared at her walking away, one of his workers entered the kitchen.

✯ ✯ ✯ ✯ ✯

"Boss, they're asking for you," Arty informed him. Then, while looking at Justice, he thought, *I know her.*

Cool as a cucumber, Justice walked away while laughing inside. *Men,* she thought.

As she stood there plating the salmon, Arty walked up on her.

"Don't I know you from somewhere?" he asked, undressing her with his eyes.

Justice pretended she didn't know what he was talking about. "I doubt it."

"Nah, I would never forget a face like that," Arty replied.

"Oh shit, Justice. Keep cool. He's just fishing," Chance said through the earpiece.

"That makes two of us," Justice responded. She tried to walk away, but he blocked her path.

He touched the side of her face. "Nah, I could never forget a face this pretty."

"Arty!" Khalidi yelled. "What the fuck are you doing?"

"Nothing, boss. I was just…checking," he began explaining as he moonwalked out of there.

As Justice stood there trembling like a leaf on a tree, Khalidi looked over at her and asked, "Are you okay?"

She swallowed hard. "Yes, thank you."

This time, Khalidi didn't respond. He just left the room, leaving Justice puzzled. She didn't see him for the rest of the evening.

*****

The following morning as Justice got ready to leave for the airport to head back home to Atlanta, there was a knock at the door. It was the bellboy with a dozen of roses.

"Good afternoon. These came for you," he said, handing her the bouquet of two dozen long-stemmed red roses.

"For me?" Justice asked while taking the flowers. "Thank you."

After Justice checked out, she stood in front of the hotel waiting to catch a cab to the airport, when a platinum-colored

Bugatti pulled up in front of her. It was Khalidi dressed in a crisp white linen suit.

"You need a ride?"

The way everyone was staring and pointing you would have thought he was P. Diddy.

What the hell is he doing here? she thought. *He must've followed me to the hotel last night. Chance was right. These people are on point.*

Justice had to think quickly. She didn't want him to get suspicious, so she walked over to the car.

"Nice set of wheels," she sarcastically replied.

"You know, the only two people who have this vehicle are myself and Jay Z. The car costs two million dollars," Khalidi informed her.

Big fucking deal, she thought. Then before walking away, she said, "Thanks for the Carfax info, but I'm off duty."

Khalidi jumped out of the car and went after her, grabbing her by the arm again. "I don't chase females. It's not even in my DNA. Now, I'm tryna be nice, but you're making this hard," he stated in a stern yet sexy tone.

Despite being turned on, she looked down at his hand and then back up at him. "And I don't take kindly to men grabbing on me," she said, removing his hand.

Khalidi laughed. No female had ever dared touch him in such a way as to remove his hand off of them. His team, who were waiting in another car parked behind him, was shocked he didn't slap Justice to the ground. But, there was something about her that Khalidi was attracted to. He didn't know why, but he wanted her.

"My apologies."

Justice acknowledged his apology with a nod.

"Ms. Justice, is it possible for you to have dinner with me?"

"Sorry, but I have to catch a flight back to Atlanta in an hour."

"I'll have my private jet fly you back."

Flattered, Justice flashed a seductive smile. "Thanks, but I really have to get going."

Unwilling to give up, Khalidi said, "Well, how about I take you to the airport? Is that okay?"

Damn, Justice thought, *if I say no, he might suspect something. But, what if I get in his car and he kidnaps me? That certainly wasn't part of the plan.* She needed to notify Chance and the rest of the girls quick. Thinking fast, she pulled out her cell phone and called Chance.

"Hey, I'm gonna be late. I missed my flight."

"What?" Chance asked, confused. Then she eventually caught on. "He's in front of you, isn't he?"

"Yes."

"Alright. Do you still have the earrings on?"

"Yes, but I need you to check what time the next flight leaves," Justice said.

"Okay, good. Put your earpiece in your ear, but make sure no one sees you. Be safe. These people are dangerous."

"Alright, thanks. I will." Justice hung up.

"Cleared it with your man, eh?" Khalidi asked, licking his lips.

"Matter of fact, I did, smart ass," she said, tossing her bag over her shoulder and getting in his car.

Khalidi smirked; he loved her sexy accent.

With his team trailing closely behind him, Khalidi drove to Sam's Steakhouse. Once there, Justice excused herself to the ladies' room to put in the earpiece.

"You there?" she mumbled, testing it.

"Yeah, but listen, do you have your watch on?" Chance asked.

"No, it's in my bag."

"There's a camera inside it. Put it on."

"Alright. Now let me get back to the table," Justice said.

Khalidi had already ordered drinks for them.

"I see you don't like to waste any time," Justice remarked snidely while taking a seat.

"Not with you. So tell me about yourself."

"What do you wanna know?"

"Everything," he replied and waited.

"You can't know everything. That spoils the fun," she told him, then took a sip from the glass of water.

"Whatever you do, Justice, don't drink the wine. He might've spiked it," Chance warned her.

Khalidi was about to respond, when one of his boys came over and whispered something in his ear. Khalidi acknowledged him with a nod and then signaled his entourage to the door.

"Excuse me for a second," he said before standing up from the table.

As he went over to talk to his boys, Justice sat there shaking inside. She wanted to talk to Chance, but she knew all eyes were on her.

"I'm here. I can see everything. You're doing great. But, be careful. This guy is nothing to fuck with," Chance stated, trying to keep Justice both calm and on point.

Justice cleared her thoughts, and moments later, Khalidi returned.

"Sorry about that."

"Something wrong?" she asked.

"Nothing I can't handle."

For the next couple of hours, Justice and Khalidi got acquainted. Surprisingly, he was the perfect gentleman, and after lunch, he drove Justice straight to the airport.

"Can I see you again?" he asked.

"I don't know. Do you have any more parties planned?"

Khalidi busted out laughing. "You're one of a kind. You know that?" he said, then pressed his body up against hers.

Aroused, Justice took a deep breath. "I know."

He looked into her eyes, leaned down, and kissed her passionately. She wanted to turn her head, but had to admit she was attracted to him. Lost in the moment, Justice pressed her body up against him more while rubbing his back.

"Come home with me," he moaned.

"I can't. I have to work."

"What they are paying you I'll double."

That comment brought Justice back to her senses. He was the enemy, a man who raped and sold children. He had killed Patra. Suddenly, her lust turned into rage, and she glared at him.

"I thought I told you I'm not for sale." She pushed him off of her.

Khalidi backed up, nodding his head. "You're right. I just thought we had something."

"In one day?" Justice sucked her teeth and grabbed her bags. "Thank you for lunch and for the flowers," she told him, then started to walk away.

Khalidi reached out for her hand. "I'm sorry. I didn't mean to disrespect you, Justice. Can I at least see you again?"

Justice pondered for a second while staring at him. "Don't think so," she finally replied and then strutted away.

Smiling to himself, Khalidi watched Justice until she was out of sight. She wasn't aware of it, but Khalidi planned to win her heart.

*****

Whew! Justice thought, glad to be back home.

"Hey," she said, speaking to the ladies who were still tuned in through the earpiece.

"Nasty girl," Chance and Seven teased after witnessing via the camera watch what had happened between Khalidi and Justice.

Justice laughed. "That wasn't supposed to happen. He just shoved his tongue down my throat," she explained in her defense.

"Yeah, sure he did!" Seven said, giggling. Then an alert popped up on the system, and Seven opened it. "Hey, guys, they're running a name search on Justice," she informed them.

Just like Chance thought, Khalidi was running a background check on her to make sure she wasn't an agent. Once she cleared, he would pursue her. The question was, for what?

"Oh my God! For real?" Justice said.

"Don't worry. I got this," Seven told her, intercepting the alert.

"Justice, for the next couple of weeks Khalidi is gonna have you followed," Chance said.

"You think so?"

"Yes, because he's interested in you."

"Yeah, he wants some of that Bajan pussy," Seven blurted out, causing them to laugh.

"It's important that you act normal," Chance added. "Keep your earrings on and your earpiece in at all times."

"Alright, but let's talk more later, because right now, I'm tired as hell," Justice replied.

"Later, girl," Seven and Chance said in unison before disconnecting the surveillance equipment.

Again, Chance was right. Khalidi conducted a full investigation on Justice. Once he got the green light, he flew out to Atlanta to see her. Justice had just started her shift at her second job at the Marriott when Khalidi checked in.

Khalidi held a few meetings and checked on a few brothels before calling it a night. He was walking through the lobby when he spotted Justice talking to a co-worker. His first intention was to walk over to her, but something told him to wait. Although the background came back clean, he wanted to make sure she didn't have a man. So, for the next couple of days, he watched her, becoming familiar with her daily routine. She worked out in the morning before going to work. She went to school on the weekends, and in her free time, she studied. Her life was simple; something like his life was before The Secret Society ruined it.

Justice had just come back from her daily run, when Khalidi pulled up on her.

"Can I work out with you?" he joked.

Trying to catch her breath, Justice replied, "Don't think you could keep up."

"Maybe not, but I would love to try," he said, getting out the rental car.

He's such a womanizer, she thought while standing with her arms folded. "So you found me?" she asked him, already knowing the answer.

"Yes, I did."

"Very good. Now what?" she said.

Dying to touch her again, Khalidi walked over to Justice, gently grabbed her by the waist, and brushed a couple of hairs from off her face.

"Now this," he said before kissing her.

Justice wanted to fight it, but he was too sexy to resist.

*****

Sleeping with the enemy, she thought. The past couple of weeks Justice didn't know if she was coming or going. Khalidi was wonderful; he treated her like a queen. He was smart, sexy, and oh, the sex. He was the only man who ever made her cum. In truth, Justice was falling for him, but she wasn't the only one head over heels. Khalidi had fallen madly in love with Justice and was even thinking about marriage in their future.

That evening, Khalidi sent a private jet to pick Justice up so they could have a romantic dinner in one of his many houses. This was unlike him since he never brought anyone to his home, and his entourage thought it was a bad idea. One of his close confidants felt Khalidi was slipping and worried the bosses would find out. But, there wasn't much he could do about the situation since Khalidi was *his* boss.

Justice arrived wearing a long, strapless, flowing dress. Her sandy blonde hair was pulled back with a headband. Khalidi watched as his henchmen escorted her in.

Damn, she looks good than a motherfucker, he thought before giving her a kiss and saying, "You look sexy, as always."

"Hello, handsome."

"Shall we?" he said, and then led her further into the house.

"Do you think this house is big enough?" she jokingly asked.

"Why, you want something bigger?"

Justice laughed. "No. I used to clean houses like this."

Khalidi swung her around. "Well, if I have anything to say about it, you will never clean another house again."

Cuddling as they waited for dinner to arrive, Khalidi gazed into Justice's eyes and asked, "Where have you been all my life?"

Justice blushed but stayed quiet.

"I'm serious," he said.

"What do you mean?"

Khalidi continued to stare, which made Justice a little uneasy. How could he trust her when he barely knew her? His mind was telling him no, but his heart and dick said yes.

"If only I had met you years ago."

"Why, what happened years ago?" Justice asked, seeking more information.

Khalidi hesitated for a second. "Let's just say I would be in a different line of work."

Justice nodded. "What is it that you do?"

"Work," he vaguely replied.

"Working doing what? Only rappers and athletes live like this," she stated.

"You didn't know I play for the Lakers," he joked, making both of them laugh.

One of his workers came in and whispered something in his ear. Khalidi kissed Justice on the cheek before excusing himself.

"Justice," Chance said, scaring the shit out of her because she forgot about the earpiece. "Justice, you need to listen to me. Ramon and Daniel just arrived."

Sipping her wine, Justice almost choked. She looked around, and while trying not to move her lips, she said, "What?"

"Yes, they just arrived. Stay put," Chance instructed.

Trembling, Justice wanted to leave. Seven and Patience noticed her fear.

"Just calm down. Okay?" Patience told her.

Justice nodded in a subdued way.

In the other room, the bosses discussed Khalidi's relationship.

"Did we interrupt?" Ramon asked.

Scared himself, Khalidi replied, "No, never."

"Is everything set for the auction?" Daniel inquired.

"Yes."

"Oh, it is? Because I'm hearing something else. I heard someone else is occupying your time," Daniel spitefully said.

Khalidi shot him a nasty look. *Damn, I can't get no pussy without someone being all up in my business*, he thought, but replied, "I'm a man with needs, if that's what you mean. Not to worry, though. Everything is covered."

Ramon was a no-nonsense person who didn't like bullshit, and he sensed some from Khalidi.

"Is she here?" Ramon asked.

"Who?" Khalidi responded, knowing he was referring to Justice.

"The pussy that has your nose open, motherfucker. That's who," Daniel snapped.

"Oh, yes…she's in the other room," Khalidi answered, signaling one of his boys to go and get her.

He didn't want Justice to be subjected to this asshole, but he knew if he refused, he and Justice were both dead.

"May I offer y'all a drink while we wait?" Khalidi asked, trying to ease the tension in the room

"Sure," the two men answered.

The room froze once Justice entered. Daniel and Ramon were having a sidebar conversation, but both lost their train of thought upon laying eyes on her. An uncomfortable Justice stood there fidgeting, trying not to make eye contact with any of them.

"Justice, unfold your arms so we can get a nice view of them," Seven said, referring to the camera in Justice's watch.

"And stop fidgeting," Chance added.

"So you're the lady that's winning Khalidi's heart?" Daniel said.

Justice looked at Khalidi and smiled nervously. Although she tried hard not to look at them, she felt them undressing her with their eyes.

How can a woman that beautiful be with someone like Khalidi? Daniel thought. Ramon, on the other hand, was always stinkin' thinking. *Yes, she's beautiful, but something ain't right.* He felt like they needed to put some eyes on her.

As for Khalidi, he felt humiliated. He knew they were checking her out and not because they wanted her to work on the street. They wanted her for their personal pleasure. He wanted to say something, but knew better. After a couple minutes of taking her in with their eyes, Ramon dismissed her.

On her way out, Arty followed her back to the private room. "You may have my man open, but I'm not gonna let you ruin what we've built," he told her.

"Khalidi is a big boy," she shot back.

Once Justice knew she was alone, she mumbled, "Guys, I need–"

"I'm already on it," Seven said. "I'm pulling up Arty's background now."

After a short pause, Chance read the information off his rap sheet.

"Justice, he's a small-town punk. His name is Arty Holmes. He's been busted a few times for petty stuff and has been friends with Khalidi for years. Khalidi brought him in. His mother still lives in the Marcy Projects. He's a nobody. He's just trying to scare you."

This was still all a little too much for Justice, who wanted to get the hell out of there. *Fuck this plan. I'm not about to lose my life over this,* she thought, while pacing the floor as she tried to think of how she could leave.

"Justice, you need to calm down. If you don't, they're gonna know something is up. Pour yourself a glass of wine and relax," Patience told her.

"She's doing it again. She's gonna fuckin' blow it," Seven said in the background.

Following Patience's advice, Justice took a deep breath, poured herself something to drink, and sat on the couch.

"Hey, I'm sorry about that," Khalidi said, entering the room.

Justice stood up to greet him. "It's fine, but maybe I should go."

Khalidi kissed her. "No. I just forgot about this business meeting. It's no big thing."

"You sure? Because we can reschedule."

Khalidi was pissed at Ramon and Daniel. He knew he was slipping, but Justice had him open. While still apologizing for what just happened, he pulled Justice to him and kissed her lustfully. Taking a second for a breath, Khalidi walked her into the other room.

Wrestling with the many emotions building up inside her, she whispered, "Khalidi…"

Ignoring her protest, he kissed her again, this time squeezing her tighter. Justice could feel his dick pressing up against her. Her nipples hardened as she sized him up. It had been a while since she felt the genuine touch of a man. Even though he was a monster in her eyes, he felt like an angel in her arms. *This is it,* she thought as he lifted her up and sat her on the table. Without saying a word, he slowly started to remove her clothing.

Nervous, Justice moaned, "Oh, Khalidi…"

Khalidi paused, then walked over to lower the lights.

"No!" Justice exclaimed. "I wanna see."

With the lights turned up, she could see why he was such a cocky bastard, and at least she could see it coming if he wanted to kill her. Shaking the negative thought, she pulled her dress over her head.

"Damn," Khalidi said, admiring Justice's breasts and then attacking them as if they were his last meal.

His dick was so hard he couldn't think straight. He figured if he was going to die, it might as well be over some good pussy. Gaining momentum from his thoughts, Khalidi removed his shirt, revealing a fresh white wifebeater, and flexed for Justice. She let out a sexy giggle, letting him know she was definitely impressed. Once he took off his pants , his dick busted through the opening of his boxers. Justice jumped down off the table, pulled his dick over the top of his boxers , and while looking him dead in the eyes, she started to deep throat his nine-inch dick like she was a snake swallowing a large animal. Khalidi's knees grew weak, and he put his hand on her shoulder to catch his balance.

"Mmm," he moaned, while looking down at Justice.

Deeply inhaling the scent of his cologne, she teased the top of his dick with her tongue and then deep throat it once more before he pulled her up to meet his tongue. As he rubbed her ass with one hand, he stuck the fingers of his other hand in her ass. She flinched, but Khalidi soothed her by grinding against her with his dick, finally meeting her freshly shaved pussy. He was ready to turn Justice out.

As Justice stood there with her panties and bra still on, Khalidi told her to spin around for him. Stroking his dick, he watched her admiringly, impressed with her choice of lingerie.

"Take it off," Khalidi instructed as he licked his lips, anticipating fucking the shit out of her.

As Justice happily obliged, she thought about his entire dick going in and out of her. Fully undressed now, she began to feel awkward as Khalidi stood watching her. So, she covered her breasts by folding her arms over them, but he walked over and pulled her hands down until they were touching his dick.

"Rub it," he demanded. "Don't be scared. He won't bite."

Smiling at his comment, Justice dropped back down to her knees and began sucking his dick as if in a contest. Lost in euphoria, Khalidi stopped her before it was too late. Justice stood up, seductively wiped her lips, and finished taking him to heaven by riding him.

Meanwhile, while watching via satellite, Chance, Seven, and Patience were concerned about Justice's safety. She was alone and inexperienced.

"I'm worried about Justice," Patience stated.

"Me, too," Seven said, monitoring their site.

Thinking, Chance just nodded.

"Do you think this Arty guy is a threat?" Patience asked.

"I don't know," Chance replied in a daze. "I really don't know."

*****

It was two o'clock in the morning when Khalidi got the call about one of his girls working with the police. He ordered them to bring her to his house.

"What's wrong?" Justice moaned, still half asleep.

"Nothing, baby. Go back to sleep," he told her while getting dressed.

By the time Khalidi got downstairs, there were two young girls in the yard. The girls were so scared that they were trembling like a leaf on a tree.

"Daddy," one of the girls cried, while the other girl stared down at the ground.

"What happened?" Khalidi asked.

"One of the tricks was a cop. He told me if I didn't give him a free one, he was gonna arrest me. So I did, but he still arrested me," she explained.

Justice heard voices coming from outside, so she got up to look out the window. Standing there were two girls, Arty, another guy, and Khalidi, who was yelling at one of the girls. Khalidi started to walk away, but then stopped, picked up a pipe that was on the ground, and knocked the shit out of the girl. He hit her so hard that she fell into the pool.

"Stupid bitch," he said while walking away.

Stunned, Justice put her hand over her mouth to keep from screaming. The girl wasn't moving; her body just floated in the water.

"Boss, what about this one?" Arty asked.

"That's your call," Khalidi replied before entering the house.

Justice wanted to continue watching, but didn't want Khalidi to catch her. So, she jumped back into the bed and pretended to be sleeping. After a few minutes had passed without him returning to the bedroom, she got up to go look for him. Instead of going back to sleep, Khalidi had decided to get some work done. Just as he was about to log on the site, Justice walked up behind him.

"Are you gonna come back to bed?" she moaned, planting a wet kiss on his ear.

Khalidi grinned. "Yeah, in a minute. I just need to check on something."

He was about to log on, but stopped when he noticed Justice watching. She laughed before turning to face the other way.

However, she stood at an angle and wrapped her arms around herself in a way that the ladies could see the username and password. She waited a couple of seconds, making sure the watch's camera captured everything. She then went to lie back down. Moments later, Khalidi joined her, and they made love all night long.

Khalidi wasn't the only one who couldn't sleep. Chance felt something was wrong, so she reopened the Secret Society file. She noticed a pattern of Ramon and Daniel always meeting with a lieutenant one last time before hiring someone to kill them. Therefore, she knew Khalidi was in danger. Chance woke Seven and Patience.

"What's up?" Seven asked.

"I think Ramon and Daniel are gonna kill Khalidi."

"What!" Seven exclaimed.

"What's going on?" Patience asked, entering the room.

"The Secret Society, they're gonna kill Khalidi," Chance explained again.

"We have to get Justice out of there," Patience stated.

"I know," Chance said.

"But how?" Patience asked.

"Wait. What if we're wrong?" Seven said. "What would make you think that, Chance? Did anything happen last night? Did Justice say something?"

"No, but I haven't checked the site," Chance responded.

"Then we may be jumping the gun." Seven logged in to retrieve the data from Justice's watch. "Chance, look at this," Seven said. "Justice recorded Khalidi's username and password."

"Get the fuck outta here!" Patience ran over to the computer.

Immediately, Seven hacked into their system and almost passed out. They were having an auction in Las Vegas, but they were not selling cars. They were selling human beings, and over a hundred pimps and pedophiles were invited to attend.

"We need to go to the police," Patience said.

"No!" Chance snapped. "Where is it being held, Seven?"

"It doesn't say, but it's gonna be held outside of Vegas."

Chance nodded. "Seven, find out the exact location. Ladies, we're going shopping."

"We're not going to the police?" Patience asked.

"For what! So they can get off on some legal technicality? Fuck that!" Chance replied.

"I agree with Chance, Patience. The law doesn't always work in favor of those who are innocent. Look at you," Seven commented.

Patience sighed. They were right; Byron was a perfect example. "So what's the plan?"

"First, we have to warn Justice," Chance stated.

*****

Khalidi was gone by the time Justice woke up, but he left a gift box with a note.

Sexy,
Had a meeting to attend. Make yourself at home.

Love ya,
K

Justice opened the box to find a diamond tennis bracelet inside. In awe, she smiled.

"Justice," Chance said, scaring her. "If you can hear me, cough."

As instructed, she replied by coughing two times.

"Listen, we need to see you."

Justice looked around the room. She wasn't sure if she was being watched. Therefore, she didn't answer. Instead, she went into the bathroom, closed the door, and turned the water on.

"Is everything okay?"

"Yes. When are you leaving?" Chance asked her.

"Tonight. Why?"

"Alright. We're flying in to Atlanta tonight. We're gonna stay at the Marriot."

"Okay. See ya there."

At Khalidi's request, Justice made herself at home. She lounged around watching TV and reading magazines. Hungry, she went downstairs to get something to eat, when Arty walked up on her again.

"It's a step up from washing dishes, huh?" he said.

"Excuse me?"

"You heard me. You were a server at that other party."

"I don't know what you're talking about. Khalidi pursued me…"

"Yeah, yeah, bitch. I know your type. I just didn't think my boy would go for it."

Pissed off, Justice responded, "Funny you're worrying about Khalidi. Maybe your wish is to be the one in his bed instead of me. You look like a bati boy."

Insulted by her remark, Arty slammed her against the refrigerator. "I should pull out my dick and have you suck it, you fucking whore." He backed away. "Yeah, that's what I'm gonna do. See why my man is so open," he griped while unbuttoning his pants.

Justice tried to leave the kitchen, but Arty grabbed her.

"Where the fuck are you going? You're gonna suck this dick."

"Get off of me!" Justice screamed, pushing him away from her and slapping the shit out of him.

"You stupid bitch!" Arty yelled, and then punched Justice in the face. "Are you fucking crazy?" He hit her again, this time knocking her to the floor, and kicked her. "Fucking bitch!"

As Justice laid balled up in a fetal position, Arty grabbed her up by her hair and was about to strike her again when Khalidi came in.

"What the fuck?" Khalidi charged Arty, putting him in a headlock until he released Justice's hair. "Get the fuck off of her!" he yelled as he tossed him across the room. "Fight me!

Fight me, nigga!" Khalidi knocked the shit out of Arty. "Fight me, you bitch!" he screamed and then hit him again.

On the floor, Arty begged Khalidi to stop, but Khalidi kept stomping him. He would've stomped him to death if it hadn't been for the other workers stopping him.

"Khalidi, chill!" they screamed in unison, trying to calm their boss.

Winded and tired, Khalidi gasped for breath. "Get that piece of shit out of my house before I kill him."

Arty was lucky. If it were anyone else, Khalidi would've put a bullet in their head. Justice had already left the room to nurse her wounds. She had a black and blue ring around her swollen eye and a busted lip. Her ribs were sore, and she swore they were broken.

Khalidi knocked on the bathroom door. "Baby, are you okay?"

Justice opened the door. "I wanna go home," she cried.

Seeing the damage inflicted upon Justice, Khalidi wanted to kill Arty. He reached out to embrace her.

"I'm sorry, baby. He will never do that again."

Still crying, she fell into his arms. "Please, just take me home."

"What happened?" he asked, while trying to comfort her. "He's never acted like this before."

"He saw me at the other party. I was a servant there," she explained through her tears. "He said I planned all of this…to be with you. But, I didn't. I swear, Khalidi," she said, then started crying harder into his chest.

"I know. I know you didn't. I didn't even see you at the last party."

Khalidi wanted Justice to stay. However, after what had just happened, and after Ramon and Daniel's bullshit last night, he didn't feel it was safe to take any more chances.

*****

After Justice left, Khalidi went to check on Arty. Something was up, and he needed to get some answers. When Khalidi entered the room, he saw that Arty's face looked worse than Justice's.

"You alright?" Khalidi asked.

"I'll live," Arty snidely responded, then took a sip of Courvoisier.

Khalidi stared at Arty. He could tell he was hurt and not just from the ass whooping.

"Arty, talk to me. Why did you attack Justice like that?"

"I don't trust her."

"Is there something you're not telling me? Because we did a background check on her, and she came up clean."

"Nah, Khalidi. Come on, man. She's a server for a catering company."

"So? Just because she's a maid, I can't date her?"

"I'm not saying that, but you can have any bitch in the world," Arty stressed. "Why her? She's beautiful and all, but the fact is she's still a fuckin' server."

Khalidi stared at Arty and his other men who were nodding their heads in agreement. "So all of you feel like this?" he yelled.

"I agree with Arty, boss. She's bad as fuck, but she's beneath you," one of his henchmen commented, expressing his opinion.

For the first time, Khalidi realized who he had around him. *These niggas don't care about me. They only care about what I represent. If it wasn't for me, half of these motherfuckers would be dead or in jail. In fact, half of these niggas were dead, the walking dead. How dare they look down on Justice because she's a server?*

Khalidi nodded. "So just because she's a server she isn't good enough? Niggas, do you know what we do for a living? Who we are? For someone like Justice to even look at me is a blessing. I don't give a fuck what she does for a living, I love her, and if any of you disrespect her, I will kill you. Y'all niggas are talking all this shit, but at least I don't fall in love with hoes," Khalidi grumbled before walking out.

*****

The icepack reduced a lot of the swelling, but it was still black and blue. Justice applied some foundation to cover it up. She thought about calling out, but her manager had already warned her about her time off.

It was a typical day at the bank, until one of Khalidi's henchmen came and talked to the manager. Moments after he left, the manager called Justice into his office and offered her a managerial position. If that were anyone else, they would've been thrilled, but knowing the reason for the promotion, Justice respectfully declined. While the thought was sweet, Justice didn't need Khalidi's help.

This is becoming a bit much, she thought. So, she planned to sit down with the other women and tell them how she felt.

Later that evening, Seven used a fake name and credit card to book the room in case someone was watching. Justice had just clocked in and started her regular routine as a housekeeper.

Knock! Knock!

"Housekeeping," Justice announced. "You called for housekeeping?" she said when Patience opened the door.

Once inside, Chance asked her, "What the fuck happened to your face?"

"Arty attacked me."

"What! What did Khalidi do?" Seven asked.

"Beat his ass," Justice replied. "So what's up? What do you have to tell me?"

"It turns out that Khalidi is having his yearly human auction."

"Auction?" Justice looked confused by Chance's statement.

"Yes, an auction. He's invited pimps, pedophiles, and any other crazy motherfucker to come and bid on the kids he has kidnapped," Chance informed her.

"What?" Justice said, still in shock.

"Yes," Seven responded.

"How do you know this?" Justice asked, causing them to give her the side eye.

"We've seen it. We retrieved the information from your watch and got his user name and password," Seven stated.

"Oh," Justice mumbled

"Just, what's wrong," Chance asked, sensing something was wrong.

"She fell in love with him. That's what's wrong," Seven blurted out.

Justice rolled her eyes at Seven's comment, but didn't deny it. In fact, it was true. Although viewed as a monster, Khalidi showed her a different side.

"Is it true? Are you falling in love with him?" Patience asked.

Justice lowered her head.

"Are you fuckin' kidding me? You get some dick and fall in love." Seven sucked her teeth in disgust.

"Justice..." Patience said, sounding worried.

"It's true. She can't even answer us," Seven exclaimed in a furious tone. "That motherfucker's organization had your cousin killed! He rapes little kids and then puts them out on the fucking street to work, you dumb bitch! How can you fall in love with a nigga like that?"

"Fuck you, Seven! Who are you to judge me or him?"

"Arty should've knocked some sense into your ass," Seven snapped.

"Why don't you come over here and do it?" Justice shot back.

"Bitch, you don't want none of this! You see this shit?" she said, looking around at the others. "The bitch said *me or him* like they're married. I knew this bitch was weak," Seven stated. "Get a little piece of dick and don't know how to act. I hope your dumb ass used condoms, silly bitch."

Justice charged at Seven and tried to take her head off. Chance and Patience had to get in between them.

"Come on, bitch, so I can show you what a real ass whooping feels like!"

"Fuck you, you dyke bitch!" Justice yelled in her strong Bajan accent.

Holding Seven back, Chance yelled, "Everyone calm down! Calm the fuck down! Seven, chill out. You guys are gonna get all of us killed."

"Chance is right," Patience agreed, holding Justice back.

"Justice, talk to us," Chance said, wanting to get to the bottom of this.

"What's there to tell? I can't lie. I do care about him. I know he's the bad guy, but I can't help how my heart feels. That doesn't mean I'm gonna let him get away with it." Justice sighed. "I don't know, Chance. My mind is all screwed up."

Chance nodded. She knew this could happen. It wasn't uncommon for assassins to fall in love with their targets. "So what do you wanna do?" she asked Justice, while taking a seat on the bed.

"Right now, I don't know. But, I'm not gonna let you girls down."

Everyone took a deep breath. This wasn't a part of the plan. Depending on how deeply Justice felt about Khalidi, it could blow their entire plan.

"Justice, I can't tell you what to do. I just want you to be careful. I got a strong feeling Arty isn't done with you," Chance warned.

"I know. Khalidi beat him up real bad."

"That shit was a front. Them niggas are probably drinking and laughing at this shit. You have a lot to learn. Money over bitches! Don't they teach you that in London?" Seven snidely asked.

"What about the auction?" Patience inquired, turning their attention back to the pressing matter at hand. "What are we gonna do about that?"

"It's a couple of months away, so we have time," Chance answered.

"You mean we can't do anything because this bitch might blow us up," Seven said, starting back up again.

"Fuck you! I'm sticking to the plan. I'm just going through something right now."

This isn't good, Chance thought. *She needs time to get her mind together.*

"The best thing right now is to pull you out," Chance stated.

"What!" Justice yelled. "What do you mean pull me out? Come on, Chance. Do you think I would turn on you guys?"

"Not willingly, but, Justice, you fell for the target. How can we be sure you're on our side? If they find out anything, we'll all be dead. If Khalidi finds out, do you think he won't kill you?" Chance pointed out. "Pull back. Give yourself some time to get your head straight. It's the best thing for all of us."

Justice glared at them. "So, in the meantime, do I see him or not?"

"It's up to you. It's also up to you if you wanna wear the wire and earpiece. Personally, I would wear it so we can track them, especially since Arty is after you."

Standing with her arms folded, Justice thought about what Chance just said. She did have a point. Right now, she wasn't thinking clearly, and the last thing she wanted to do was put the girls' lives at risk.

"Alright, I will pull back a little. I'll still wear the earpiece just in case, though. I'll make up some excuse about not wanting to see him. But, I want it to go on record that I never planned for this to happen, and I would never cross you guys."

"We know," Patience and Chance answered. Seven, on the other hand, glared at her. At that moment, she wasn't feeling Justice.

Chance changed out Justice's spy devices just in case someone was watching her. With these guys, it's the little things they noticed. After taking one last look at the ladies, Justice left.

As they watched her leave, Seven asked, "What do you think?"

"Only time will tell," Chance responded.

"What if she crosses us?" Patience said.

"Then we kill her. Fuck it!" Seven exclaimed.

CHAPTER 7
WWW.JEREMIAH.COM

While Justice took a step back from things, the ladies worked on a plan for Jeremiah. Jeremiah Samuels was different from Khalidi; he didn't trust anyone. He had that "don't fuck with me" attitude. He was forty years old and raised in the streets of Brooklyn. Coldhearted, he didn't have a problem killing anyone. To him, women weren't anything but hoes and tricks. They only served one purpose, and that was to bear children and make money. Patience was about to make him eat those words.

Jeremiah wasn't flashy or boisterous. He felt being those things only brought unneeded attention to a person. For him, a pair of Timbs, some jeans, and a crisp button-up was good enough for him. He only wore a suit for business meetings and exclusive parties. Jeremiah rode around in a bulletproof black SUV with six heavily armed men. When not being chauffeured, he drove a black Acura Legend Coupe fully loaded with secret compartments.

Jeremiah was a loner. When he wasn't conducting business, he preferred to be by himself. Having several luxury apartments throughout the state, he spent most of his time at one of his homes in Arizona with his twin boys, who he was raising after having killed their mother. She was a stripper he had been involved with. One night in his drunken state, he forgot to bag it up and became pissed off when she announced she was pregnant. When he told her to have an abortion, she refused. After the DNA confirmed they were his children, Jeremiah stepped up. He moved them into a nice house, bought her a car, and provided her with a monthly allowance. Her only responsibility was to take care of the kids. Once a hoe always a hoe, though. When Jeremiah found out she was fucking dudes in the house where he was paying the rent, and while his kids were in the other room, she had to go. So, Jeremiah drove up to the house, shot her in the head, took his kids, and never looked back.

In his line of work, Jeremiah didn't take any chances, especially with Ramon and Daniel. Those motherfuckers would kill their own mother and father if they ever thought about crossing them. That's why Jeremiah made sure all of his ducks were in a row. He needed to be around to watch his kids grow up.

Today, he was attending a pharmaceutical seminar in Chicago. Ramon and Daniel thought they should start recruiting more doctors and pharmacist since the ones they had were starting to get greedy. Patience, who volunteered for one of the companies once she knew Jeremiah would be at the seminar, stood there handing out pamphlets. Unlike Justice, Patience took the time to study the women in Jeremiah's life. He was straightforward and liked his women to be the same way.

"Would you like a pamphlet?" Patience asked him.

"Sure. Thank you," Jeremiah replied without bothering to look at her before walking away.

During the seminar, Patience watched Jeremiah from afar. He had three bodyguards with him, and he didn't interact with people much. When he did, the conversation was brief.

Patience was in the cafeteria when Jeremiah walked in with some food from the buffet.

"Is someone sitting here?" he asked in deep voice.

"No…no," Patience said, while pretending to read a magazine.

As Jeremiah texted away on his BlackBerry, he noticed the name of the magazine.

"You like reading that?" Jeremiah jokingly asked, referring to the *Source Magazine* in her hand.

Pretending to be embarrassed, Patience looked away. "Guilty pleasure."

"Nah, I like that, too," he stated. "Who's on the cover?"

"Rick Ross…Rosa," she sang.

Jeremiah laughed. "Let me find out you like Rick Ross."

"I'm selling dope straight off my iPhone," she said, spitting the lyrics from one of his songs. "Yes, I think he's nice."

Jeremiah bopped his head to her words and laughed again before introducing himself. "Jeremiah."

"Patience Green," she said, extending her hand.

"You come here often?"

"Sometimes. I like learning about new medicines since I can no longer practice."

"You're a doctor?" he asked.

"I use to be, but that's a long story."

"Oh, so which company you work for?"

"None. I'm just volunteering for the people who are giving the seminar."

"Why?" he inquired.

"I get to travel for free, meet good people, and the food is great," she replied.

After lunch, Jeremiah went back to the seminar, and he didn't say another word to Patience. As part of the plan, Patience stayed in the same hotel as Jeremiah. As she dined alone in the hotel's restaurant, Jeremiah came in with his crew and posted up by the bar. Patience was leaving when Jeremiah spotted her.

"Rosa," he sang.

Patience turned around, waved, and kept walking. Jeremiah was about to let her go, but his boys were telling him to holla at her.

"Yo, you see the ass on her? Dawg, you better go holla at that," they teased.

It didn't help Patience had on some boyfriend ripped up jeans, a wife beater tank, a blazer and some six inches pumps. Her hair pulled off her face with a clip.

Jeremiah hesitated for a second. Hollering at chicks in public wasn't his style. Then he thought, *Fuck it. Who knows? Maybe I'll get some pussy tonight.* That's when Jeremiah got up and went after her.

"Excuse me," he called out to her.

Patience turned around, batting her eyes. "Patience," she said, reminding him of her name.

"Yes, Patience." He smiled. "What's up? You wanna go have a drink?"

"Nah, I'm kinda tired. Maybe some other time," she told him and then started walking away.

Jeremiah looked back at his boys, who were signaling him to go after her.

"Patience, come on. We can talk about Rick Ross," he said charmingly.

Patience laughed. "Alright."

They went to a local Chicago club, and once inside, Jeremiah headed straight to the VIP section. When a crowd started to gather, he fell back from talking with Patience. Despite her being the prettiest chick there, he didn't talk to females in public. Patience didn't seem to be bothered by his change in attitude because the plan was already in motion. After having one drink with him, she called it a night.

Back at the hotel, Patience checked her earpiece. "Hey, are y'all there?"

"Yes," they answered in unison.

"Is he gay?" Seven asked. "Because he's tough."

Patience giggled. "I don't think so. I just think he's cautious."

Just then, several knocks interrupted their conversation.

"Wait. Someone's at my door," Patience told them. She looked through the peephole and saw Jeremiah standing there. "Oh shit, it's him," she whispered, informing the ladies.

"Hey," she said upon opening the door.

"I wanted to make sure you got to your room safely," he said.

"How did you know which room I was staying in?"

"I have my ways," he said, flashing a sexy grin.

Apprehensive, Patience gave a half grin in response. "Well, thanks. It got kinda crowded, so I just made an exit."

Jeremiah laughed. "Yeah, it did. Well, a'ight. You gonna be at the seminar tomorrow, right?"

"Yep, handing out pamphlets."

"Maybe we can have lunch tomorrow."

"Maybe," Patience repeated.

*****

The next day, Patience and Jeremiah didn't have lunch. Instead, he invited her to dinner. Over dinner, they laughed and talked about how bored they were at the seminar. Jeremiah lied, claiming he was an investor who invested in pharmaceuticals. Patience chose to tell him the truth about her being an ex-doctor, but left out the part about Byron and The Secret Society. She noticed how Jeremiah's eyes lit up when she shared this information with him. He pulled out his BlackBerry to type a message.

"Jeremiah just asked them to run a background check on your name," Seven informed her through the earpiece.

Patience wasn't worried, though. She had lost her license due to malpractice, and she hadn't mentioned Byron's name.

Throughout the evening, Jeremiah kept checking his phone, waiting for Patience's background to come back. Just like Khalidi, once he got the okay, he would press her some more and offer her a job.

"So where do you live?" he asked.

"Maryland," she said.

"By yourself?" he inquired.

Patience laughed. "What's up with all the questions? Are you gonna do an article on me or something?"

Jeremiah laughed along with her. She was on point, and he liked that about her. "Nah, I'm just making conversation."

Patience sipped her drink. "Well, let me make it short and sweet for you. My mother is white and worked at a correctional facility, where an inmate who she was having an affair with impregnated her. Because he was black, she gave me up for adoption. So, I spent my childhood and teenage years in and out of foster homes. Despite all that, I managed to finish school, get my degree, and become a doctor, but lost it all over some sick dick and a promise."

Jeremiah was speechless at her bluntness and thought he was the only one who had it rough growing up. All he could manage to say was, "Damn."

Patience reached across the table to touch his hand. "It's cool. I finally learned the truth and even got to spend time with my father before he passed."

He wanted to share his life story with her, but it was too soon. "So will you ever get back into the medical field?"

"Only if I can perform the duties as a doctor. Other than that I have no desire. Why?"

"Just curious."

"What about you? What's your story?" she asked.

Jeremiah looked around and then replied, "Maybe one day you'll find out."

A few minutes later, Jeremiah had to leave, but he made sure he got Patience's contact information.

A couple weeks had gone by and Patience was about to give up, when she received a text message from Jeremiah asking her if she was busy. When she replied no, seconds later her cell phone rang.

"Hello?" she answered.

"Yo, come outside," he instructed.

"Huh?"

"I'm outside of your house. Come out."

Patience jumped out of bed and looked out the window. Sure enough a black SUV was parked right outside of her house. "Boy, have you lost your mind?"

"A little. Now, are you coming out or what?"

"Can I get dressed? Thank you!" She struggled to throw on some clothes.

Not sure if Jeremiah had tapped her phone, she put on her earpiece and watch, and prayed Chance and Seven were watching.

Chance was sleeping, but Seven was awake and reading up on Zhang.

Still unsure if her house was safe, Patience started singing Diana Ross' "I'm Coming Out".

"I'm here," Seven said, letting her know that she was monitoring everything.

When Patience stepped outside, Jeremiah, who was standing in front of his SUV like a boss, greeted her.

Dressed in jeans, a button-down blazer, and some Timbs, he smiled and said, "Let's talk."

Apprehensive, she paused and looked over at his henchmen before asking, "Where?"

Jeremiah noticed her nervousness and laughed. "You're good, ma. I just want us to go someplace private and talk."

"Okay."

A short while later, they were pulling up to a strip club and entered through the back door. Jeremiah told his men to go enjoy themselves while he kicked it with Patience. A server came over to offer him something to drink, but Jeremiah declined. As for Patience, she wasn't drinking anything until she knew what was going on.

"Is this some kinda joke, bringing me here to a strip joint?"

Jeremiah looked at the girl on stage shaking her ass, then turned and faced Patience. "Nah, ma. I conduct my business in different places. That's just me."

"So this is a business meeting?"

Jeremiah licked his lips. "Why, you want it to be more?"

Patience couldn't front. After watching Khalidi put it on Justice, she was curious to see if Jeremiah could deliver the same thing.

"No. I just hope you're not gonna ask me to get up there and shake my ass."

Jeremiah laughed. "Not yet."

"Don't bet your life on it. So what's up?"

While stretching his legs, Jeremiah signaled for one of the waiters, and after placing his drink order, he asked her, "You want something?"

"No thanks," she replied. The only thing Patience wanted was to get the fuck out that place that smelled like smoke and sweaty pussy.

"I wanna offer you a job."

"Doing what?" Patience asked.

"I'm setting up some pharmaceutical companies in Maryland and DC, and I want you to run them for me."

"I told you I'm not a pharmacist"

"You don't have to be. Just run my operation for me," Jeremiah said, staring her down.

Patience stared right back at him. "You're serious?"

After taking a sip of his drink, he replied, "One thing you will learn about me is that I'm serious about my sons and my money. So what's up? Are you gonna work for me or not?"

"Well, can I think about it?" she asked.

"No," Jeremiah said, turning his head back to the stage.

"I guess I don't have a choice then."

"I guess you don't."

*****

The following morning, they discussed the details further. As for Chance and Seven, they didn't like the idea. They felt Jeremiah was up to something, but Patience convinced them it was the only way into his operation.

Within two weeks, Patience had learned everything there was about the operation. On the outside, it appeared to be a pharmacy, but behind closed doors, it was a drug stable. Jeremiah's companies were grossing millions. Doctors would write prescriptions for patients, and the pharmacist would fill it, giving them illegal drugs. The best part was the government was paying for all of it.

To gain his trust, Patience gave Jeremiah great investment ideas, advising him on new technology and government funding. She also suggested that he open up pharmacies in high-infected HIV areas and sell Atripla, an HIV medication that required the patient take one pill a day instead of ten. Uninsured patients would buy these pills by the boatload with the government's help.

Patience helped Jeremiah expand his business, and it was all perfectly legal. Not only did he consider her an asset to his operation, he was slightly attracted to her. She always conducted herself in a professional manner, never asking too many questions and looking good in her suits.

Ramon ordered Jeremiah to fly out to Columbia to check on things. Normally, Jeremiah would fly out by himself, but this time, he decided to take Patience along. Chance and Seven were dead set against it. They didn't have eyes and ears out there and felt like Jeremiah was up to something.

It was the night before they were supposed to leave, and Patience was in the office gathering her things when Jeremiah entered.

"You busy?"

"No…no. Come on in," she told him.

"So you're okay with this trip?" he asked.

"It's for business, right?"

"Yeah…yeah. I just wanna make sure you're good with the traveling thing," he said, walking closer to her.

Nervous, Patience nodded. "Yes, I'm fine with it. I have some ideas for the company. You wanna hear about them?" she said, picking up a folder.

Jeremiah snatched the folder out of her hand and tossed it across the room. "Not now," he said, then kissed her in the mouth.

Stunned by his approach, Patience kept her mouth closed. When she tried to speak, he made one more attempt, this time palming her ass. Patience surrendered, kissing him back.

Meanwhile, Seven and Chance, who were watching, thought she was losing her fucking mind.

"Patience," Seven whispered through Patience's earpiece, "what the fuck are you doing?"

"Patience," Chance said.

"She's becoming like Justice?" Seven snapped.

Patience ignored them as she guided Jeremiah to the loveseat in her office, pushed him down, and stood in front of him. She then kneeled down and gently kissed him on the neck.

"Is this part of the job?" she asked.

Horny, Jeremiah gasped. "Tonight it is."

Wanting to see his rock-hard penis, she started to unbuckle his pants, but Jeremiah stopped her. While kissing her, he unbuttoned her blouse.

"I've been dying to suck these titties," he moaned.

After indulging on her titties like a breastfed baby, he flipped Patience over on her back, lifted her skirt, and pulled down her stockings and panties. Patience swore it was the best head she'd ever experienced. Wanting to return the favor, she flipped him on to the couch and yanked down his pants.

With Seven and Chance in the background trying to discourage her from going there, Patience searched for his dick, but she couldn't find it. There was a bunch of hair but no penis. *Where the fuck is it?* she thought, while massaging his pubic hairs.

In her ear, Patience could hear her cohorts laughing their asses off.

"Let me find out he doesn't have one," Seven managed to get out.

After a couple of minutes, Patience finally found it. At first, she thought it was a cyst because it was so small. When Seven and Chance saw this, they almost died.

"Oh my God! Is that his dick?" Chance screamed, laughing.

"That's not a dick. That's a nipple. I know babies who were born with bigger dicks than him." Seven cried in laughter.

Patience tried so hard not to laugh as she started sucking it. Completely disgusted, she wanted to stop, but knew it would be a problem. Jeremiah would be so embarrassed he would probably kill her.

Meanwhile, Jeremiah had a full erection and had the nerve to moan, "Suck this big cock."

Patience wanted to laugh. *Is he serious?* Nonetheless, she gave him head until he came. She couldn't believe someone with such a little dick would have so much cum. As for Jeremiah, he was good and felt relaxed.

Patience was the first girl who Jeremiah didn't have to pay or threaten to have sex with him. He had been born with a micropenis, which of course is smaller than the average man's penis. That's why Jeremiah never pursued women, afraid of what they would say about his manhood.

Chance and Seven were stunned. It was the first time either of them had ever seen such a thing.

"How can a man who wears a size fourteen shoe have a dick that small? What the fuck is that about?" Seven asked.

"Shit, I'm still trying to figure out how Patience sucked that little shit," Chance said, still laughing.

Seven giggled. "Yeah, Patience is one bad bitch. I don't think I could've done that."

*****

Patience was horrified at what she witnessed in Columbia. Women and children were working in cocaine fields for hours. The ones not working in the fields were used as mules, carrying drugs across the state line. They kept the children and fed them little food so they could work longer hours. They even performed surgery on two small children, inserting two bags of coke in them, and if the parents objected, they were killed on the spot. Patience couldn't believe her eyes.

During the plane ride home, Patience couldn't get those images out of her head. She looked over at Jeremiah, who was on his laptop conducting business. She wanted to cut him open and watch him bleed slowly to death.

While they were out of town, one of his stash houses was robbed. They took over a million in cash and drugs. They blamed it on one of the lookouts for bringing a crackhead to the house. So, instead of going home after the plane landed, Jeremiah ordered his driver to take him to the 59th Street Bridge where they were holding the worker.

The boy was about sixteen years hold. They had his mother, sister, and baby under the bridge. Patience watched as the boy begged for his life, crying and saying it was a mistake. Unmoved, Jeremiah lifted the toddler over a burning garbage can, looked at the boy, and dropped the baby inside it.

Patience covered her mouth to keep from screaming. Chance and Seven, who were also watching, were traumatized. The boy pleaded for Jeremiah to just kill him and let his family go, but that's not how they operated. Everyone had to pay for one's slipup. Jeremiah looked at one of his henchmen, and after giving them the signal the beast put the shotgun to the back of the mother and sister's heads and fired. Their heads exploded like cantaloupes. Patience looked around frantically, praying someone would hear them and call the cops. Jeremiah's boys noticed Patience's reaction and shot her a dirty look.

"Patience, chill out before they shoot your ass," Seven said, noticing it, too.

Jeremiah mumbled, "This is what happens when you fuck up my money." Then he gave one final nod to have the young man killed.

In the car during the ride home, Patience didn't look at him or say a word. She was beyond scared.

"Who knew a motherfucker with a little dick had such huge balls," Seven humored.

After Jeremiah dropped Patience off at her house, the car peeled off.

She wondered why Jeremiah would kill someone in front of her, and figured either he really trusted her or he was sending her a message not to cross him. Patience wasn't aware of it, but there was a method to Jeremiah's madness.

Yes, he enjoyed her company and was impressed by her knowledge of the business, but he didn't trust her. He knew no woman that beautiful would be with a man who couldn't satisfy her in bed. Jeremiah wasn't stupid; he knew she was up to something. That's why he wanted her to witness firsthand that he was nobody to fuck with.

Days had passed, and Patience still found herself saddened by what she had witnessed. Needing to get away, she went to visit Chance and Seven.

"Hey, girl. How are you holding up?" Chance asked.

"He just dropped the baby in burning garbage," Patience cried. "He's a fucking monster!"

"I told you these motherfuckers are ruthless," Chance said.

Seven was messed up behind it, as well. "You wanna pull out for a while?" she asked.

With tears rolling down her cheeks, Patience didn't know what to do. "He wanted me to see him kill that family for a reason, right?"

Chance nodded.

"Which means he's either on to me or doesn't trust me," Patience added, wiping her face.

"That's what it's looking like. Jeremiah is evil," Seven said.

"So I see. Oh, here," Patience said, handing them a flash drive. "These are the files I recorded in Columbia. Those bastards use children as mules."

The ladies could see Patience was fired up, so they just listened to her vent as Chance changed out her devices.

While Seven checked the website, an alert popped up. "Check this out, guys."

"What?" they said.

"Arty just emailed Justice's picture to one of his boys named Lamar who lives in Vegas."

"So?" Patience said.

"So that means one thing. Either they're gonna kill her or try to put her on the street to work," Chance replied.

"Or they're fishing for shit. Didn't you say Justice visited her cousin out there? Someone might have recognized her," Seven said.

"Damn! What do we do now?" Patience asked.

Chance thought for a moment before speaking. "Jeremiah might be on to you, Patience. So, it's best you go back to work. He's gonna watch you for the next couple of days just to see how you react. Whatever you do, don't lie to him. He'll sense it and kill you. Seven, stay here and keep an eye on Patience. Also, reach out to Justice and warn her," she instructed, then pulled out her gun and cocked it back. "I'll handle Arty."

Chance was on point about Jeremiah. He played Patience close the next couple of days. She was just about to leave work, when Jeremiah entered her office.

"Going home?" he asked.

"Yeah. Why, you need me to doing something before I leave?"

Jeremiah looked down at his penis and then up at Patience, who stood there with a disgusted look on her face. *Just what I thought,* Jeremiah thought.

"You know that song by Snoop Dog that goes, Bitches ain't shit but hoes and tricks?" he asked. "I figure you would since you love rap so much."

Not knowing where he was going with the conversation, Patience played along. "Yes, I know the song, just like I know *Ruffneck* by MC Lyte, but what's your point?"

"Do you think there's some truth to those songs?" Jeremiah asked, staring at her with guarded eyes.

Patience smirked, but she knew one of two things could happen. Either she was going to walk out there alive or be carried out in a bag.

"Sometimes, but you didn't come here to talk about rap music."

Jeremiah chuckled. "Nah, I didn't. How do you feel about what you saw the other night?"

"I wouldn't want it to happen to me, if that's your question."

Jeremiah nodded at her witty and smart response. "You think I would do that to you?"

Mind games, Patience thought. "I think you would do that to anyone who crosses you. Is this conversation going someplace?" she asked, annoyed.

"That depends on if you tell me the truth. Why are you really here?"

"Because I need a job and you hired me," she plainly stated.

Jeremiah walked over to her. "Really? That's it?"

"And you needed someone to suck your little dick?"

Jeremiah wasn't hurt by Patience's comment. He knew he had a little dick; he just wanted to see if she had the balls to say it to his face. If she had made that statement in front of his boys, he would've had no choice but to cut her tongue out, but since it was just the two of them, he was cool with it.

"So my dick is little?" he asked, repeating her comment.

"That's what you were waiting for. You wanted to see if I would say it. This will determine if you can trust me or not. It's called reverse psychology," Patience stated while gathering her things to leave.

Jeremiah grabbed her by her arm. "I see why Byron hired you," he said, scaring the shit out of her. "Oh, you didn't think I would remember you. I knew who you were the first day I saw you."

"Well, if you did, then why did you hire me?" Patience shot back, trying to hide her fear.

"I like you. I like that you were honest. You didn't lie about who you were, and I needed someone like you on my team."

"And now?"

"Well, that depends on you." Jeremiah gently brushed her hair off her face. "Now that we cleared the air about everything, how about you suck my little dick?" he said, dropping his pants.

Patience was steaming inside. If his dick were big enough, she would've bitten it off.

After performing her sexual duty, Patience sped all the way home. "Can you believe this motherfucker?" she said, talking to Seven through her earpiece.

"Girl, I thought he was gonna shoot your ass. He's a coldhearted little dick bastard."

"Yeah," Patience said.

Jeremiah made Patience feel like a molested child, but she kept telling herself that his day would come.

*****

Once word got back to Ramon and Daniel about Jeremiah taking Patience with him to Columbia, they immediately scheduled a meeting with him. They were in Zhang's office, when Jeremiah arrived.

"Jeremiah," Ramon said, greeting him.

"Ramon...Daniel," Jeremiah replied, unbuttoning his coat and taking a seat.

"How's business?" Daniel asked.

"Great. We're expecting a huge shipment in a few weeks," Jeremiah informed them with a smile.

Ramon and Daniel looked at each other and then back at Jeremiah.

"Wonderful. So there's nothing else we should know?" Ramon said with a mysterious look.

Oh shit, Jeremiah thought. Just by the tone of Ramon's voice, he knew something was up. He figured they had heard about him taking Patience to Columbia. Jeremiah swallowed hard. He had to think fast.

"Well, I did take a trip to Columbia, if that's what you mean?"

"Did you go by yourself?" Daniel inquired.

"I took a lady friend," Jeremiah answered.

"Is this the same lady friend Byron was messing with?" Ramon asked.

Ramon and Daniel looked at each other again, which made Jeremiah more nervous. He started to say something slick, but thought about his sons.

"I checked her out, and she's cool. Actually, her ideas brought in a lot of money."

"And?" Ramon asked.

Jeremiah cleared his throat. "And she's doing her job. I'm keeping her close to me. Trust, if I even suspect anything, you know she's outta here."

Ramon stood up, buttoned his jacket, and walked over to the window. He then placed his hands in his pockets. This is why he didn't like to hire fake-ass street thugs. They always thought with the wrong head. It's the same problem he was having with Khalidi.

"Her name is Patience Green, right?" Daniel said.

"Yes."

"Was her knowledge or her head game the reason you hired her?" Ramon asked, turning around. "Because there aren't many women who would suck a dick your size."

Mortified by Ramon's comment, Jeremiah felt like stomping the shit out of him. "I didn't know the size of my dick was an issue," Jeremiah replied.

Ramon looked at his bodyguard, who then yoked Jeremiah up from behind. Jeremiah could barely breath. Ramon walked over and got in Jeremiah's face.

"The next time I hear about you doing anything without my approval, I'm gonna put a bullet in your kids' fucking heads," Ramon grumbled before knocking the shit out of Jeremiah. "Release him," he ordered.

"Jeremiah, you know we have eyes and ears everywhere." Daniel smirked.

"That's what we get for hiring illiterate street punks," Ramon commented. "After the next two shipments, I want you to slit that bitch's throat and the throat of anyone related to her."

Jeremiah rubbed his throat while nodding his head.

Once other business had been discussed, Jeremiah left the meeting fuming. After all the work he had put into the operation, those bastards wanted all the money. Now he understood what the last lieutenant was saying about them. They didn't have any loyalty. All they cared about was the money. *Damn, I should've seen this coming,* Jeremiah thought to himself. It's because of him the last lieutenant lost his life. Ramon and Daniel came to him with an offer he couldn't refuse. They suspected Joe, Jeremiah's predecessor, had been skimming the books. Therefore, they asked Jeremiah to keep an eye out. Thirsty, Jeremiah lied and said Joe was cooking the books. So, Ramon ordered a hit on Joe, which Jeremiah carried out.

Ramon and Daniel also ordered Jeremiah to check on operations in other states, which meant they were looking for a new lieutenant to run their operation.

"What do you think about Khalidi and Jeremiah?" Daniel asked Ramon.

"Just wait. We need them for a couple more months. After that, fuck them and their bitches, too."

CHAPTER 8
WWW.COWELL.COM

What the fuck is wrong with everyone? Patience is sucking small dicks. Justice is falling in love with molesters. I have to get a hold on everything before we all get killed. What was I thinking recruiting these ladies? Chance thought.

Chance landed in L.A. It had been almost eight months since she'd been home. She also needed to check in with the Bureau. Chance dropped her bags in the living room and then sighed. The house brought back many memories. After staring at the family portrait located on an end table, she grabbed it and took a seat on the sofa. No matter how hard she tried to get over it, the wounds were still fresh. She missed her family so much. Then she glanced up at a picture of her and Linda. *Sometimes to catch a crook you must become one*, Linda used to say.

"You're right about that," Chance said out loud as she got up to pour herself a drink.

A couple hours later, she checked in at the office to make sure everything was good. She stopped in to see Burgos, but he was in Washington at a meeting. After leaving there, Chance ran a couple of errands before getting ready for tonight. When she checked in with the girls, she learned Seven had warned Justice and Patience was still working with Jeremiah.

According to Seven, Arty checked into his hotel and then made his rounds to check on a few different things. Later, he would be meeting up with Lamar at LAVO, a club where Patra use to work.

It was three o'clock in the morning when Arty and Lamar left the club with two underage girls. From the looks of it, the girls didn't want to go with them. Right there in the parking lot, Arty slapped one of them in the face, unzipped his pants, and forced her head down while everyone pretended not to notice. When she refused, he backhanded her. Lamar and the other girl got into the car. Arty was a piece of work; he believed he was untouchable. They raped the girls right there in the parking lot. When they were done, they left them in the alley.

Chance waited to see if anyone pulled off after them. Once she saw they were alone, she followed them but made sure to keep a safe distance so she wouldn't be noticed. These guys were merciless and armed. If Chance ran up on them, there was no doubt in her mind they would fire back, and she wasn't about to get into a shooting match with them. Therefore, she had to make this killing clean.

Chance waited for them to exit the highway, and once they were on a dark road, she activated her siren, signaling them to pull over. She put her gloves on as she approached the car and took out her badge so they would know she was a cop.

Arty rolled down the window. "Is there a problem, officer?"

"Yes, you were speeding," Chance replied.

"Sorry. I didn't realize it."

"Step out the car, sir," she told him.

"Come on now, officer. I'm sure we can work this out."

"Maybe, but I just need you to step outside of the car."

"Man, go on and step out the car so we can get the fuck on," Lamar said, slurring.

Arty sighed when he realized it was too late to hide the gun tucked inside the waistband of his jeans. If he couldn't bribe her, he would be spending a night in jail.

Chance backed up so Arty could get out. While patting him down, she found the .9mm Glock. "What do we have here?"

"I have a permit for that," Arty explained.

"I bet you do."

Chance unlatched the safety lock and then fired two shots into the car, hitting Lamar in the neck and temple.

"Oh shit!" Arty said, realizing it was a hit. He tried to disarm Chance, but she was too quick for him. "What do you want?" Arty asked, scared to death.

"Your life," she simply responded.

"Huh? Yo, how much you want? I'll pay you anything."

"Money is not an option."

Starting to cry like a bitch, Arty yelled, "Yo, man, do you know who I work for? They gonna kill you! You hear me!"

Unmoved by his threat, Chance laughed before firing three shots into Arty's head. "That's a chance I'm willing to take," she said while looking down at his lifeless body.

Before leaving the scene, she removed their cell phones and identification. She thought about leaving the gun, but decided it would come in handy later.

*****

Chance checked in with Seven again to make sure everything was still good. It seemed that Arty and Lamar weren't high enough in the organization for The Secret Society to react. In fact, Ramon and Daniel were happy because they didn't like the way Arty and Lamar handled business. It was only a matter of time before they had them killed, so actually, Chance had saved Ramon and Daniel the trouble of having to do it themselves.

Khalidi, on the other hand, offered a fifty-thousand-dollar reward for any information regarding Arty's murder.

Gee, only fifty thousand? Chance thought.

Frustrated about everything, Chance decided to stay in L.A. and hit the shooting rage. She'd just finished up, when a gentleman who had been observing her from the private room walked up behind her.

"Nice shooting," he said.

Chance turned around to see who was speaking to her. It was Nigel Cowell.

"Didn't know anyone was watching," she snidely responded.

He smiled. "A little."

Cowell stood six feet tall and had a nice build with a militant type haircut. "Where did you learn to shoot like that?" he inquired, trying to make conversation.

Chance looked around. "Why are you so worried about where I learned to shoot?"

He raised his eyebrow and asked, "FBI?"

Chance glared at him for a second, then while remaining quiet, she finished gathering her things.

"Look, I won't waste your time. I can use someone like you on my team," he said.

"Team?"

"Yes, and no one has to know," he said, leaning closer. "I know the Bureau isn't paying you what you're worth."

Chance nodded. "You're right; they're not. What's your point?"

"My point is which side are you gonna be on? The haves or the have-nots? I served this country for what? All I got is a fucking gold medal star. So, it didn't take much for me to join the team," he vented.

She looked him up and down. "Keep telling yourself that," she said, then proceeded to walk out.

"Linda would've taken the deal," Cowell said, causing her to stop in her tracks. He walked over to her. "Linda was your partner, right? She was killed along with your husband and daughter," he added, shaking his head. "And I bet the FBI doesn't have a clue who's behind it."

Chance looked around, spotting the several cameras in the room. *He's lucky, because I was about to add some lead to his diet. Is he on to our operation? Is this a set-up? Damn, I don't even have my earpiece.* She had to think fast. *Fuck it! I have to go with my gut.*

"How do I know you're not trying to set me up?" she whispered.

"That's the thing; you don't. But, I'm pretty sure after we leave, you're gonna do some homework on me to see if I'm legit before you make your decision."

"You sound like you already know my answer?"

Cowell just smiled confidently.

"Let's talk," she said, leading him outside.

They went across the street to a grab a cup a coffee.

"So you just happened to be at the range today? Don't you think that's ironic?" she asked once they were seated.

"Ironic?" He chuckled. "Let's just say it was fate that brought us together."

Humored, she asked, "Okay, why me?"

"Because you lost your family, and look at what the Bureau did. They relocated you to a bullshit office where you push paperwork. That's what they do, Agent Cohen."

"So who are these people you work for?" Chance inquired, getting to the point

"You mean besides the government?" Cowell sarcastically responded. Realizing Chance didn't find the humor in his comment, he continued. "The people who I work for are businessmen. They take care of business and their employees, unlike the government."

"If you're pissed about your pension, you should write your congressman," she stated spitefully.

Cowell laughed at her comment. "You and I both know, Agent Cohen, the government is the biggest organized crime family in the world. These are the same people who will put a gun in your hand, tell you to kill a man, and then turn around and sentence you to life for killing a man. See my point?"

Chance nodded and then said, "They didn't choose you, though. You chose to work for them, just like I did. So, don't feed me that bullshit about the government."

Cowell nodded; Chance had a valid point. "Is that what you think, that I chose them? I suggest you do your homework before making such comments. There was a time when a black man didn't have a choice. Enlisting in the military was the only way for us to get a college education. So, you're right; I did choose."

"And chivalry is dead," Chance said with an attitude.

He took a sip of his coffee, while thinking maybe she was too young to understand his point.

"Chance, I don't want you to do anything you don't want to do. But, let me tell you something about our government. My father fought in the Vietnam War, and he came back all fucked up. You know what his country did for him? They provided him with free health care and eight hundred dollars a month. That's all they gave a man who put his life on the front line. I'm just getting mine early. Maybe you aren't the person for the job after all."

As he started to get up, Chance blurted out, "If you didn't think I was the person for the job, we wouldn't be having this conversation?"

Cowell smiled and sat back down. "True."

"So what do I have to do, and how much will I get paid?"

Guess that fifty-thousand-dollar a year salary isn't enough, he thought while smirking. "Straight to the point, eh? I like that," he commented.

"Me, too," Chance responded.

"But, I want you to give it some thought, because once you're hired, there's no backing out," he told her. "Here's my card. Call me when you're ready."

After meeting with Cowell, Chance considered calling the entire operation off, assuming their cover had been blown.

Uncertain if Cowell was having her followed, Chance waited a couple of days before flying out to see the girls. Knowing him, he was, especially since he offered her a job. He didn't just pick her name out of a hat. There was a reason why he approached her. She needed to get to the bottom of this before everything blew up in their faces.

She thought about calling Burgos to let him know what was going on, but what if the leak was from their office. While pacing back and forth, she decided she had to let the girls know. Unsure if her phone was tapped, Chance left out and used a payphone.

"Hey, it's me," Chance said.

"Girl, where the fuck were you?" Seven asked. "You had us worried sick."

"Cowell approached me with a job."

"What?" they said in unison.

"Who's that in the background?" Chance asked.

"Patience and Justice. I called them when I didn't hear from you. So why didn't you check in?"

"Yeah, Chance! You had our asses scared as hell?" Patience yelled.

"Sorry, ladies. Stay put, though. I'm catching the next flight out there. Seven, run a trace on Cowell, and let me know if he's on to us."

Seven sighed. Since he was the next target on their list, she had already started researching him. She hacked into his email and found Chance's profile saved on his hard drive. But, she couldn't tell Chance that over the phone, so she simply replied, "Okay, I'm on it."

If they were following Chance, she was going to run circles around them. Chance flew to DC and then took a bus into New York. From there, she took the train into Burlington County.

"Hey," Chance said, entering the warehouse.

"What's up?" Patience greeted.

"Hey," Seven said, coming out of the surveillance room.

"Where's Justice?" Chance asked.

"She went to get us something to eat," Seven told her.

"Did you find anything on Cowell?"

"Yes. I hacked into his computer and found your profile," Seven replied, while leading them back into the surveillance room.

"I figured that."

"The crazy part is he searched for you three years ago."

"What?" Chance said. "Three years ago?"

"Yep." Seven showed her the email she retrieved from his computer.

"We weren't even in operation at that time."

"I know. He also obtained a history of your financial records. Chance, someone in the Bureau has been feeding him information about you."

Too angry to respond, Chance just glared at them.

"Hey, what's going on?" Justice said as she entered the surveillance room.

Everyone looked at her, but no one responded.

"Okay. Well, let's eat," she mumbled as she went back out to the main area of the warehouse, with the ladies following behind her.

During dinner, everyone ate in silence, consumed with their thoughts. Again, Chance started to have second thoughts about their operation. She felt it had been a bad idea from the start, and now it was time to end it.

"I'm dismantling the operation."

"Dismantling? What? Why?" Patience asked.

Chance got up to get something to drink. "It's best. We're in over our heads."

"Why, because someone got your profile?" Seven said.

"This *someone* isn't some young kid who's trying to sell my identity, Seven."

"Exactly, Chance. So fucking what he got it? It makes it even better because now he knows what you're all about."

Chance turned to face the ladies. "You guys just don't get it. These people are always a step ahead. They have killed judges, federal agents. They won't care about killing us."

"No, we get it, Chance," Patience jumped in. "I've seen it firsthand, and that's even more of a reason why we need to stop them. Seven is right. We've managed to stay a step ahead of them thus far. We shouldn't give up now."

Justice nodded. "True. You knew they were gonna run a background check before they even did it."

"You guys are missing the point. Yes, I knew they were going to run a background check on me. I just didn't think it would be beforehand. Someone on the inside is working with them, someone from the Bureau."

"And this surprises you?" Patience said. "Why you think you chose us and not anyone in the Bureau? It's because you couldn't trust them."

They did have a point, but something just didn't feel right to Chance. If it were one of her fellow agents deceiving her, she wouldn't have a problem with it, but just because these ladies had trained for months, it didn't make them experts.

Tired of hearing the bullshit, Seven stood up to leave. "You know, you're so fucking selfish. You came to us seeking information. What we didn't have, we either got it for you or offered to help you get it. Did you ever stop to think how this would affect our lives? We just can't stop and go back to the way we were living. It's not that simple. Khalidi is talking marriage, and Jeremiah likes Patience sucking on his newborn penis!" Seven exclaimed, making the ladies giggle.

"Seven…you don't understand," Chance pleaded.

"No, you don't understand. For the past couple of months, we turned our lives upside down. Yeah, we all knew the risk involved and still said fuck it. My father is six feet underground because of these people. Ramon and Daniel may not have pulled the fucking trigger, but they are damn sure gonna join him. Now, get your shit together, and let's finish what we started," she ordered before walking back into the surveillance room.

Chance looked at the other two ladies, and by the looks on their faces, they weren't ready to give up, either.

After cracking open a Heineken, Chance told them, "Let's get back to work."

The ladies stayed up most of the night trying to devise another plan. They also shared updates on their targets with each other. Khalidi was taking Arty's death hard. He was also upset that Ramon and Daniel didn't acknowledge it. Khalidi was so open off of Justice that he was taking her to see a mansion in Las Vegas. Jeremiah was a different story. He kept Patience close to him, but it was only for his sexual pleasure. However, Patience still found out about shipments of heroin and cocaine coming in to the West End Piers on boats. Seven had done some research on Zhang Lee and learned she worked out three times a week at Equinox. In addition, she loved reading Mark Twain.

Amazed at how these ladies stayed on point, Chance thought, *How can I give up on them now?*

"Sorry about getting cold feet early. It's just when Cowell approached me, it freaked me out," Chance said.

"It's fine," Justice replied.

"Alright, let's focus. Seven, I need you to add more surveillance cameras around the warehouse. Also, I got some more spy devices because we need to switch up. From now on, we keep everything close to the vest. If they're on to us, we're not going down without a fight. Patience, find out when the next shipment comes in. Justice, find out if that's where Khalidi is holding his auction."

"And you?" Patience asked Chance.

"I'm about to start a new job," she told them.

*****

Chance waited a couple of days before she reached out to Cowell. They made plans to meet in New York City for drinks. Cowell picked one of The Secret Society's restaurants for them to meet, which the ladies had already figured. They made sure Chance's devices were hidden properly. Since Chance was certain Cowell was familiar with all espionage devices, she took extra precautions. Her wedding ring would serve as a microphone and the chain had a camera. Inserted in her ears was an earpiece the size of a pea.

By the time Chance arrived, Cowell was already there. In fact, they were the only two people in the restaurant. Chance looked around and took a deep breath. There were two men at each exit with guns. To her right were two more men armed with machine guns.

"You think you have enough security?" Chance smirked and took a seat.

"One could never have too much security. You should know that."

Chance acknowledged his statement with a nod. "So let's get down to business."

Cowell signaled for the woman at the bar to come over. "Before we continue, there's something I need you to do," he stated as the lady walked over to them.

"What?" Chance asked.

"Strip," he said, ogling her.

"Excuse me?"

"Before we go any further, I want you to go in the bathroom and strip for her. If you're clean, we can move on, but if we find any devices on you, she's gonna cut your throat from ear to ear."

Chance stared at him for a second, while praying Seven could hear and see everything.

"I'm here, girl. I got this," Seven said through the earpiece, as if she could read Chance's mind.

Seven knew they were going to scan Chance's body for devices, so she turned them off so no signals would be picked up.

Chance laughed once Seven responded. "No need to go in the bathroom, Cowell," she said, then stood up and started to disrobe while staring directly into his eyes. She removed every piece of clothing. To humor him, she bent over, squatted, and then coughed like an inmate being searched.

She attributed her fierce body to her grueling daily workouts. Every man in the room, including Cowell, got aroused.

"Are we finished here?" she asked as the lady checked her clothing.

After the lady nodded to Cowell, he licked his lips and said, "Yes, you can get dressed, although I prefer you like this."

Watching, Seven mumbled, "Calm down, girl," fearing Chance might go off on him because of his comment.

"Now that I've passed your security check, can we get down to business?"

Cowell nodded. "Certainly. Chance, I'm looking for a person who I can trust, someone to be a part of my team. Trust is very important to me."

Already pissed off and somewhat humiliated, Chance interrupted him. "Let's skip the Godfather speech. You

approached me for a reason. Considering you did your homework, you think I'm the right person for the job."

Cowell got up, walked over to the bar, and poured them a drink. "You're right. I did do my homework. You're not like other agents. You are straightforward…not a 'yes' man. Sorry, you're not a 'yes' woman."

"You forgot one thing. I don't like bullshit," she said, taking a drink out of his hand.

"Neither do I, so let me get straight to it. I need an inside person."

"Inside?" Chance answered, playing dumb.

"I need to know if the FBI or any other federal agency is watching me."

"That's all?"

"I have a few shipments coming in," he informed her. "I need a Federal clearance."

"When do you need this by?" she asked.

"The shipment will be here in three weeks. I'll let you know the drop location. As far as the report, I need that in a couple of days."

"How much is my fee?"

"A hundred thousand if…" Cowell paused to take a sip of his drink. "…everything goes well." He stared directly in her face.

After dinner, Cowell had his men escort Chance to her hotel to make sure she wasn't being followed. Chance knew Cowell didn't quite trust her, but that would soon change. Once alone in the room, Chance didn't talk. She wasn't sure if he had her room bugged, so she coughed, signaling Seven.

"Yeah, girl, I'm here. These motherfuckers are crazy. But, I gotta admit, you looked good naked."

Chance wanted to laugh, but instead, she yawned to let Seven know she was calling it a night.

At three o'clock in the morning, Chance awoke to the sound of someone messing with the door to her hotel room. She grabbed her gun and tiptoed over to stand to the side of the door. The door's handle kept moving as if they were trying to get in.

Quietly, she looked through the peephole and saw it was only a drunk guest.

"Wrong room!" she shouted, then took a deep breath. "I have to calm down."

*****

At the last minute, Cowell told Chance to fly out to Maine. The ladies didn't think it was a good idea, but Chance knew if she refused, she was as good as dead.

Using someone's password from the Bureau, Seven obtained delta-level clearance, the highest clearance in the FBI. The clearance gave Seven access to every law official database, even facial recognition. Chance would need this. Seven didn't have a good feeling. She feared that after Cowell got what he wanted, he would kill Chance.

Cowell and Chance arrived at a huge warehouse as the trucks were being loaded. He instructed Chance to ride back with them, but before she would be allowed in the truck, she had to remove all her clothing again and put on a uniform. After Chance removed her clothing, one of the workers noticed she was still wearing her pendant and wedding ring, and he ordered her to remove them. When she refused, the worker called Cowell into the room.

"What's the problem?" he asked.

Angry, Chance grinded her teeth and said, "I guess you're gonna put a bullet in me after all, because I'm not removing my wedding ring or my pendant."

The tone in Chance's voice said it all. He knew she was at the point of not giving a fuck what happened.

Cowell looked her up and down, met her stare, and said, "Let her keep it on." Then without another word, he left.

On the outside, Chance was sizzling, but inside, she said a silent pray.

"Girl, don't you do any shit like that again," Patience said, watching everything.

It was a long drive to Baltimore. There she was riding down I-95 with enough ammunition for Pearl Harbor.

Just before they arrived, Cowell gave the order for Chance to be blindfolded prior to entering the warehouse. Once inside, the blindfold was removed.

While standing in front of her, he sarcastically said, "So you made it here alive?"

"Yes. Now what?"

"Well, there's one more thing I need you to do. You see that gentleman over there?" He pointed.

"Yes."

"I want you to put a bullet in his head."

Chance looked at him as if he were crazy. "May I ask why?"

"Nope. I want you to tell him to face you and then put a bullet in his head."

Chance swallowed hard. She felt Cowell was testing her again.

"So you just want me to kill him?" Chance said, stalling.

"Would it make it easier if I told you that we just found out he was an FBI agent working out of Washington?"

"Sorry to hear that."

"Not as sorry as he's gonna be. So the question is; will it be him or you?"

"What do you mean?" Chance asked, although she knew what he was saying.

"If you don't put a bullet in his head, I'm gonna put one in yours."

No way in the world could Chance kill a federal agent. She had to think quickly, because Cowell was standing with the gun in his hand, waiting for her to take it. After coughing to make sure Seven was alert, Chance took the gun out of his hand, walked over to the guy, and instructed him to turn around.

"What agency are you from?" she asked, while pointing the gun at his face and praying Seven was running a facial scan.

"Hold on, girl," Seven told her. "I'm running it now."

"Huh?" the guy said, with his hands up and staring at the gun.

"Chance, he's not a FBI agent. He's one of them. His name is Juan Rodriguez. He's wanted for murder and rape, among other things. His rap sheet is a mile long. Kill him, and get the fuck outta there."

With a sense of relief, Chance looked at Cowell, winked, and then fired a single shot into the guy's head.

One down and an organization to go, she thought.

CHAPTER 9
WWW.ZHANG.COM

The ladies were meeting that night to provide updates. Justice believed the mansion Khalidi had taken her to would be where he held his annual human auction. Patience found out the exact date when Jeremiah's drug shipment would come in. Chance, on the other hand, was feeling remorse. She wasn't upset about killing that guy. She was upset about Cowell using her as his puppet.

Next up was Seven, and she couldn't wait. She would show the other girls how it should be done. Zhang was the target, and all that falling in love, scared bullshit wasn't in her equation. Especially since Seven had studied her for weeks; she studied her so closely that she damn near knew when Zhang's menstrual cycle was due.

"What's up?" Seven said, greeting each lady with a kiss on the cheek.

"Hi, Seven," Patience replied as the girls smiled.

"Are you ready?" Chance asked.

Seven smiled and nodded. "Been ready. While y'all were out there running crazy, I was doing my homework on this hoe."

"Don't underestimate Zhang. She's a very smart and powerful woman," Chance highlighted.

"Which makes it even better. At the end of the day, she bleeds once a month like the rest of the hoes," Seven pointed out while doing a two-step dance.

The ladies looked at each other and laughed at the nastiness of Seven's mouth.

"Alright, since Seven is up next, we have to take turns monitoring the system," Chance told Patience and Justice.

"Not really," Seven said, while reaching into her bag and handing them each a cell phone. "We can listen and record from our iPhones."

Confused, Chance, Patience, and Justice looked at each other and then at Seven, who stood there laughing at their expressions.

"What, y'all think I just sit here all day playing with myself? I'm on my job. I downloaded an application on all of our phones that will allow us to monitor each other and record. It even has a GPS tracking device. And get this? Should any of us misplace or lose the phone, it automatically locks, and the info would be erased if the voice isn't recognized."

Shaking their heads, they examined the phone. Seven was obviously good at what she did.

"The information is remotely transmitted to the server in the backroom. Trust me, I've thought about everything with these people," Seven stated, winking at them.

"Alright, I need updates, Justice and Patience," Chance said, switching the subject.

"Khalidi is still messed up about Arty, but he's moving forward. He told me that he's not going to be in town next week, claiming he has a huge business meeting to attend," Justice informed them.

"Does he suspect anything?" Chance asked.

"No. I try not to see him much, and when I do, I just act normal."

Chance turned. "Patience…"

"Jeremiah met with Ramon and Daniel. I don't think it was good. He's been checking on his operations in different states. Jeremiah is moving such a large quantity of drugs it's sad. He killed a few more people in Texas because the DEA raided some of his spots, and he's making room for a shipment he's getting in a couple weeks."

Chance nodded. "Good. Cowell's been quiet, which mean he's thinking about my next assignment."

"Have y'all noticed the lieutenants don't interact with each other's businesses?" Justice asked.

"I've never heard Khalidi mention any of the others' names. Have y'all?"

"That's why they're so successful. Ramon and Daniel are not stupid. Never tell the left hand what the right hand is doing," Chance answered.

"That's how they stay on top," Seven said.

The ladies continued with their regular routine of drinking, laughing, and changing out their devices. After Patience and Justice left, Seven stayed behind gathering her things to go home, when Chance walked up behind her.

"I guess you answered my question about being ready."

Flashing her sexy smile, Seven replied, "I guess so. Have a good night, Chance."

*****

Zhang Lee was powerful, and at thirty years of age, she was the youngest of them all. After graduating with a Master's in Business Finance from McComb's School of Business, many of the top accounting firms in the world had extended job offers to her.

Being one of those women who were serious about her body and health, she worked out at least three times a week at the Reebok Sports Club on Columbus Avenue, where Seven got a job as a receptionist. Zhang liked to work out in the morning just before she went into the office. Her phone stayed glued to her ear the entire time, and unlike the other lieutenants, Zhang never traveled with an entourage.

One morning, the gym was short staffed, so the manager asked Seven to clean the boxing studio area.

"How long are you going to be?" Zhang asked, standing with her arms folded.

"Not long," Seven replied.

"Not long? What's not long? Five minutes, ten minutes?" Zhang questioned in a snobbish tone.

Not intimidated, Seven faced her. "Like I said, not long. What part don't you understand ?"

Appalled, Zhang walked over to her. "Excuse me? What's your name?"

"Seven."

Zhang grilled her up and down, while Seven continued with what she was doing.

"There you go. Nice and clean." Seven smiled as she walked about to inspect her work.

Days had gone by, and Seven still hadn't made any progress with Zhang. Maybe *Chance was right. Zhang isn't easy after all,* Seven thought. With it being her day off, Seven decided to workout in the private boxing room area at the gym. Zhang walked in and watched her.

When Seven stopped for a water break, Zhang snidely remarked, "I didn't know they allowed employees to use the gym."

Seven took a deep breath. "I'll be done in a couple of minutes."

Zhang rolled her eyes as she put on her gloves.

"It's all yours," Seven said. "Try not to hurt yourself," she sarcastically added before leaving the studio.

After their little encounter, Seven caught Zhang checking her out. She could tell by the way Zhang acted around her that she was definitely interested. So, she decided to put Zhang to the test. Since she liked watching, Seven was going to give her something to look at, and she had just the right person.

She called up Deputy Young and invited her to New York for a couple of days. Thrilled at the opportunity to see Seven, Deputy Young caught the first flight out. Deputy Young and Seven had just finished working out and were on their way to the sauna, when Seven spotted Zhang.

Seven knew Zhang used the sauna after every workout. Right before Zhang walked in, Seven started kissing and caressing

Deputy Young, who found herself instantly lost in another world. Caught up with Seven, Deputy Young didn't even notice Zhang. Seven waited to see what Zhang would do with the opportunity. Either she would make some noise to let them know she was in the room and then report Seven later. Or she would sit and watch, praying no one caught her.

Once Seven saw Zhang hadn't left out of the sauna, she gave her a show she would never forget. Enthralled, Zhang fully entered and locked the door. Deputy Young's moans made her moist. As Seven licked and stroked Young's clitoris, she stared up at Zhang, who was now biting on her bottom lip.

"You like that?" she asked indirectly talking to Zhang.

"Yes," Young loudly moaned.

Zhang's vagina tingled, and she subconsciously started touching herself. Seven laughed inside. *Deputy Young isn't the only one I brought to a climax,* she thought.

Afterwards, Zhang was so embarrassed that she hauled ass out of there.

Seven smirked and quietly whispered to herself, "It's on."

*****

For the next couple of weeks, Zhang avoided Seven like the plague. Then one day, Seven noticed someone staring at her; it was Zhang. Seven flashed a half smile and entered the sauna with Zhang following and closing the door behind her.

Their eyes briefly met before Zhang quickly turned away. Seven strutted up to her.

"You like to watch?" she asked, teasing.

Zhang looked around, trying to avoid the question. "I don't know what you're talking about."

"Bullshit," Seven said. "You loved it. Probably the best nut you ever had."

"Don't you—" Zhang blurted out and then stopped.

"Don't I what?" she asked, touching her shoulder. Seven then leaned close to her ear and whispered, "I don't mind. I like an

audience." With those words, she walked out of the sauna, leaving Zhang speechless.

After that last episode, Zhang could not get Seven out of her mind. There was something so wicked yet intriguing about her. While Zhang wasn't gay, she found herself fantasizing about the scene in the sauna between Deputy Young and Seven.

"Do you box a lot?" Zhang asked upon entering the steam room a few days later, attempting to make small talk.

Seven opened her eyes and saw Zhang sitting across from her. "When time permits," she flatly answered, then closed her eyes again.

"Are you a trainer?"

Not wanting to be rude, Seven sat up. "You know I'm not a trainer."

"I don't know that for sure. It seems you do a lot of stuff around here," Zhang replied with a hint of sarcasm.

Seven smirked while undressing Zhang with her eyes. "And it seems you like to watch the stuff I do. Curious?"

"Curiosity killed the cat," Zhang said.

"But satisfaction brought him back," Seven responded with a wink.

Silence filled the area as Seven stared seductively at Zhang. After a few minutes, she got up to lock the door.

"What are you doing?" Zhang asked nervously.

Without saying a word, Seven pulled Zhang to her feet and started kissing her.

"What..." Zhang gasped.

While licking her collarbone slowly, Seven moaned, "This is what you wanted. You can't stop thinking about it."

"No," Zhang said, trying to fight the urge, but then released a moan of her own when Seven removed Zhang's towel.

Zhang didn't know if it was the steam from the sauna or Seven making her sweat like a virgin in prison. Proactively, Seven licked Zhang's lips with the tip of her tongue. Still trying to fight the temptation, Zhang closed her eyes.

Seven stopped and backed up, causing Zhang to open her eyes.

"What's wrong?" she asked, confused.

"Nothing," Seven said, walking back up to her.

Without saying another word, Seven gently kissed her. This time, Zhang didn't refuse.

She didn't know it, but Seven was about to turn her out. Zhang was so horny that if Seven wanted, she could've fucked her right then. But, Seven wasn't ready; she wanted Zhang to beg for it.

Pulling away again, Seven told her, "Just something for you to think about."

*****

After that kiss, Zhang went out of her way to get Seven's attention. As for Seven, she was tickled pink watching her act like a schoolgirl. *Dangerous and powerful, eh?* she thought.

Seven was at the front desk when Zhang found the courage to approach her.

"You're really good at boxing," she said in admiration.

"Thanks," Seven replied, then continued checking a guest in.

"Can you teach me how to box like that?"

"Didn't I tell you that I'm not a trainer? I thought we had this conversation already," Seven said, while swiping the member's card.

"I know, but I like the way you box. My boyfriend thinks I'm too skinny. He wants me to build more muscles."

Seven looked her over. "Your boyfriend?" she said, raising her eyebrow.

"Yes," Zhang said in a stern tone.

Seven paused, looked around, then leaned over the counter and whispered, "Does your boyfriend know you like to watch?"

Zhang sighed. "Are you gonna teach me or what?"

"Yeah, I can see why he wants you to box. You're all skin and bones."

Offended, Zhang retorted, "Really?" Then she smirked. "That's funny considering I've seen your type." She'd had enough of Seven's shit.

Seven giggled.

"You're getting a kick out of this, aren't you?" Zhang asked with anger.

After checking another member in, Seven responded in a calm tone, "No. What I get a kick out of is a stuck-up bitch who has no clue what she wants."

"Fuck you! Do you know who I am or what I'm capable of?" Zhang shot back.

"A woman who's dying to be fucked?"

"Don't worry, you'll never have the chance," Zhang snapped.

Seven simply smiled while watching her walk away.

*****

After that last encounter, Seven and Zhang had grown close. Although it had only been a little over two months, Zhang found Seven to be an honest friend.

Unlike the other lieutenants, Zhang didn't have a life. Though on the outside she portrayed herself as a tough businesswoman, she was really insecure and lonely on the inside. Since The Secret Society had alienated her from family and friends, being around Seven made her feel human again.

Seven finally convinced Zhang to hang out with her at 1 Oak Club. At first, she declined, claiming the club scene wasn't her cup of tea, but Seven persuaded her anyway. Zhang was in the VIP area when Seven arrived. Instead of Seven joining her, she played the bar. Zhang noticed it and went over to her.

"You didn't see me? I'm in the VIP section."

After taking a sip of her drink, Seven responded, "I saw you, but VIP is not my style."

"Why?"

"Because you can't live in the VIP section. Why come to the club and sit in VIP all night poppin' bottles? People who do that just wanna be seen. Me?" She paused to take another sip. "I'm low. Just wanna have fun."

Zhang stood there, not sure if she should stay or leave. One thing for sure, Seven wasn't joining her.

"So what do you wanna do?" Zhang asked, confused.

Seven put her drink down, grabbed Zhang's hand, and led her to the dance floor. They danced all night until their feet were killing them.

They were having so much fun that before they knew it, it was almost four o'clock in the morning, and the ladies were starving. Seven knew a place where they could get some breakfast, and with Zhang too fucked up to drive, Seven drove.

"This is a Mercedes SL," Zhang pointed out. "Have you driven one before?"

Irritated, Seven replied, "No, but a car is a car. Do you wanna go or not?"

"Sure."

Seven lowered the drop top and jumped on the Westside Highway.

"Weee!" a drunk Zhang yelled as the wind blew through her hair.

For the first time in her life, she felt free. She was having so much fun, Seven had to pull over and strap her ass in.

"Chill out. I'm not tryna get a ticket."

But, Zhang was in heaven. "God, I wish we could do this every day," she exhaled.

"What do you mean?"

"I mean...I just wish I chose a different career," Zhang expressed with sadness.

Seeking more information, Seven responded, "Girl, are you fucking crazy? You know how many people would kill to have your life? Yeah, you work a lot of hours, but it pays off."

"Things aren't always what they seem, Seven." Zhang's eyes started to tear up. Realizing the seriousness of the moment, Zhang changed the subject. "You know what? I don't wanna talk any more. Let's just listen to some music," she said, then blasted Ashanti's "Rock Wit U (Aww Baby)".

Seven pulled up to Junior's Restaurant in Brooklyn.

"Where are we?" Zhang asked, hesitating to get out of the car.

"Junior's Restaurant. It's known for its famous cheesecake."

"Never heard of it," Zhang said.

Seven giggled. "Girl, get your ass out of the car. No one is thinking about you."

Pouting, Zhang obliged. "Is my car safe?"

"No, so I hope you have full coverage," Seven joked with a wink.

As they waited for their food, Seven asked, "Did you have a good time tonight?"

Smiling like a teenager, Zhang replied, "I actually did. It's been a long time since I had this much fun."

"Why?"

Much sadness could be seen behind Zhang's eyes. Before she started working for Ramon and Daniel, Zhang had a good life. It wasn't much, but it was hers, hanging out with her friends and going to family functions. Now, all she did was work and fuck Ramon when he requested it. Like the other lieutenants, Zhang wanted to leave, but once you were in, there was no way out.

"I work long hours. So, I don't have time for a social life," she said, lowering her head.

"All work and no play isn't good for you," Seven pointed out. "You only get one life to live."

"I know, but..." Zhang started to reveal her secret, but caught herself. "Let's just say my line of work can be very dangerous."

"May I ask what is it that you do?"

"I'm an accountant for Shark Enterprise, a very powerful firm," she replied.

That's what they're calling it? Seven thought.

"And I hate it there," Zhang blurted out.

"Then quit."

Zhang rolled her eyes. "I wish it were that easy, trust me."

Seven stared at her, but didn't bother to comment. She didn't want to push the subject. Still, she felt Zhang wanted to talk.

"What about you, Seven? What's your story?"

"I don't have one. I'm an only child, and both my parents are dead. I'm working at the gym until I find something better. You know, the usual. Same shit, different day."

"No friends? No love life?"

"Nah, I don't fuck with bitches too tough. They're grimey. As for my love life, I don't have one. What about you?"

"Oh, I lost touch with my friends years ago," Zhang responded. "And I'm not in a relationship. I just get fucked occasionally."

"Thought you had a boyfriend?" Seven asked.

"Like I said, I get fucked occasionally," Zhang repeated.

Seven's eyes widened from her bluntness. "You get fucked?" she repeated.

Zhang laughed. "What do you call it when a guy calls you over when his dick is hard, fucks you, and puts you out?"

"A fuck," Seven said, agreeing and causing Zhang to laugh. "Why do you accept it? You're a pretty girl. I'm pretty sure you can get someone better. Is the dick that good?"

Zhang shook her head. "No. He's good in bed, but I've had better. There's more to it. I just can't say right now."

"Fair enough," Seven responded, backing off.

"What about you? Why are you single?"

"By choice. I just don't know what I want. Sometimes I wanna eat pussy, and other times, I wanna suck dick," Seven explained, causing Zhang to choke on her coffee.

"Excuse me?" Zhang said, patting her chest. "You've messed with men *and* women before?"

"Yes. No one knows your body better than a woman."

"So I've heard, but I'm not into that."

"Really? So what you call us?" Seven asked, undressing Zhang with her eyes.

Their food came, and for the rest of the morning, the ladies laughed and talked shit.

Afterwards, Seven caught a cab back home.

*****

Zhang woke up with a hangover and Ramon standing over her.

"Nice evening?"

"What are you talking about?" Zhang asked in a tone laced with fear.

"I'm talking about you hanging out all night."

Zhang jumped out of bed. "Yes, I went out last night. Were you looking for me?"

"Who were you with, a guy?" Ramon asked.

Zhang glared at him. *This bastard has a lot of nerve questioning me when he's out there fucking everything that moves.*

"No, a girlfriend of mine."

Ramon smiled. "Can I meet this girlfriend of yours?"

"Sure, I'll set something up," she said, then walked toward the bathroom.

Ramon snatched Zhang by the arm as she walked by him, scaring the hell out of her. He doesn't say anything. He just sniffed her like a dog and shoved her away. Without saying a word, he exited the room, leaving Zhang shitting in her pants.

The next couple of days, Zhang avoided Seven. She didn't go to the gym or call her. Zhang knew if Ramon met Seven, he would want to fuck her or put her on the street. Either way, it wouldn't be good. It's what happened with her friend Janice. Ramon took her out a few times, had sex with her, and then put her on the street to work. When Janice wanted out, he had her drowned in a hot tub.

Zhang was in a meeting, when she thought about her and Seven's conversation about only having one life to live. She played it over and over in her head before excusing herself to call Seven.

"Hello, stranger," Seven answered, bringing a smile to Zhang's face.

"Hi. Are you busy?"

"Swiping cards," Seven teased.

Zhang laughed. "I wanna go out again."

"It's Tuesday," Seven reminded her.

"And? You said live a little, right? So, let's go."

"Okay. Think of something to do," Seven said, giving in.

"Alright, I'll meet you in front of my building at nine."

"See ya then," Seven told her and ended the call.

As always, the ladies had a ball laughing, talking, and flirting with guys on the street. Once again, Zhang got drunk. Even Seven felt tipsy, but she still managed to get Zhang home safely.

During the ride to Zhang's apartment, she leaned over and whispered in Seven's ear, "Thank you."

"For?" Seven responded.

"Making me feel alive again."

Seven giggled. "You're welcome," she replied, while jumping out the car. "Come on, lady." She helped Zhang out of the car.

In her drunken state, Zhang stumbled, falling into Seven's arm. For the first time, she really stared into Seven's eyes. She was so beautiful and confident, something Zhang yearned for.

"You wanna come upstairs?"

"Zhang..." Seven muttered, looking around.

Zhang leaned forward and started to kiss Seven. Like a dude, Seven palmed her ass and tongued her down.

"Let's go upstairs," Zhang said after breaking their kiss.

As bad as Seven wanted to turn her out, she declined. Before doing so, she sucked on her bottom lip, sending chills through Zhang's body.

"I would love to, but I don't like drunk pussy. When I make love to you, I want you to be sober so you can remember it the next morning." Seven planted a wet kiss on her neck and then on her mouth. "Good night, sexy," she said and walked away, leaving Zhang horny and baffled.

Chance and the girls were amazed with Seven's skills.

"You're a bad bitch," Chance mumbled in her ear.

Seven laughed. "You ain't seen nothing yet," she told them as she walked to the nearest train station.

*****

As Seven sorted contracts in the office, Zhang knocked on the door and entered.

Seven paused and looked up. "You again? What's up with you popping in and out? You have one helluva job."

Zhang looked around and then asked, "Can we go somewhere and talk?"

"I'm listening," Seven said, counting the applications.

"Please," Zhang whispered.

Seven took a deep breath. "Sure. Follow me," she replied and led her to a private area in the gym.

Fidgeting like a little girl, Zhang looked around trying to think of what to say. Finally, she blurted out, "I don't want you to get the wrong idea about me."

Nonchalantly, Seven replied, "About?"

"Us. I was—" Zhang stressed.

"Oh that," Seven said with a subdued nod, cutting her off. She walked up to Zhang, making her heart race. "Why are you breathing so heavy?"

Nervous, Zhang tried to avoid Seven's gaze by lowering her head, but Seven lifted it up so they were staring into each other's eyes.

"Seven…" Zhang mumbled. "I'm not a les—"

"I never said you were," Seven said, cutting her off with a soft kiss on the neck. "Live your life, Zhang," she added, while massaging her body.

Oh my God, this feels so good, Zhang thought. Unable to control her desire anymore, she grabbed Seven by the waist and kissed her deeply.

"Let's go back to your place," Seven moaned.

"When?" Zhang gasped, trying to catch her breath.

"Now."

"What about work?" Zhang asked.

"Oh, I'm about to put that work in," Seven replied with a seductive smile.

Zhang lived only a hop, skip, and jump away from the gym in the Bloomberg building on 59th Street. Her penthouse was gorgeous and well furnished, like something straight out of an interior decorating magazine.

"You want something to drink?" Zhang offered.

At that moment, Seven noticed although Zhang was pretty, there was nothing sexually attractive about her. Next, she looked at the clock on the cable box. *It's not even eight o'clock in the morning yet. I'm definitely gonna need a drink.*

"Yes," she replied. "Pour me some vodka straight up."

To ease her nerves, Zhang poured herself one, too, before joining Seven on the couch.

"Cheers," they toasted, and after a couple sips of their drinks, they started with the kissing again.

"I want you so bad," Zhang moaned, kissing Seven on the neck.

"And you will have me," Seven responded, getting in the mood. But, first, go freshen up."

"Why don't you join me?" Zhang suggested, and Seven agreed.

After they stripped out of their clothes, Seven playfully chased Zhang to the bathroom. Once in the shower, she washed and kissed every part of Zhang's body. Dripping wet, Seven led Zhang into the living room and sat her on the couch. She opened up the drapes, allowing the sunlight to shine in on their naked bodies. Seven stood over Zhang, who anxiously stared up at her. Seven kneeled down between Zhang's legs.

"Calm down," Seven told her, trying to comfort a shaking Zhang.

Seven pushed her back onto the couch and placed her legs on her shoulders, positioning herself face to face with Zhang's nicely trimmed pussy. Seven softly blew on it, causing Zhang to jump. Seven could tell Zhang was on fire by the way her juices were oozing out of her. Seven gently pecked her vaginal lips, teasing her almost into an orgasm.

"Oh God, Seven, please," she moaned with pleasure.

Seven wasn't ready, though. She rose up and started to suck Zhang's titties, making her nipples rock hard, while Zhang massaged her hair. She'd been with many men, but they never made her feel like this. Seven licked Zhang from her neck down to her pubic hairline, while massage her wet pussy with her fingers.

"Fuck me, Seven. Please fuck me," Zhang begged.

Smiling, Seven played in Zhang's pussy a little more, making it wetter. *Oh yeah, she's ready. I'm gonna make her beg for it.*

Seven hadn't even started, and Zhang had already climaxed. She parted Zhang's lips and teased her clit with the tip of her tongue. Zhang softly moaned.

Seven's licking, teasing, and sucking caused her moans to grow louder. Once Seven knew Zhang was nearing another climax, she stood up and stared at her.

"Tell me what you want me to do," she said.

With her passion-filled body tingling all over, Zhang replied, "I want you, Seven."

"Where's your dildo?" Seven asked.

"In the top drawer of my nightstand on the right side of my bed."

Seven ran to get it. It was long and thick. *Nice,* Seven thought as she prepared to turn Zhang out.

When she returned to the living room, she instructed Zhang to play with herself while she watched. New to this level of freakiness, Zhang felt a little uncomfortable, but did as she was told. Wanting another taste, Seven pushed Zhang's hand out of the way and began tickling her clitoris with her tip of tongue, causing Zhang to scream out in ecstasy.

"Oh God, what are you doing to me?" Zhang moaned as Seven started to thrust the dildo in and out of her.

Zhang's body began to tremble, and her pussy was soaked after about twenty minutes of pounding.

"Seven, I'm cumming! Oh God, I'm cumming!"

Seven pulled out the dildo, shoved it in Zhang's mouth, and made her taste her own juices.

Then she went back down on her. All of a sudden, Zhang squirted her hot juices onto Seven's face while screaming out her name. Seven licked her lips and climbed on top of her.

"Look at me. This is your cum," she said, kissing her.

Out of breath, Zhang laid on the couch, while Seven gathered her clothes, took a shower, and got dressed.

"Where are you going?" Zhang asked, wanting more.

"I gotta get back to work. I have bills to pay."

"I'll pay them. Stay," Zhang said.

Seven took both of Zhang's hands. "I don't need you to pay my bills. I'll call you later, okay." Then she kissed her in the mouth.

Disappointed, Zhang responded, "Okay, but you're gonna call, right?"

"Of course," Seven said, while walking toward the door. *I should've been a dude,* she thought as she exited, leaving Zhang lying there with her thoughts.

Watching from his home camera system, Ramon found himself impressed with Seven's skills. Even he had to admit Seven was a motherfucker. *She'll make a good weapon. Hell, maybe it's time to replace the entire team,* he thought.

Zhang, on the other hand, was in lust, and for the first time, she contemplated leaving the organization.

CHAPTER 10
WWW.KHALIDI.COM

Justice confirmed that Khalidi would be holding his auction in a couple of days, which gave them more than enough time to come up with a special plan. To avoid the possibility of Khalidi getting suspicious, Chance and the ladies thought it was best for Justice to return to Atlanta in case he popped up on her.

Seven and the other girls caught the next flight out to Las Vegas. The auction would be held outside of Vegas in an abandoned mansion. Since public records showed the owner had a termite problem, the ladies decided to pose as exterminators, and Patience created prosthetic disguises for them so they wouldn't be recognized.

They were greeted by one of Khalidi's men. "What's up? How may I help you?"

"We're from the Department of Health. We have an order to exterminate the premises," Patience said, handing him some papers.

After reviewing them, he said, "Oh yeah. A'ight, follow me." While guiding them inside, he asked, "How long is this gonna take?"

"Three hours tops. We have to do the inside and outside," Chance replied.

"A'ight. Well, let me know when y'all are done," he said before exiting.

Once the coast was clear, Chance looked around and began barking orders. "Make sure you seal off all exits. I don't want these motherfuckers escaping."

Meanwhile, Ramon and Daniel had flown to Miami to go over the final details before the big event. Khalidi felt it was unnecessary, but he met with them anyway.

"Gentleman," Khalidi said, greeting them outside on the lanai.

"Is everything good for the auction?" Daniel asked.

"Yes. Emails were sent out to buyers. Trucks are on the way. Everything is good."

Ramon nodded. "You won't be there, right?"

"No, I'll be far away. With all due respect, gentlemen, I'm the one who started this auction, so I know what I'm doing," Khalidi stressed to them.

"We never said you didn't know. We just need to make sure you *still* know what you're doing," Daniel told him.

"Understood," Khalidi answered, nodding.

"Very powerful people are attending this meeting," Daniel added. "So, it's very important that everything goes well."

"I'm aware of that, and trust me, I'm on it. Seth sent out an encrypted file with the location, date, and time."

"Alright. Make sure Zhang gets the final numbers. How are we looking on the street?"

"Good…we're looking real good. We just got a shitload of new things, young and fresh."

Daniel looked at Ramon and then over at Khalidi. "I heard about Arty? Any leads?"

"Nah."

"I guess his mouth finally wrote a check his ass couldn't cash," Ramon snidely remarked, while staring at Khalidi and looking for a response.

Khalidi smirked. *Ramon is such a punk,* he thought, but unless Khalidi wanted to join Arty, he knew to keep his mouth shut.

So, he simply replied, "You're probably right."

Ramon and Daniel hung around for a couple more minutes before leaving. On their way out, Daniel turned to Khalidi and asked, "How's your girlfriend? I bet she'll bring us in a ton of money. When this is done, I want you to bring her by my place for dinner."

"Sure," Khalidi answered.

Khalidi knew Daniel was trying to get under his skin. From day one, they never cared for each other. Everyone in the organization knew Daniel didn't run anything. He, too, was Ramon's bitch.

Instead of getting upset, Khalidi called Justice.

"Hey, baby."

"Hi," Justice said, smiling over the phone.

"I miss you."

"Same here."

"Fly out to Miami," he told her.

"Awww, I can't take off any more days. My boss is up my ass already about my attendance."

"So quit."

"Khalidi, you know I can't quit," she said with seriousness.

"Why?"

"I have bills."

"I'll pay them," he stated in a tone that matched hers.

While the offer was great, Justice wasn't about to accept any money from him, especially since she knew how he got it.

"Did I tell you I don't need a man to take care of me?"

Khalidi sighed. He felt she could be so difficult at times. "Alright then. Work yourself to death with your independent ass."

Justice giggled at his comment. "Since you miss me so much, why don't you fly down here?"

Damn, Khalidi thought. He still had a lot to do in preparation for the auction, and Ramon and Daniel were already on his ass. Now wasn't the time for him to fly anywhere, but he missed her.

"I can't right now…"

"That's fine," she said, cutting him off. "I have some studying to do anyway."

Khalidi thought about it again. *Fuck it. I can finish up here tonight and then fly out to Atlanta in the morning.*

"I tell ya what. Let me finish up here, and then I'll fly out to be with you."

"Wonderful. I'll be waiting," Justice said before hanging up.

As for the ladies, they finished up and flew back to New Jersey.

*****

Things took longer than Khalidi anticipated. Unable to fly out to see Justice in the morning, he decided to surprise her by taking a later flight and picking her up from school alone. Justice giggled like a schoolgirl when she saw him standing out front with flowers in hand.

"What are you doing here?"

After kissing her, he responded, "I wanted to see you."

"Oh really? Without your entourage?"

"I gave them the day off. It's all about you and me today," he moaned, kissing her again.

"What if I was with my man?" she said, kissing him back.

"Then I would tell your man to step off 'cause daddy's home." He laughed.

Instead of going home, Khalidi and Justice did some sightseeing around Atlanta, visiting historical places. Being with Justice made Khalidi realize what he was doing wrong. He knew if Justice ever found out he would lose her.

For a perfect end to a perfect day, Khalidi planned a romantic dinner for them at Bacchanalia Restaurant.

"This place is nice," Justice stated, sipping her water.

Khalidi smiled. "Nothing but the best for you."

Justice was about to say something in response, when his cell phone rang.

"Yo," he answered.

"Everything's good. Trucks are in route, and buyers are starting to arrive," the caller stated.

"Good! Keep me posted," Khalidi said before hanging up.

Aware of what was going on, Justice's demeanor quickly changed. When she thought about all those children cramped inside those trucks, it made her sick to her stomach.

"Is something wrong?" Khalidi asked, noticing the expression on her face.

Justice forced a smile. "No…no."

"You know I enjoy being with you, right?"

Justice lowered her head. While she did care about Khalidi, there was no way in hell she could be with someone like him. "Khalidi…I care about you, too."

Because of her hesitation, he sensed something was up with Justice. Then again, maybe he was being a little paranoid. So, he decided to back off.

"So how's school?" he asked, changing the subject.

"It's tough. I'm a little behind in my studies."

"Because of me?"

"Yes, and working two jobs. But, I don't mind," she said, flashing a smile.

Khalidi blushed. It had been a long time since he felt like this. While he portrayed a tough-talking pimp, he was actually a gentle, loving, caring man.

For most of the dinner, it was quiet, until Justice broke the silence between them.

"What are you thinking about?" she asked.

"Thinking about if I had only met you a couple of years ago."

"What would've changed?"

"A lot…a lot…" Khalidi's voice trailed off.

After dinner, they headed back to Justice's house. She glanced down at her watch and thought, *It won't be too long now.* Khalidi was impressed with Justice's house. It was simple, yet nice. It had that homey feeling, like your grandma's home.

"Nice," he commented while looking around.

"Thank you. Make yourself at home."

In the living room, Khalidi noticed Patra's pictures. When Justice entered and saw him looking at them, she told him, "She's me cousin."

"She lives here?" he asked, seeking more information.

"Nah, she's dead."

"What happened?"

Justice glared at him. *Motherfucker, don't act like you don't know. One of the bastards in that organization killed her,* she thought.

"She was kidnapped from Barbados and sold as a sex slave."

Searching for a reaction, Justice looked right at Khalidi, who appeared to be remorseful.

"Damn," he said, shaking his head.

"Yeah, but at least she's at peace."

"Did they ever find her killer?" he asked.

"No," Justice said, hoping he would reveal more information.

Khalidi got up and walked over to the picture. He remembered Patra; she had been Daniel's bottom bitch. Khalidi wasn't a lieutenant when she was alive, but he remembered when Daniel ordered the hit on Patra.

"Is something wrong?" Justice asked.

Feeling guilty, Khalidi put his head down. For the first time, the evils of The Secret Society were this close to him. To them, it was about money, and they didn't care how it was made. Sadly, that's how they lured Khalidi into their web. Life wasn't great for Khalidi, but it was his life. That all changed when Ramon made him an offer he couldn't refuse, the three most powerful tools: money, power, and sex.

During the first two years, Khalidi felt like he was on top of the world, untouchable. However, just like with most good things, there was a catch. Khalidi had to become a monster, selling little girls and boys to pedophiles. He thought about refusing, but no one dared defy Ramon.

As he stood shaking his head at the picture, Justice hugged him from behind and whispered, "Are you okay?"

"Yes," he said, turning to face her.

*****

Meanwhile, Chance and the other ladies were on the job. As the worker stated, the trucks were in route. However, they would never make it to their destination. There were five trucks carrying over a hundred children. They were less than ten miles away and ahead of schedule, so all the drivers decided to get something to eat. Patience and Chance pulled into the parking lot behind them. They watched as the men ate and laughed, while kids were in the truck suffering.

"Can you believe this shit?" Patience said in disgust. "These motherfuckers are having a good time while some child might be dying in one of these trucks."

Shaking her head, Chance replied, "I know." Then she pulled out her iPhone and called Seven. "Hey, how's everything going?"

"Good on my end. Justice is with Khalidi. How about you?"

"We're fine. They left the trucks in the parking lot while they went to eat."

"Get the fuck outta here!"

"Exactly! Alright, I'll see ya when we get back."

"Be careful. Later," Seven said, ending the call.

"So what you wanna do?" Patience asked.

"There's only one thing to do." Chance put on a pair of gloves, then grabbed the Uzi off the backseat.

"I was thinking the same thing," Patience said, matching her comrade's actions.

Chance asked her, "Do you remember how to fire this?"

"We will see tonight," Patience replied.

Thank God the diner was empty, and the waitress was in the back. The guys were still laughing and talking, until one of them noticed Chance. Sadly, he didn't have a chance. She pulled out her gun and let a barrage of shots loose in the crowd. *Tah, tah tah!* Patience followed her lead. The shots were so powerful that they lifted their bodies out of the booth.

When the waitress came out screaming, Chance and Patience looked at each other and then fired a round of shots into her. There could be no witnesses. Patience went into the back and found the cook hiding underneath the counters. She stared at him, contemplating what to do. If she killed him, she was no better than Ramon and Daniel, but if she let him live, she was as good as dead.

"Sorry," she said before sending him to heaven.

After they checked to make sure the entire diner was empty, they looked for an office to see if there were any surveillance cameras. Once they made sure no clues were left behind, they ran out to the trucks where the sound of little voices crying for help could be heard. Realizing they hadn't grabbed the keys, Chance ran back into the diner to get them off each of the drivers' dead bodies. Just as she was about to open the back of one of the trucks, Patience grabbed her hand.

"No. Let's leave the keys for the cops."

"What?" Chance asked, confused.

"We can't afford for these kids to see our faces. Let's call the police and give them the location."

Chance thought about what Patience said and agreed. So, she went back into the diner, notified the police, and then they drove off.

"How do you feel?" Chance asked.

"About?"

"What just happened."

"I've seen dead bodies before, if that's what you mean," Patience replied.

"And about killing?"

"If it means saving thousand of others, I feel great."

Chance looked over at Patience. "My sentiments, too," she said, and then placed a call to Seven, giving her the go-ahead.

*****

Meanwhile, Justice and Khalidi were getting it on. As she grinded on top of him, she knew it would be only a couple more minutes before justice was served.

Back at the warehouse, Seven watched as the convoy of pedophiles arrived. She waited until the last guest checked in and decided to have some fun. She could not believe who was attending the auction. Sadly, they weren't regular pimps off the street. They knew some government officials would attend, but never in a million years would they have suspected judges, teachers, police officers, and even priests to be there. What disgusted Seven the most were the women there to purchase a child.

Seven cleared her throat, grabbing everyone's attention. The attendees looked around, wondering where the voice was coming from.

"Good evening, ladies and gentlemen. I am tonight's entertainment!" Seven quoted from the movie *The Dark Knight*. She burst into laughter at the looks on their faces.

"Is this some kind of joke?" someone quietly asked.

"No, this isn't a joke. Welcome. Welcome to WWW.COM. Unfortunately, there will be no auction tonight."

Questions and voices of confusion echoed throughout the room, while some attendees tried to make their way toward the door.

"Ut uh," Seven said. "If you go through that door, it will explode. How does it feel to be trapped and caged like an animal?"

"What are they paying you? Maybe we can work something out," one of the judges asked.

"Not today," she said, releasing a crazy laugh.

Ignoring her warning, they tried to run for the door.

"Stupid motherfuckers." Seven shook her and then pressed the button, setting off the bombs.

As the house exploded, so did Khalidi.

Then, while holding Justice in his arms, he told her, "I love you."

CHAPTER 11
WWW.JEREMIAH.COM

The explosion was all over the news. Ramon and Daniel wanted to move on the shipment even though a lot of the buyers were hesitant. *Figures*, Jeremiah thought.

After the hijacking incident, Ramon and Daniel started micromanaging everyday activities, having the lieutenants provide them with an update every hour. Jeremiah and Patience were in the office going over the books, when Daniel and Ramon walked in. Patience tried to excuse herself, but Daniel told her to stay.

Both men had to admit Patience was a nice piece of ass and that Jeremiah had to be paying her well. *There's no way in the world a women that beautiful would fuck this little dick motherfucker,* they thought.

"Don't leave on my account. We won't be staying long," Ramon stated.

Jeremiah and Patience glanced at each other, wondering what was going to happen.

"Is everything still on?" Ramon asked.

Jeremiah looked at Patience and then at Ramon. *Is he trying to be funny?* Jeremiah thought.

Ramon never discussed business in front of someone he didn't know. Jeremiah remained quiet for a second, not knowing whether to respond.

"Right on schedule," he finally replied.

"Good. I want you to take Dr. Green with you." Ramon smirked, looking at Patience. "That's your name, right?"

"The last part is correct. My name is Patience M. Green; it's no longer Dr. Green," she said sarcastically.

"May I ask why?"

This bastard has a lot of nerve. Because of you, motherfucker, she thought while smirking inside, but replied, "I was young and did something stupid, but you probably already know that."

"Sorry to hear that. Any plans to get your license back?" Daniel asked.

Patience shrugged her shoulders. "It's up to the board."

"So you're working for Jeremiah now?" Ramon inquired, raising an eyebrow.

"Yes," she said, wondering what he was getting at.

He then asked, "Do you know who Jeremiah works for?"

Patience looked over at Jeremiah, who was almost pissing on himself. "No, I don't, but if my paycheck ever bounces, I will ask." She smiled, causing everyone to laugh.

"Sense of humor. I love that in a woman," Daniel expressed. "What else do you do for Jeremiah?"

Confused, Patience said, "Excuse me? What do you mean?"

Daniel looked at Ramon from the corner of his eye. *Is she fucking kidding me?*

"Well, I can't lie. You are beautiful, and if I know Jeremiah, he didn't hire you for your head. Or did he?"

Patience lowered her head and took a deep breath. She could see where this was going. She looked over at Jeremiah, who stood there with a scared little boy look on his face. While Ramon and Daniel may have intimidated Jeremiah, they were not about to do to the same to Patience.

"What are you getting at? Jeremiah hired me to do a job, and that's what I do."

Daniel felt his dick getting hard. "I bet you are. Too bad he can't fulfill your needs," he mumbled.

"Who said they weren't?" She looked over at Jeremiah, who now had a humiliated look on his face "I don't think you came

here to talk about my job functions, though. So, I'm gonna step out and let you gentlemen talk privately. Sounds like you need to clear some things up. Excuse me, gentlemen."

Patience got up to walk out. When she looked over at Daniel, who was still gazing at her, she noticed his erection. "Now you might have an unfulfilled problem," she said before exiting the room.

Jeremiah wanted to bust out laughing. *Good for your punk ass. That's what you get for tryna play me. Who's the bitch now?* he thought, looking at the expression on Daniel's face.

Even Ramon smirked at Patience's comment. He told Daniel many times not every woman wanted him. As for Daniel, he wanted to cut the bitch's heart out. He started to get up and go after her, but Ramon shot him a "sit the fuck down" look.

"I like her," Ramon said. "She's smart, witty. Too bad we can't keep her. You know what to do with her after this is done."

"Yes, but I was hoping she could stay on for awhile. Ramon, she's bringing in a ton of money and has a lot of great ideas on how to move the drugs."

"Is it the ideas that impress you?"

Jeremiah smirked. "Well, that's not the only thing," he admitted.

"I think we need to get rid of her," Daniel said, adding his two cents. "She was Byron's piece of ass, but then again, you look like a man who likes sloppy seconds. I mean, considering that's all you can get with the tool you have. She might be trying some bullshit, and this little dick motherfucker is too open to notice."

Jeremiah brushed Daniel's slick comment off, knowing he didn't run shit but his mouth. Jeremiah knew that Daniel was jealous of him and Khalidi because he could never get women like Patience or Justice on his best day. Jeremiah didn't have to pay or threaten Patience to suck his little dick. She wanted him.

Ramon stared at Jeremiah. For some strange reason, he respected him. He respected his honesty about wanting to keep Patience around because he enjoyed fucking her, and if the shoe were on the other foot, he would do the same.

"Alright, it's your call, but keep her close to you. Understand?" Ramon instructed.

"Ramon, are you fucking—" Daniel started to say, but Ramon quickly shut him down.

"I said she stays on. Do you have a problem with that?" he yelled while looking at Daniel.

"No," Daniel mumbled.

"I didn't hear you," Ramon said, wanting him to speak up louder.

"No!" He nearly bit his tongue when he responded.

Jeremiah glanced at Daniel with a smirk on his face, while thinking, *And I thought you ran shit.*

Patience waited for Ramon and Daniel to leave before coming back into the office.

"Thank you," Jeremiah told her.

"For?" Patience asked.

"For sticking up for me."

"I was just doing my job. Besides, that guy is an asshole, worrying about another's man dick. You sure he isn't gay?"

Jeremiah shook his head. Patience had a lot of heart and didn't allow anyone to walk over her. He liked that about her.

"You have a lot of balls. You know that?"

"Growing up in and out of foster homes makes you a survivor by any means necessary."

Jeremiah could relate. He had also spent time in foster care while his mother went through rehab. "Yeah, I guess so."

After a few moments of silence, Patience asked, "Hey, have you ever thought about having surgery?"

Until now, Jeremiah had never talked about the subject. He had always been too embarrassed.

"I'm not inserting anything in me."

"Insert what? Do you know how many men have surgery to make theirs bigger?" Patience said, referring to Jeremiah's penis.

Jeremiah's eyes widened. "Get the hell outta here. I'm not walking into no doctor's office and telling them I need a bigger dick," he protested.

Patience laughed. "Contrary to what people say, not all black men are hung," she stated, making both of them laugh.

"Nah, you know what I'm sayin'. What I look like going into a place and saying 'Doc, make my dick big'?"

"The same way you told me to suck that shit," she shot back and then continued. "You already got the swag of a big-dick nigga. Next time Ramon or that faggot-ass Daniel talks that shit, you can pull your dick out and let it hit the floor," she said, speaking in ghetto slang.

Jeremiah started cracking up; he didn't know Patience could talk like that.

Patience walked over to him and got serious. "All jokes aside. Either you can continue to walk around here feeling ashamed and having people humiliate you, or you can do something about it. I know some good doctors who can perform the surgery. It's called phalloplasty. They take the fat from one part of your body and inject it into your penis. It leaves a small scar, but no one will even notice it."

That was the first time Jeremiah had heard of such a thing. For years, he had been too ashamed to get undressed in front of people, and now to hear there was a cure for his "little" problem, he felt like kissing Patience.

"Jeremiah, I know you can't be happy with the way you are, because every man needs to feel like a man. Why don't you at least consider it?"

He agreed; he felt like less than a man when it came to his performance in the bedroom.

"A'ight, do the research for me so I can read up on it," he told her.

She smiled. "Okay. Now let's get back down to business."

Jeremiah stared at her for a second, thinking, *She would make a good wife and mother to my boys. Damn, if only we would've met under different circumstances.*

"Why are you staring at me?" Patience asked while laying documents out for them to review.

"Daniel said he knew your ex-fiancé…Byron?"

"Byron was a piece of shit, just like your boss," Patience stated nonchalantly.

Jeremiah laughed. She did have a point. Besides, he never met Byron and couldn't care less; she was fucking him now.

They spent the rest of the day going over inventory. However, Jeremiah wasn't comfortable sharing the plans for the shipment with her just yet, so he didn't.

*****

"I need a drink," Patience said as she entered the warehouse to find Chance alone.

"What happened?"

"Daniel. He's such an ass."

Chance giggled. "Huh?"

Patience kicked off her shoes and poured herself something to drink. "He's a prick. Today, he came in the office and indirectly asked me if I'm sucking Jeremiah's little dick. Who does that?"

Chance burst into laughter. "Daniel came by himself?"

"No, of course not. He was with Ramon."

"What!" Chance yelled.

"Yes, and he made me stay for the meeting. In fact, they know I use to be a doctor for them and that I was engaged to Byron. Don't worry, though. I didn't deny anything."

Now Chance had a concerned look. "Patience, don't sleep—"

"I know, Chance. I was scared as shit. I damn near shitted on myself, but I had to play along. Ramon was cool. It's that fat motherfucker Daniel. The way he talks to Jeremiah is crazy. If he were my boss, I would've killed him years ago."

Patience didn't understand that there was a method to everything Ramon and Daniel did. They didn't do anything without thinking about it twice. Patience noticed Chance's hesitation.

"Chance, don't worry. I'm not sleeping on these guys."

Right when Chance was about to reply, Seven and Justice entered.

"What's up?" they said.

"Hey," Chance and Patience answered.

"How's Khalidi?" Patience inquired.

"Not good. I haven't seen him since that night. He hasn't called or nothing," Justice replied.

"Is he still alive?" Chance asked.

"Yes," Seven said. "I checked to see if pics of his dead body were uploaded and found nothing."

Justice's heart stopped for second. Although he was a monster, she did care about him.

"What's up with you and lil' dick?" Seven questioned, causing the other ladies to laugh.

"We're getting ready for the shipment to arrive. How about Zhang?" Patience asked.

Seven shook her head. "Shiiiit, that bitch is looking for me with a flashlight and a mattress strapped to her back. I got that pussy locked down."

The ladies looked at each other, then at Seven and fell out. Seven was such a dude.

"Oh my God, Seven," Justice stressed. "Must you be so graphic? Geesh!"

"What?" Seven held her hands up. "You asked me a question, and I answered it."

While still laughing at Seven's statement, Chance asked, "Seven, have you ever been with a man?"

"Of course! I make them lose their minds, too. I just like watching women cum. It's the best thing."

"So you prefer a woman or a man?" Justice asked.

"For me to cum, I need both," Seven replied, silencing them. "I mean, God gave women holes to be poked. But, for me, I need some good-ass head and then a huge fat dick to seal the deal. That's the only way I can cum. But, if I had to choose, it would be a guy. Patience, you're good, 'cause I could never fuck a nigga with a dick that small. My pussy would dry up with the quickness." Patience laughed and shook her head. "And what's up with you, Chance? Did Cowell get any of that pussy?"

Chance shook her head at Seven's vulgarity. "Hell naw!"

"Not yet," Justice said.

"Not ever!" Chance snapped.

"What! Are you fucking kidding? You wouldn't give any to his fine ass?" Patience snapped. "If I can suck Jeremiah's little dick, you can fuck him."

Seven and Justice nodded their head in agreement.

"I didn't say I wouldn't," Chance said in a defensive tone, changing her response. "He just hasn't asked me."

"Would you?" Justice asked.

Chance lowered her head. "Um, I would have no choice, right?"

The ladies dropped the subject and focused on briefing each other on their targets and working new plans for them. Hours passed, and it was getting late. Seven was meeting with Zhang for drinks later that night, while Chance would fly back to L.A. to check with the office.

Justice and Patience were left in the warehouse alone to talk.

"Can you believe how our lives have changed?" Justice asked.

"Not in a million years," Patience replied. "I always wondered about people who live double lives."

"Yeah, me too. I keep telling myself we're doing the right thing," Justice stated.

"I guess."

"How did it feel shooting that cook in the diner?" Justice asked.

Patience paused for a second before answering. "I didn't feel a thing. I don't have nightmares or any guilty thoughts. It scares me to think of what I may have become."

"Wow! What about your feelings for Jeremiah?"

"What do you mean?" Patience asked wanting to be sure she understood her question.

"You mean to tell me that you're fucking him and there's no feelings involved?"

Patience looked at Justice as if she had lost her mind. "Yes. Men do it all the time. Justice, when I was younger, one of my counselors raped me. When I lived with one of my foster parents, their sons took turns raping me. One time, they gave me a STD, and the next time, I got pregnant. They were fucking me so much that I didn't even know which one of them was the father. When I got older, men would promise me the world just to get in my pants. Byron charmed me just to get what he wanted. So, I would say my feelings died a long time ago," Patience explained while pouring another drink.

"Sorry…I didn't know," Justice mumbled.

Patience sighed; she didn't mean to be so harsh with Justice. In fact, this was the first time she ever told anyone besides her father.

"Hey," she said, taking a seat next to her, "I didn't mean to snap at you, but when I think about how many little girls I've treated when I was a doctor because of them, it makes me angry. When I went to Columbia, I saw mothers and fathers give up their children to become mules. I had girls die in my arms because one of the bags burst in their system."

As Justice listened, she thought about her feelings for Khalidi.

Patience looked at her. "So, yes, we are doing the right thing."

Justice took a deep breath. "I think I'm pregnant."

"What!" Patience shouted.

"I'm only a couple days late, but I've been feeling so tired lately."

Patience looked at Justice, who was crying, and hugged her tight. "It's gonna be alright, girl. It's gonna be alright."

"I know, Patience. I can't help it, though. I love him." Justice broke down, crying hard.

Patience sighed. *Shit's about to hit the roof for sure.*

CHAPTER 12
WWW.COWELL.COM

Chance wasn't in L.A. twenty-four hours before Cowell called to meet with her. She planned to meet him later that night at the gun club, but first, she had to check in with Lieutenant Burgos.

"Agent Williams! Wow, it's so good to see you." He kissed her on the cheek as she entered his office.

"Lieutenant Burgos, it's great to see you. How's it going?" She hugged him.

"Busy. Did you hear about the mansion that blew up in Vegas with all them government officials."

"Yeah, yeah," Chance replied, nodding with a somber look, "but they didn't give any details."

"Let's go outside and talk," Burgos told her, grabbing his coat.

It was a high-profile case that had everyone on pins and needles.

"Sorry, the walls have ears," he said once they had exited the building.

Chance nodded. "Don't they always?"

Burgos released a slight chuckle. "It's rumored they were part of a sex slave trade. They found five trucks with children inside ten miles away."

"What!"

"Yep, somebody tipped off the police to the location of the truck. Can you believe that? Now they're up our asses, wanting us to track down this lead," Burgos stated. "How are things going with you? Any leads on your family and Linda's killers?"

"None. Every lead turns up dead, but I'm not giving up hope," Chance lied.

"Don't worry. Something will turn up."

They talked for a couple more minutes before Chance went back inside to fill out her timesheet and check in her weapon. Then she headed out to meet Cowell.

"Agent Cohen," he said, flashing a wicked smile.

"Nigel Cowell. Do you have my money?"

He reached into his pocket. "A deal is a deal."

"I thought I was gonna have to kill you?" Chance snidely said with a smile.

Cowell led Chance upstairs to the private area to discuss her next assignment. He went through the usual routine of frisking her to make sure she didn't have any wires.

"Anything on the radar I should know about?"

"No. I just checked in, and everyone is working that case in Vegas," Chance replied, looking to see if Cowell's expression changed.

"Oh yeah, I heard about that. Some government officials were killed, right?"

"I don't know. They're still identifying the bodies. It's not my case."

Cowell and Chance talked about her next assignment in which he wanted her to accompany him while he conducted a weapons transaction overseas.

"Overseas where?" Chance exclaimed.

"Russia," Cowell casually replied, then asked, "You want something to eat?"

"Russia? And no, thank you," she said, responding to both the trip and his offer of food.

Cowell laughed. "Agent Cohen, you need to lighten up. I was joking about Russia, but I do need you to accompany me on my next assignment."

"When?" she asked.

"Now."

Chance smirked. It was typical of Cowell to pull a stunt like this. Even though she had proven herself many times, he didn't fully trust her.

"Let's go," she said, calling his bluff.

Cowell paused for a second. Her response shocked the hell out of him since he wasn't expecting her to go along with it. Chance, on the other hand, stared dead into his eyes while laughing inside. If Cowell thought she was going to crack, he had another thing coming. Once he realized Chance was hip to his games, he stopped playing them and got down to business. In a couple of days, he would be meeting with some powerful people from Russia who were interested in buying some guns and explosives. He wanted Chance to be there at the meeting.

"This is not your typical meeting," he informed her.

"What's so special about this meeting?"

"Well," he said, leaning back in his chair, "we're going out to dinner, and you'll be my date."

"Date?" Chance repeated.

Cowell laughed. "Don't worry. It won't be that painful. Wear something sexy, and I'll let you know the rest of the details later." He then reached out and grabbed Chance's wrist. "Your husband was a lucky man."

"Yes, he was. Too bad you will never have the pleasure of knowing such luck."

"Don't be so sure, Agent Cohen. Don't be so sure," he said, releasing her so she could leave.

It didn't make sense to fly back to New Jersey since the dinner meeting would be in a couple of days. Instead, Chance checked in with the girls and hung out in L.A. It'd been a long time since she visited her family and Linda's gravesites. So, she got up early the next morning to pay her respects. Although it had been over two years since their deaths, it still felt like it was yesterday. She smiled at her daughter's picture on the tombstone. She looked just like her daddy.

Once she left there, Chance headed over to the cemetery to pay her respects to Linda and her family.

"I guess you were right, Linda. It takes a crook to catch a crook," she muttered to herself.

*****

The day of the meeting, Cowell informed Chance of a change of plans. Instead of having dinner in L.A., they would be having dinner at Spiagga Restaurant located in downtown Chicago.

Chicago, the Windy City, she thought. All she could do was laugh because this was typical of Cowell, always changing shit at the last minute.

Chance caught the first flight out to Chicago, but not without informing the girls. She made sure Seven would be streamlining everything back to the command center.

As she walked through the airport, Cowell called on her cell phone.

"Are you here?" he asked.

"Yes."

"Well, there will be a black Lincoln Town Car waiting for you. It will take you to the hotel," he told her, then hung up abruptly.

Chance sighed. She didn't know how much more she could take. She walked out of the airport, where she was met by a big, bald, muscular man. Acknowledging her with a nod, he sensed Chance's hesitation.

"It's okay, ma'am. Cowell sent me."

Chance looked around and then followed him to the car.

Once inside the hotel room, she found a black, strapless Carolina Herrera cocktail dress laying on the bed and a pair of black Manolo Blahnik pumps. In the closet hung a Chinchilla Stole from Lafayette. Chance looked at the price tag; it cost over twelve thousand dollars. Most women would've been thrilled, but Chance was disgusted for many reasons. One, she wasn't materialistic and was insulted that Cowell thought her clothing wouldn't be good enough for the meeting. Two, she didn't like where the money had come from to purchase the things. And three, she just didn't like his ass.

As she was getting ready, there was a knock at the door. It was Cowell looking like a million bucks in his tuxedo.

"Wow! Don't you look good," he complimented.

"You don't look bad yourself," she said as she grabbed her stole. "Really, did you have to buy me this outfit?"

Gawking at her, Cowell licked his lips and replied, "Tonight I wanted you to look special. While I admire your choice of clothing, nothing accentuates a woman's body better than European clothing."

"European? Carolina Herrera is from Venezuela," she said in an annoyed tone, then walked to the door.

*****

Dinner was wonderful. Cowell was a true businessman. Too bad it wasn't being used for good. He really didn't need Chance at the dinner. The whole evening, Chance just laughed at all their stupid jokes.

When Chance excused herself to go to the ladies' room, she looked at the time and wondered how much longer it would be. By the time she came back, everyone was ready to leave.

"So tomorrow, Nigel?" the Russian said, using his first name.

"Yes." Cowell stood up and shook the man's hand.

Chance looked at Cowell, who sat back down. Confused, she asked, "We're not leaving?"

"No. I thought you and I should have one more drink."

Chance exhaled and then sat back down, also. "Did everything go well tonight?"

Sipping his red wine, Cowell smiled. "It's too early to tell."

"Okay," she mumbled, while looking around and praying for someone to shoot her.

"So tell me about your husband?"

"What about him?" Chance said in a quizzical tone.

"Oh, I don't know. What did he do for a living?"

"I thought you did your homework. I'm sure you know what he did for a living," she replied, rolling her eyes.

"Yes, I do," he admitted. "How old was your daughter when she died again?" he asked, getting underneath Chance's skin.

Chance leaned over closer to him and whispered, "There's three armed men around us. By the time they pull out, I would have already put a bullet in your head. Don't you dare speak my daughter's name. My family is off limits."

"What if I told you that I knew who ordered the hit on your family? Would it be off limits then?"

Chance laughed once again. *He's lying. Ave already told me who put the hit out on Linda. My family was only collateral damage.* Still, she decided to allow Cowell to humor her.

"Maybe. It depends."

"I'll tell you in due time, Agent Cohen," Cowell told her.

"Time is of the essence when it comes to the truth. Remember that." Chance winked and took a sip of her drink.

Cowell glanced at his watch. "Shall we?" he said, standing up and buttoning his coat.

During the car ride, Chance didn't say a word; she was sick of Cowell's mind games.

"Where are we?" she asked when they pulled up to a heavily guarded warehouse.

"Asking questions like that can get you killed."

"Playing with a woman's emotions can also get you killed," she replied.

When Chance entered the warehouse, she could not believe her eyes as she looked around at the cargos full of guns, missiles, and the Russian standing close by. She looked at Cowell, thinking it was set up.

"Nigel, this is a boy's only meeting," he voiced in his Russian accent.

"Then why are you here?" Chance sarcastically said.

The Russian guy walked up to her. "In my country, women are good for two things, bearing children and cooking meals."

"You're not in your country," Chance coldly replied.

"Don't worry about her. She's good," Cowell said, wanting to get this over with.

The Russian looked back at his men and then at Chance before he slapped the shit out of her, causing her to stumble.

"Stupid bitch," he said, spitting on her.

The slap she could've dealt with, but the spitting was a total violation. Chance came back and punched the Russian so hard that she knocked out two of his teeth. His men drew their guns, which were cocked back and loaded.

"Whoa, whoa!" Cowell said. "Come on, let's play nice, gentlemen. Put down your weapons."

Bleeding from her bottom lip, Chance had her weapon drawn and pointed at the Russian's temple. She wanted to shoot him so bad her nipples were hard.

"Cohen, put the gun down!" Cowell yelled, but Chance was like a cheetah focused on its prey. Realizing Chance wasn't about to follow his orders, he stood in front of her. "Put your weapon down," he repeated.

Cowell knew if he allowed the Russian to live he was going to send someone from his team after him and Chance, or even worse, Ramon would come looking for them. Just as the Russians lowered their guns, Cowell looked over at Chance and then fired two rounds into the Russian's head, causing a war. Sadly, the Russians didn't have a chance since Cowell had men placed in every corner of that warehouse.

Afterwards, Cowell ordered his men to dispose of the bodies. He then turned to Chance and asked, "Are you alright?"

"Yeah," she said, holding her face.

Ramon couldn't get wind of this. He would kill Cowell for bringing her along and for fucking up their money. In truth, Cowell didn't like doing business with foreigners. But, Ramon would sell NASA secrets to terrorists if it meant making a buck.

The bodies weren't even cold before word got back to Ramon. It was four o'clock in the morning when he got the call.

"Boss...sorry to wake you, but something went wrong."

"What?" Ramon asked in a groggy voice.

"Cowell brought some chick along that had words with the Russian connect. Before I knew it, Cowell had put a bullet in his head."

"What!" Ramon yelled, tossing the sheets off of him and jumping out of the bed. "Who is this woman?"

"I don't know, boss. I didn't get a good look at her face."

Without saying another word, Ramon hung up. To calm his nerves, he threw on his rob and went downstairs to pour himself a drink. He then called Daniel.

"Get Cowell's ass here now!"

*****

Chance knew shit was about to get hot, so she hopped on the next plane to New Jersey.

"What the fuck happened to your face?" Patience asked.

Shaking her head in disgust, she responded, "You don't wanna know. Where's Seven and Justice?"

"Oh my God!" Seven yelled as she and Justice entered the room as if on cue.

Patience walked over to examine Chance's face. "How does this feel?" she asked, touching the bruised area.

"Sore, but it's not broken," Chance replied.

"What happened?" Seven said.

"I don't know. Cowell invited me to a business dinner with some Russians. They left and Cowell followed. I think he was gonna stick them up. Anyway, one of the Russians insulted me, calling me a bitch and spitting in my face. So, I knocked the shit out of him. Next thing I know, everyone pulled out their weapon."

Seven shook her head. "Chance, this is not good."

"I know. Anything pop up on the site?" Chance inquired.

The ladies looked at each other and then at Chance.

"We think Ramon is gonna kill Jeremiah and Khalidi, and Cowell probably just got added to the list," Seven said.

"What!"

"Yes. Seven intercepted a message from Ramon to Seth," Justice told her.

Confused, Chance asked, "What message?"

Seven led the ladies into the surveillance room. "Ramon sent an email to Seth that said in a couple of weeks he's gonna announce some new leaders." Seven said, bringing it up on the screen. "Ramon and Daniel are gonna kill Jeremiah, Khalidi, and now Cowell."

Chance sighed. Her face really hurt now. "This is not good. Who's in line to take their places?"

"Don't know…" Seven responded

Chance went over to the monitor. "Then let's find out."

*****

Meanwhile in New York, Cowell was doing some serious explaining to Ramon and Daniel.

"What the fuck happened?" a pissed Ramon asked.

"They were tryna make a move," Cowell said.

"I've been doing business with the Russians for years, and there's never been a problem."

Cowell sighed. "Well, you know, Ramon, I told you before not to trust those foreigners."

"It's not the foreigners I'm worried about."

"What are you trying to imply?"

"There's one thing you clearly don't understand," Ramon said while looking at one of his bodyguards, giving him the signal to put Cowell in a headlock and place a gun to his head. "I'm here for a reason, you understand? If you shit a different color, I'll know about it," he growled. "Now…I'm only gonna ask you one more time. What the fuck happened?" he said, watching as Cowell tried to wrestle his way out of the headlock.

Cowell had fought in wars and been beaten by terrorists, so this shit Ramon was trying to pull wasn't going to work on a solider like him.

"Like I said, they tried to make a move," he griped, remaining calm.

Ramon stared into Cowell's eyes. Unlike most, he didn't sense any fear. Ramon walked over to Cowell, grabbed his bodyguard's gun, and shot him in the hand.

"Next time, it's gonna be your head."

As blood gushed out, Cowell bit his bottom lip. He was too angry to scream.

Daniel handed Cowell a towel. "Stop fucking bleeding on the damn rug."

In pain, Cowell just glared at them. Ramon and Daniel were lucky they had disarmed him before the meeting, or there would've been a bunch of dead motherfuckers in that room.

While on his way to the hospital to have his hand looked at, Cowell thought, *So there's a leak in my crew. Someone is always looking to get ahead.* He should've seen this coming, though. It's how Ramon and Daniel operated, divide and conquer. Well, Cowell had something for their asses.

Pulling out his cell phone, he called and left a message for Chance to call him.

CHAPTER 13
WWW.ZHANG.COM

Zhang found herself daydreaming about Seven all day. It wasn't just the sex Zhang loved; it was Seven's confident attitude and words of wisdom. She made Zhang feel comfortable with herself, reminding her that everyone has flaws. When they were together, Seven made her feel like nothing mattered.

Zhang glanced at her watch. She wished Ramon would hurry up. At the last minute, he wanted to go over some numbers with her. Shaking her head, she thought, *Ramon is something else. He thinks when he calls everything should stop.* Finally, her assistant announced he was on his way upstairs. Zhang made sure she had all the files on the table; she wanted this meeting to be quick.

"Zhang, my love," Ramon greeted her with a smile and kissed on her cheek.

"Ramon." Zhang flashed a fake smile. "So what can I do for you, boss?"

For starters, you can tell me about that gorgeous dyke you're fucking, he thought while staring her up and down, but instead, he replied, "We can start with the new numbers."

"Anything in particular?" Zhang asked, not wanting to prolong their meeting.

"Is there someplace you have to be…or someone?" Ramon asked with a wicked look.

Zhang coughed, clearing her throat. "No…no, Ramon. Don't be silly."

He screwed up his face and nodded. "Well then, let's order some dinner and get on with this."

Zhang glared at him for a moment. She wanted to toss the folders at him and tell him, *Look over them your damn self*, but she thought better of it.

Forcing a smile, she said, "What would you like to eat?"

"Chinese is fine with me," Ramon replied as he smiled and grabbed one of the folders.

Zhang took a deep breath, laughed to herself, and then called her assistant to order the food.

She glanced at her watch. "Excuse me for a second. I gotta run to the ladies' room."

Ramon continued reading, ignoring her. On her way out, she glanced at him from the corner of her eye. *Bastard!* Once in the bathroom, Zhang phoned Seven.

"Hey, babe. Sorry, but I have to cancel tonight. My boss is here, and he wants to go over some fucking numbers."

"It's cool."

"No, it's not. He thinks the world revolves around him and this bullshit company."

The sound of Zhang's voice let Seven know she wasn't happy.

"I tell ya what. Call me when you're done. I'll come over and give you a tongue bath."

Seven's words gave Zhang goose bumps all over her body.

Smiling, Zhang sighed and whined, "Alright…I miss you."

"I miss you, too, but I can't take care of both of us right now," Seven said, being humorous.

"I can," Zhang stated.

"Zhang…"

"It was just a suggestion," she whined, when her assistant knocked on the door to let her know Ramon called for her. "Babe, let me get back to work," she told Seven.

"Okay. I'll see you later." Hanging up, Seven mumbled to herself, "Well, my date has canceled."

With nothing left to do, she decided to snoop around The Secret Society's website. When she did, she came across some video footage someone had uploaded. At first, she was going to ignore it, but something told her to click on it. Seven almost vomited at what she saw. It was Khalidi having sex with a girl who appeared to be about thirteen years old. She was crying, begging him to stop, and screaming about how he was hurting her. Seven saved the file and then clicked on another, which showed a drugged young boy being gang raped. Furious, Seven searched for the IP addresses of people who had uploaded videos. Three of the videos were sent by a user who lived in lower Manhattan. Seven sent him a message asking him to meet her in Prospect Park because she had some young fresh meat she wanted him to see. The person immediately replied, giving her the location where to meet them.

"So you like to have sex with kids?" she uttered, picking up two nine Glocks.

As Seven was on her way out, Patience was coming in.

"Where are you going dressed in all black?"

"To catch a predator," Seven snapped.

"Huh?" Patience responded, confused.

Deciding to show and not tell, Seven went back over to the monitor and started the video for Patience.

"Oh my God," Patience mumbled, putting her hand over her mouth. "Is this real?"

"Yep," Seven said, turning it off.

"You need some help?" Patience asked.

"Let's go hunting."

While Seven went on her mission, Zhang was bored out of her mind. Ramon went over every lieutenant's account. If he didn't understand something, he called them on the phone and asked them to explain. When most of them couldn't, Ramon realized he hadn't hired Ivy League men to run his business.

Finally! Zhang thought once they were finished.

"What are your plans for tonight?" Ramon asked.

"Nothing. I was going home," she lied.

She's not a good liar, Ramon thought, smirking inside. "I'll give you a ride."

"No, don't be silly," she said, waving her hand and flashing a fake smile. "I kept you long enough."

"It's not a problem," Ramon replied in a stern tone. "Not unless someone else is driving you."

Zhang swallowed hard. "No...no. Let me get my purse, and we can leave."

*****

Patience and Seven arrived at the park first. They pretended to be a couple taking a romantic stroll in the park, when Seven noticed a middle-aged man sitting on a bench. She paused when she noticed he was wearing the same shirt that he had on in the video.

"What's the matter?" Patience asked, noticing the change of Seven's facial expression.

"That's him." She looked over in the direction of the man. "He's wearing the same shirt."

"Okay," Patience said, confused.

"Which means the video was probably done a couple of hours ago. Those kids are still in danger. If we kill him out here, we may never find the kids." Quickly, she pulled out her iPhone.

"What are you doing?" Patience asked.

"I'm sending him an email to tell him that I can't make it."

"Are you crazy? From your iPhone?"

"Don't worry. He'll never know it's from me," Seven said, typing the message. "Sent! Now let's wait and see where he goes."

The guy pulled out his BlackBerry, and after reading the message, he looked around, got up, and started walking out of the park.

Seven turned towards Patience. "Don't ever doubt my skills," she said while walking to follow the man.

It seemed like they followed the guy for hours. He took them on a wild goose chase on foot in the freezing weather and then finally stopped at the corner. After looking around at his

surroundings, he disappeared around the block. The ladies waited a few seconds before entering the block behind him.

"Damn, we lost him," Patience grumbled.

Refusing to give up, Seven started looking all around to see where he went. As they walked down the block, they heard a loud bang as if someone dropped something. Seven glanced at Patience right before they put on their gloves and leaned against the wall like they were cops chasing down a criminal.

"You ready?" Seven asked.

Although scared, Patience nodded her head.

Just as they were about to kick the door down, they noticed the doorknob turning. They looked at each other, thinking, *Oh shit!*

The gentleman didn't even clear one foot over the threshold before Seven kicked him back inside.

"Where are you going?"

In a state of shock, all he managed to do was grunt from the force of the kick that landed in his stomach. The ladies started kicking him again, knocking him down.

"Get the fuck up, you sick bastard!" Patience yelled.

Halting her assault, Seven grabbed the man by the collar and yanked him up to his feet.

"Are you the police? If so, I want my lawyer," he snapped.

Patience connected her right fist to his face, knocking the shit out of him. "No, we're worse than the police."

"Help! Someone please help me!" the man cried, attempting to draw the attention of those passing by on the main street. "Look, I can explain," he said, panicking.

"Where are they?" Seven asked, anger lacing her tone.

The man led them down the stairs into a dark cellar. The stench of death lingered in the air, but the smell wasn't a clue to what they were about see. The sight was something straight out of a horror flick. Children were caged up like animals. They were dirty and lying in feces, some as young as three years old. Patience almost threw up.

The man faced them. "I just house them," he lied.

Seven looked over the man's shoulder and saw the little boy from the video. He was lying motionless.

"Open that gate," she told him, pointing at the cage.

Scared, the man opened the gate. Patience checked the little boy while Seven kept an eye on the man.

"Are you okay?" Patience asked.

"I want my mommy. Please take me home," he cried, lying there in a long, bloody t-shirt.

Patience smiled. "I'm gonna take you home." Exiting the cage, she asked, "Where's the video equipment?"

"Huh?" the man said, trying to play dumb.

Seven didn't have time to play games. Spotting a pipe on the floor, she picked it up and knocked his front teeth out. He screamed as blood gushed from his mouth.

"Where is the fucking videotape!" she yelled, raising the pipe.

The man held up his hands like he was praising God. "Okay...okay...I'll show you."

He took them into a room where they found a bloody mattress on the floor.

"You sick bastard!" Seven shouted, hitting him again. "So this is where you raped them?" She swung the pipe once more, busting him in the head.

Pleading for his life, he cried, "Please...I'm sorry!"

"Yeah, you're sorry you got caught!" Patience yelled.

Then Seven had an idea. "So you wanna tape children, eh? You like being in videos?" She turned on the camera.

"What are you doing?" Patience asked.

"Sending these sick bastards a message," Seven angrily said. "Get that chair over there."

"Please...I'll do whatever you want. I'll tell you whatever you want." The man continued crying as they tied him to the chair.

"Tell us what?" Patience inquired.

"There are more places like this. I can take you there."

Patience looked over at Seven, but she was too busy setting up the footage.

"Seven, he said there's more places like this one."

"Where?" Seven asked.

"If you let me go, I'll take you," the man offered in desperation.

"Not an option. Either you tell us or I'm gonna play baseball with your head," Seven stated.

"Let me go and I'll take you," he repeated.

While setting up the computer, Seven came across a folder that had a list with the other locations where they kept the children. She looked over at the man and smiled.

"No deal. I found them," she told him.

Patience placed the bag over his head and tied it.

"Stand behind him," Seven instructed Patience. "I wanna see if I can see your face."

Patience did as she was told.

"Okay," Seven said, adjusting the equipment so Patience's face wouldn't be seen. The man fidgeted while struggling to breathe. While knowing he was going to die, the scary part was not knowing how painful it would be.

Once Seven had everything set up, she went and got another pipe, handing it to Patience.

"You like to rape little kids, huh?" Seven said, bashing him in the face.

It was the first of many blows to the head that he would suffer as they took turns venting their aggression out on him. By the time they were done, they had split his head in two.

The ladies removed the laptop and video equipment before calling the police. Meanwhile, Ramon had invited himself inside Zhang's apartment. He took his jacket off, tossing it over the couch, and then grabbed her into his arms. Although the sex wasn't great between them, Zhang settled. However, now since she had experienced Seven, just the thought of Ramon touching her made her ass cheeks tight.

"Why are you so tense?" he asked, kissing her on the neck.

"Work," Zhang said, trying to enjoy it.

Before she knew it, Ramon was on top of her. Normally, it took him about fifteen minutes, but tonight, it felt like forever. Zhang tried her best to enjoy it, but couldn't. His skills were nowhere near what Seven possessed.

After Ramon busted off, he got up and went into the bathroom. He could tell Zhang hadn't been into it, but neither had he. Ramon was just bored and needed something to pass the time before catching a flight to L.A. Now, if he'd had Seven and Zhang together, it would have been a different story.

"Can I get you something?" she offered, knocking on the door.

Ramon opened the door. "No thanks. I gotta get going," he said, brushing past her and walking into the bedroom.

Normally, Zhang would've been upset, but she couldn't wait for him to leave.

Ramon called his security to let them know he was ready.

"Zhang," he called out to her as he walked toward the door.

"Yes, Ramon?" she said, coming out of the kitchen.

"You know, there is one thing you can do for me," he said, walking up to her.

"And what's that?"

"You know that blonde girl you're fucking? I wanna meet her. Make that happen." Ramon smirked and kissed her on the lips before exiting.

Stunned, Zhang couldn't even respond. One thing for sure, there was no way she was letting him touch Seven.

*****

A couple of days went by, and it was still on the news. People were calling them secret heroes for saving the children. As for the man whose skull they split open, he was a teacher that had been married for twenty years and had two kids in college. Seven didn't feel like a hero. To clear her head, she took a little break from the operation. The fact that she took a man's life didn't bother her; it was the children she couldn't get out of her head. Having grown up without a mother and losing her father, she felt like she had been handed the short end of the stick. It wasn't until she saw those kids that she counted her blessings.

Knock! Knock!

Seven wasn't expecting anyone, so she didn't bother to answer the door. The person knocked again, this time harder. When she looked through the peephole, she saw it was the girls.

"We can hear you. Open the door," Chance said.

Seven really didn't feel like being bothered, but after taking a deep breath, she unlocked the door.

"What's up?" Seven said, opening the door.

Not responding, Chance barged in.

"What's going on with you?" Justice questioned, walking inside.

"Patience told us about the other night. Are you alright?" Chance asked, taking a seat.

Seven closed the door and joined the ladies in the living room. At first, she thought about lying, but she needed to get this off her chest.

"Talk to us," Patience coaxed.

Seven wanted to, but she couldn't. Filled with so many emotions, she burst into tears. Patience, Chance, and Justice rushed over to console her .

"I know, girl," Patience said as tears began to roll down her cheeks, also.

Chance knew something like this was bound to happen. This was the one thing she couldn't train them for. In the midst of all the planning and plotting, the ladies had forgotten one thing; they were human.

"I'm okay," Seven said, taking a seat on the couch. "I'm fine, but those kids…" She paused, getting choked up. "Those kids will never be the same."

"I haven't been the same either, Seven," Patience told her.

"It's my fault. I shouldn't have involved you guys," Chance said.

"We wanted to do this. Chance, you can't blame yourself," Seven said. "How can someone hurt an innocent child?" Seven

stood and started pacing back and forth. "They were babies," she cried.

"I don't know. There are a lot of monsters out there," Patience stated.

Going through drama of her own, Justice blurted out, "I'm pregnant." Her news caused the room to freeze. "I'm pregnant by a monster," she whispered.

While Patience already knew, Chance and Seven looked at each other with an expression that said, *Oh shit!*

"Pregnant!" Chance exclaimed.

"Yes," she said with a sigh of relief, glad to get it out in the open.

"You didn't use protection, Justice?" Seven asked in disgust.

"We did, but the condom broke."

Seven looked at the other ladies, thinking, *Yeah, right!*

"This is not good," Chance mumbled, wanting to kill the entire operation that seemed to be going down the drain.

"I know...I know," Justice said, sensing Chance's disappointment.

"Does Khalidi know?" Patience asked.

"No!" Justice shouted.

"Then get rid of it!" Seven yelled. "You better not have that motherfucker's baby."

"I'm not getting rid of my baby!" Justice snapped back.

Seven looked at the other girls and then back at Justice. *Is this bitch crazy?* she thought.

"Seven, chill. Justice, what are you gonna do?" Chance asked, annoyed.

"I don't know," Justice cried.

Chance sighed. "This changes everything."

"How can you even consider having that nigga's baby? He rapes and sells children!" Seven yelled. "Are you out of your fucking mind or just as sick as him?"

Justice jumped up. "Fuck you, Seven! I'm sick of your shit!"

Seven was about to punch her in the face, but remembered the video she had of Khalidi raping a little girl.

"You wanna have that monster's baby?" Seven said, pulling out her laptop. "Well, let me show you what your baby's father might do to your baby."

Seven played the video. Khalidi was pounding the young girl so hard that she started bleeding from her vagina. When he was done, Khalidi let other men come in to have their turn.

"That's what your baby's father does to children. You still wanna have his baby?" Seven spat, glaring at Justice who was speechless.

"Justice, are you okay?" Chance asked.

While staring into space, looking like Sissy Spacek in the movie *Carrie,* Justice replied, "Yeah, I'm fine."

The room grew silent, everyone lost in their own thoughts until Justice finally spoke.

"Chance, for the past couple of months, we've been watching these motherfuckers ruin people's lives, and we haven't done anything to stop them. When I agreed to do this, I thought we would be making a difference, but we're not. In fact, we're no better than them. Do you know how that makes me feel watching a man whose baby I'm carrying rape a child?" Justice stated in a tone so calm that it was scary.

When Chance attempted to say something in response, Justice held up her hand, cutting her off.

"Mi cousin Patra was raped every night as a child by men like these," she said in her Bajan accent. "Mi tired of playing house! Mi want him dead! Mi want to see his spirit leave his body!"

"I agree. Chance, we've been playing house a little too long. It's time to send Ramon and Daniel a clear message," Seven said.

"Yeah, Seven and Justice are right. It's time to take the gloves off," Patience added.

Chance shook her head in agreement.

"Starting with Khalidi," Justice snarled.

As the ladies were working on the perfect plan, Seven's cell phone rang. It was Zhang. Seven started not to answer, but the girls told her that she should.

"Hello."

"Oh my God, you're alright. I've been trying to call you for a while now." Zhang exhaled, holding her chest.

"Yes, I'm fine. Sorry, didn't mean to worry you."

"No, baby, that's fine. I'm just happy you're okay."

"Yeah, but can I call you back? I'm kinda in the middle of something," Seven told her.

"Oh sure, but I just wanna ask you something. My boss wants to invite you to dinner."

"Your boss?" Seven repeated, getting the other girls' attention.

"Yes. It's a long story. Will you come?" Zhang asked, praying she would say yes.

"Sure, just let me know when and where."

"Yes! Thank you." Zhang smiled.

"Alright, I gotta go."

"Okay, call me."

"Will do," Seven told her. After hanging up, she flashed the ladies a wicked smile. "Guess who's coming to dinner?"

CHAPTER 14
WWW.KHALIDI.COM

Khalidi had been keeping a low profile after the incident in Vegas. He was surprised Ramon didn't kill him, but it wasn't his fault. He had done everything they said. In fact, he told Ramon and Seth not to send out the location of the auction until a couple hours before the event. However, Ramon's thirsty-for-money ass ordered Seth to send it out a day before.

Quiet as kept, Khalidi was happy. *Good for Ramon's bitch ass, always thinking he knows everything. You would think Ramon would learn his lesson and be easy, but nope. Instead, he opens up more brothels and sex shops.*

Khalidi went along with it for the time being. He knew it wouldn't be long before Ramon replaced him. Hopefully by then, he and Justice would be long gone.

The only thing bothering Khalidi was not being able to see Justice. She was the best thing that ever happened to him, but he didn't want her to be around those motherfuckers, especially Daniel's hating ass. Every time Daniel saw Khalidi, he asked about Justice. Little did Daniel know, Khalidi would lay down first before he let that fat motherfucker touch her.

Justice smiled, while thinking, *Timing could not have been better.* First, she got an abortion. Just the thought of carrying his baby made her sick. Then, along with the other ladies, she hit every brothel house in the tri-state area, knowing for sure Ramon was going to kill Khalidi.

In a matter of weeks, Justice and the girls managed to save

over five hundred children. Many of the kids had been missing since Hurricane Katrina. Justice understood what Seven meant about the smell of death in the brothel. Young boys and girls were being forced to have sex with multiple men just so Khalidi could make a buck. All Justice could think about was how Patra probably prayed for someone to rescue her from the same nightmare.

Ramon and Daniel didn't have a clue where the heat was coming from, so they sent out an email to all the lieutenants to start relocating the product and shut down shops. During one of the raids, one of the workers, while on his deathbed, gave the location of the houses in New Jersey.

"Alright, there are five stash houses," Seven said, showing them on the screen. "They are guarded by six police officers."

"Is this live?" Patience asked.

Seven smiled. "Of course."

"Remind me to cancel my cable," Chance said, causing everyone to laugh.

"Unfortunately, this is your tax dollars," Seven told her.

"Fucking Republicans," Justice said.

"Let's go over the plan one more time. Justice and Patience, you guys are gonna relieve the two cops outside."

"Chance, won't they see our faces?" Justice asked.

"Who cares? They will never live to tell anyone. Once you relieve the two officers standing in front, Seven and I got it from there," Chance explained.

"What about the other two?" Seven questioned.

"Don't worry about them. Justice can man the front while Patience takes the other two out. We just need to make sure everyone has their iPhones and devices on. Oh, and don't forget to put the silencer on your weapon," Chance told them.

Justice sighed. "Well, we need to get going. It's gonna be a long night."

As usual, everyone was lost in their own thoughts. Justice thought about her aborted baby and Patra, while Patience and Seven reminisced about their dads and Chance about her family.

Before heading out, they held hands and said a small prayer. Since a different team worked every night, it made it easy for the ladies to fit right in dressed like police officers without anyone being suspicious.

When Justice walked up to the two male officers, one of them asked, "You're our relief?"

"That's what it looks like," Patience said.

He smiled and started gathering his things. "Great! I wanna get out of here."

Leery, the other cop looked the ladies up and down. *They don't look like officers*, he thought before asking, "Hey, what squad are you from?"

Uh oh, they both thought.

"Squad means precinct," Chance said in their earpieces. "Say you're from Newark."

"From Newark, and you?"

"Patterson," the officer responded.

Although the other officer still had an apprehensive feeling about them, he went along with it anyway. He didn't care. He just wanted to go home.

"Have a good tour," the officer said as he and his partner walked off.

Justice and Patience looked at each other while breathing a sigh of relief.

A block away, Chance and Seven were waiting for them. They waited until the officers were in the car before coming over.

"Good evening, officer," Chance greeted.

"Hey," the cheery officer responded.

Seven stood on the other side of the car smiling. Just as they were about to say something else, Chance and Seven sprayed them with bullets.

"It's all yours!" Seven announced into the earpiece to Justice and Patience.

Originally, Patience was supposed to take down the officers, but Justice wanted this.

"Wait. You stand guard. I'll go in," Justice told her.

"Hey, are you new?" the first officer asked when she entered.

Justice didn't waste her breath responding. She just shot him at point-blank range in the head.

The second officer was in the room getting a blowjob from a young boy.

"Oh!" he shouted, jumping as she entered.

Sickened, Justice shot him in the head and dick. Then she told the young boy to be quiet. The boy smiled with a sigh of relief as she motioned for him to come out and close the door behind them. She finally came upon the last two officers. One was reading the newspaper, and the other was sleeping in a chair. Justice didn't bother to alert them. She simply raised her gun and shot them both. In her mind, justice had been served.

Patience ran back to see the dead cops on the floor. She looked at Justice, who had a blank look on her face.

"On to the next one," Justice nonchalantly said.

Since they had a few more stash houses to go, the ladies decided to wait to call the cops. They were at the last location, when they came across two workers horsewhipping three of the children. You could hear the sound of the whip ripping through their skins as they begged them to stop and promised to bring in more money. Their cries brought goose bumps to their skin. Justice closed her eyes and said a silent prayer, asking God to forgive her for what she was about to do.

This particular location was an abandoned factory right off the highway.

"Get the fuck up!" the guy ordered the crying young girl. "Get the fuck up, stupid bitch!" he said, hitting her again.

Unable to stand it any longer, Justice jumped out with her gun drawn. From a distance, she fired several shots, hitting the guy in the neck and arm. She didn't bother to put her silencer on. Chance knew for sure the other workers were going to come out blazing. In fact, the other workers probably assumed it was just one of the children being killed. Chance, Patience, and Seven, who were hot on Justice's ass, reached her before she got to the last door.

"Are you fucking kidding me?" Chance snapped, grabbing her by the arm. "You're going in blindsided. I know you're angry, but this is not how you do it."

In the meantime, Seven and Patience heard the footsteps of one of the guys walking toward the door.

"Yo, man, what the fuck are you doing out there? Don't kill all their asses," he said, laughing.

As he opened the door, he didn't even see it coming. Seven splattered his brains on the door. This wasn't good; this wasn't a part of the plan. Patience ran over to one of the wounded girls who was bleeding from her head and legs.

"How many men are in there?" she asked her.

"There's three more," the child mumbled.

"Alright." Patience started to walk out, but the little girl grabbed her.

"Please don't leave me."

"I gotta rescue the other children. I'll be back, okay?" she said, brushing the girl's hair back. "Promise," she added, and then smiled before running back to the other ladies.

"The little girl said there's three more."

They all looked at Chance for guidance. "Fuck it," she replied and entered the building, looking like something out of a Jack Wu action film.

With Chance in the lead, the ladies didn't get off a single shot. She executed all three men.

"Seven, check for any hidden cameras and other devices. Justice, make the call. Patience, check on the children," she ordered, while making sure the guys were dead.

Once alone, Chance released a troubled sigh. If she hadn't taken over the situation, they all would've been dead.

With Justice acting like Laura Croft, they took their asses home.

Back at the warehouse, Chance yelled, "What the fuck was that out there, Justice?" She slammed her gun down and removed her bulletproof vest.

"Chance..." Justice started.

"Chance, my fucking ass! I told you bitches this isn't some fucking movie you're acting in. This is real life. These people are deadly. But, most of all, I'm in fucking charge," she shouted, getting in Justice's face. "Your stupid ass almost got us killed out there."

"I'm sorry. I'm sorry," Justice cried, then ran into the other room.

"The operation is off," Chance stated, moving her hands like a baseball referee motioning that a play is safe.

"Chance, chill the fuck out. She got hotheaded. It happens," Seven said.

"That's the problem. We don't have room for mistakes. If I didn't act fast, we all we've been dead. Justice didn't follow the plan, just like you and Patience didn't," Chance snapped. "You guys just don't fucking get it. You can't go out and kill people. It's not that simple."

Chance was right; these women were doing stuff on their own without thinking and discussing it with her.

"Listen, I'm not saying everything must be run by me." She looked up and saw Justice coming back in the room. "When we started this operation, I stated from the beginning that I was in charge, and not because I wanna be the head bitch in charge. It's because I'm the most experienced. I trained for shit like this. If something should happen to any of you, I will never forgive myself. You know why we were able to stay ahead of them? It's because we are a team. Everyone can't be Jordan," Chance humored.

"She's right," Justice stated. "What mi did was wrong, and I could've gotten all of us killed. I guess I felt like killing them was my way of killing Khalidi."

Chance glared at Justice and nodded. "It's cool."

"Alright, let's check the web. Shit's about to get real hot," Seven said.

"I agree. Let's lay low for a while and focus on Khalidi," Chance suggested. "Remember, guys, there's no such thing as tough. It's trained and untrained."

"So what's the plan?" Patience asked.

Justice smiled. "It's time for us to give Khalidi a taste of his own medicine."

If Ramon didn't kill Khalidi, stress would do the job. In a couple of months, someone managed to hit fifteen of their stash houses, ruin his auction, and kill his best friend. Khalidi wondered if Ramon and Daniel were behind this since he didn't think no one was crazy enough to run up in their spots. Khalidi brought in more money than any of the previous lieutenants, and he had been the one to come up with the auction idea. All Ramon and Daniel cared about was money. So, it was not unthinkable to Khalidi that they would run up in their own spots.

Khalidi called an immediate meeting with his entire comrade to put the word out. He instructed them to keep their eyes and ears open. He knew one more fuck up, and he was as good as dead. Ramon wanted him to meet with Zhang to discuss their profit lost.

Zhang's a stuck-up bitch who need to get fuck, Khalidi thought.

Since they didn't know where the heat was coming from or who was watching, Ramon told them to meet in Greenwich, Connecticut, at his home.

"Khalidi..." Zhang greeted him with a kiss.

Shocked, Khalidi just smiled.

Since Zhang had plans to meet with Seven later that night, she got right down to business. They went over the books with a fine-tooth comb. Even though the brothels were being raided left and right, business was still up. In fact, Khalidi was bringing in more money than he ever did. Right now, that was the only thing keeping him alive.

"I guess sex still sells, huh?" Zhang snidely stated.

Khalidi sighed. "I'm trying...tryna please the powers that be."

She twisted up her face and said, "Tell me about it."

Zhang's comment made him want to say more, but he kept his mouth shut just in case she was fishing for shit. He knew one could never be too careful in this organization.

After crunching numbers, they stood in the driveway awaiting Zhang's ride, while she stared at the mansion and wondered if it was all worth it.

A car pulled up, and just as Zhang was about to get in, she stopped and turned around. "Khalidi, let me ask you a question, and this is strictly off the record."

Khalidi nodded. "Shoot."

"If you could do it all over again, would you work for Ramon and Daniel?"

Khalidi laughed. "You mean Ramon? Because..." He allowed his voice to trail off.

Zhang giggled and waved her hand. "Alright, would you work for Ramon?"

With curious eyes, Khalidi said, "Why you ask me that?"

"Considering all the bullshit that's going on in your shops, it's gotta make you ask yourself is it all worth it."

Khalidi stared at Zhang. If only she knew how much he regretted working for those motherfuckers.

"What about you?" he said, answering her question with a question.

"I used to think money, power, and respect were all you needed in this world, but there's so much more."

"Yeah, it's so lonely at the top."

"That's why we gotta cherish the important things, like love," Zhang stated.

Khalidi smiled. "Uh oh, someone is in love."

She poked her lip out and playfully tapped Khalidi on his arm. "Shhh."

"Ramon got you open, huh?" he said.

"Ramon? No, Ramon ain't got shit. I'm talking about my boo Seven. She's like a breath of fresh air."

Confused, Khalidi replied, "You're fucking with girls now? Let me find out you have a little freak in you."

Zhang laughed. "Shut up! Yeah, I'm on the other side of the fence now. Sorry, but she knows how to put it down in the bedroom. She makes me feel so good, takes me away from all of this bullshit."

Khalidi could relate. "Tell me about it. That's how I feel about my baby Just."

Zhang sighed. "Hopefully, we all can hang out one day away from this…" She pointed to Ramon's house. "…bullshit."

"Fo' sure. We can do that."

Zhang kissed Khalidi once more before getting into the car. Khalidi stood there for a second. Until now, he always believed Ramon had her hypnotized, assuming Zhang breathed, ate, and shitted Ramon.

Guess she got tired of the bullshit, too. And to think another female stole her from him, he thought.

Talking to Zhang made Khalidi think about Justice. It had been weeks since he'd seen his boo. The ringing of his cell phone disturbed his thoughts. The call was from an unknown number. He started not to answer, but it might be Ramon.

"Speak to me," he said.

"Yo, if you wanna see your bitch again, bring two hundred thousand to Vegas. I'll give you the exact location once you get here. Oh, and come alone. Any signs of your crew, and I'm gonna cut this bitch into a thousand pieces."

"Khalidi!" Justice screamed in the background.

"Yo!" he yelled, but it was too late. The caller had already hung up.

The call left Khalidi stuck for a few seconds. Was this some kind of joke? Who in their right mind would take something he owns? Screwfaced, Khalidi ordered his driver to take him straight to the airport. First, he needed to get the money from his safe. Then he would catch the next flight out to Vegas. On fire, Khalidi closed his eyes, praying for Justice's safety.

The dudes who kidnapped her will never live to spend a dime of my money, he thought to himself.

Khalidi was on his way to the airport when Ramon called. He looked at the phone and then sent the call to voicemail. Right now, he had no time for Ramon's bullshit. He needed to save Justice. However, Ramon called again. Khalidi thought of

sending it to voicemail again, but knowing Ramon, he would send a team after him.

"Yeah," he answered.

"How did everything work out?"

"Good. Numbers are good. We just need to tighten up the shops a bit, but everything is good," Khalidi said, wanting to get off the phone

"That's good to hear. So are you still at the house?" Ramon asked.

Is this nigga bored or something? Khalidi thought while looking at the phone. "Nah, I had to leave. I'm on my way to Miami for a quick second. You need anything?"

"Actually, I wanted you to meet me in New York at Joe's Steak House for dinner."

"Can't. Tonight I have plans," Khalidi told him.

"I'm sure you can put your plans on hold for your boss," Ramon stated in the form of a demand and not a question.

"Alright, maybe ten o'clock," Khalidi lied.

"No, let's make it nine. I have some place I need to be afterwards."

Click!

Rude bastard! Yeah, you wait, faggot, Khalidi thought.

It was going on six o'clock when Khalidi arrived in Miami. He jumped in his awaiting car service and headed to his mansion. By the look on Khalidi's face and tone of his voice, his crew knew not to say a word to him. Khalidi rushed into his office, opened his safe, got the money, and ran back out.

"Where to, boss?" the driver asked.

"Back to the airport," Khalidi instructed.

It would've been impossible for Khalidi to pass security with all that money. So, he was thankful for the connection he had with the baggage check clerk.

During the plane ride, Khalidi tried to remain calm, but he was a nervous wreck. All he kept thinking about was what they were doing to Justice. For the first time, he thought about all the women he had raped and abused. Suddenly, he thought about his mother and how she was probably looking down on him disgusted.

Khalidi stopped by one of his spots to wait for the call and to get a weapon. There was no way he would show up unstrapped.

Why the fuck haven't they called? he thought, while trying to look cool.

Then he felt his phone vibrating. The caller ID flashed the word "Unknown".

"Hello, hello," Khalidi answered in a panic.

"Come to 7490 Esteem Street. Come alone or we're gonna show your girl a good time."

Click!

"Are you okay?" one of his workers asked, noticing the look on Khalidi's face.

"Yeah..." Khalidi patted him on the shoulder. "Yeah, man, thanks for asking," he said, picking up the bag filled with money.

"You need a ride?" the worker asked.

Khalidi stared at his worker while fighting back tears. "Nah," he said, swallowing hard. "I'm gonna take this ride alone."

By the time the cab driver pulled up to the house, Khalidi was shaking like a set of dice. *What the fuck am I doing here? It's not like this is my wife or daughter. This is a bitch I was fucking. I'm Khalidi. I can get another bad bitch,* he thought.

"Yo, turn this taxi—"

The sound of a bullet smashing through the windshield and hitting the driver in the head interrupted his request.

"Oh shit!" Khalidi exclaimed, ducking down in the backseat.

Just as he reached for his pistol, a lady's voice told him, "I wouldn't do that if I were you."

When he looked up, he found himself staring down the barrel of three shotguns.

"Hand us your weapon, and we'll let you and your bitch outta of here," Chance said in a deep voice.

Khalidi did as he was told, "Where is she? Where is Justice?" he asked, giving up his gun. "Where is Justice?" he repeated, trying to get out of the car.

Seven shoved the shotgun against his head. "Get out and walk," she instructed, leading him to the house.

In the foyer, Justice was tied and gagged.

"Oh my God, baby, did they hurt you?" Khalidi asked, running over to her.

"She's fine," they said in unison, surrounding him.

When Khalidi realized they were only women, he stood up with his chest puffed out. "A bunch of bitches. I tell ya what. Y'all let her go and come work for me," he said, licking his lips.

The ladies looked at each other and then burst into laughter.

"You really have no respect for women."

Khalidi paused at the sound of the voice coming from behind him. He slowly turned around and froze when he saw Justice standing with a shotgun in her hand and aimed at him.

"What the fuck?" he said.

"Bumbaclot pussy hole," she uttered.

"You fucking bitch! You set me up!" Khalidi said, charging at her.

Boom! Chance released a warning shot, blowing a hole in the ceiling.

"The next one will be in you," Chance informed him.

Justice laughed when she saw the fear in his eyes. "What's wrong, Khalidi? You look a little …nervous." The other ladies giggled. "Look at him. He's shitting in his pants," Justice said.

Khalidi threw his head back. "Whoa!" he shouted, then started laughing.

"What's so funny?" Patience asked.

"You tell me? How much is Ramon paying y'all?" The ladies looked at each other.

"What are you talking about?" Seven said.

"Come on!" Khalidi shouted. "I know Ramon is behind this. I know about the new lieutenant. I just didn't think he would send some bitches to do his dirty work. But, that's Ramon for ya. Just be careful he doesn't send some henchmen for y'all."

Damn, so Khalidi knew about his replacement, Chance thought. "How did you find out?" she asked him.

"That's how they do. Use us and then throw us away. No lieutenant has ever lasted more than three years with them. So what happens now?" he continued. "You're gonna shoot me in the head? What?" he said in an uncaring tone.

Khalidi's confession silenced them.

"What makes you think we work for Ramon?" Chance asked.

"Because no one has the balls to go up against The Secret Society. It's like signing your own death certificate. Only Ramon and Daniel would pull something like this."

Patience was about to tell him the truth, but Justice cut her off.

"You're right. Ramon did send us." Justice's statement caused the other ladies to look at her with confusion. She winked for them to follow her lead.

Khalidi surrendered without a fight. Why bother? All Ramon would do is send another team after him. For the rest of his life, he would be living in fear. Deep down inside, he was happy it was over.

After ordering him to strip, they led him downstairs.

"Remember this?" Justice said. "This was one of your stash houses where you kept children caged up like animals."

Khalidi looked around. *Damn it is,* he thought, not recognizing it at first.

Patience took a deep breath. "Ahhh...you smell that? That's the smell of dead bodies, the children you killed."

The stench was too much. Unable to hold his breath any longer, Khalidi vomited.

"Look at this pussy. Fucking loser! Mi sorry mi let you touch mi," Justice shouted.

They put him in a 10x10 room with no bed or blanket, but which had five gallons of water and five loafs of bread inside. The room was dark, cold, and gloomy.

Khalidi smirked before squatting on the floor. To him, there was nothing left to say. He remembered his mother saying, *What goes around comes around*, and it was at that moment when he believed her.

Standing over him were four women. Khalidi giggled. He always said when he died he wanted to die in the company of women. *Guess, I got my wish,* he thought.

"Khalidi, do you know who's taking your place?" Chance asked

"Rich Soji. He lives in Vegas." Khalidi laughed. "I'm not even in the ground yet, and those motherfuckers already replaced me," he grumbled, sucking his teeth. "Boy, I tell ya. They won't let anyone get in their way of making money. That's all they care about."

"What do you mean?" Justice questioned.

"Ramon..."

"You mean Ramon and Daniel?" Chance said.

"No, Ramon. Daniel doesn't run shit but water. A few years ago, Ramon was gonna kill him over some girl," Khalidi told them. "It's all about money with Ramon. He won't let nothing stop him from getting it."

The ladies looked at each other. They actual felt sorry for Khalidi, but not sorry enough to let him live.

"Seven…" Chance said.

"I'm on it," Seven responded, referring to researching Khalidi's replacement, Rich Soji.

"Let's get rid of the cab driver. Patience, you need to get back to New York. Seven, let's go pay Rich a visit. Justice, go home. We'll handle it from here," Chance directed. "Patience, do your thang."

Patience walked over to Khalidi. "You might feel a little sting," she said, then stuck him with a syringe.

Khalidi's heart started racing and the room spun. A couple seconds later, he fell over. Patience touched him to make sure he was knocked out.

"He'll be out for a couple of hours."

"Chain both of his hands over his head," Chance ordered.

"Justice...are you okay?" Seven asked, noticing her glaring at Khalidi.

"Mi good!" she shouted.

*****

The ladies grabbed something to eat while going over the plan again.

"Justice, are you sure you're okay? I know this can't be easy for you considering…" Seven asked out of concern.

"Mi don't know. I can't lie. I still have feelings for him and seeing him naked…" She quivered. "…it brought back so many memories."

"Shit, I bet. You see the dick on that nigga? The camera ain't add shit. That boy's hung," Seven remarked, licking her lips. "I know you miss that shit," she added, sipping on her soda while the ladies laughed.

Chance reached into her pocket and handed Justice a key. "Here, go back and get some closure. Trust me, you'll feel better."

"Chance," Justice exhaled.

"Take it," Chance repeated.

Seven interrupted. "Chance is right. Jump on that big dick one more time."

Justice laughed. "You're so nasty."

"What happened to the Bajan accent?" Patience inquired.

"It only comes out when I'm pissed off," Justice explained.

"Or getting fucked," Seven said, raising an eyebrow.

"Well, I don't care if she fucks until the sun burns out. She just better not let him get away," Chance said defiantly, staring at Justice.

"I'm good," Justice sighed.

*****

The sun was setting when Khalidi finally woke up. Justice sat in a chair staring at him all day.

She kneeled down over him. "Here, drink some water."

At first, he turned his head, refusing. Tied up like an animal, Khalidi wiggled, trying to break free.

"Come on, drink," Justice slowly said.

Helping him, she held his head so he could reach the cup.

"You hungry?" she asked.

"I'm good," Khalidi replied, wondering why he was still alive. "Are we alone?"

"Yeah, the others left."

Both of them silently stared at each other for a few moments until Justice spoke.

"Just so you know, I was pregnant," she informed him. "But, I got rid of it."

"Why?"

"Why do you think, Khalidi? How could you? I saw what you did to those girls."

"You think I wanted to? Justice, I had no choice. If I didn't rape them, Ramon would've thought I was working with the police."

"Bullshit!" Justice yelled. "I saw the video."

"What? That was all an act."

Justice began to cry. Even on his deathbed, she expected Khalidi to tell the truth. Once Khalidi saw Justice's tears, he wanted to hold her.

"Just," he called lowly. "Look at me. Please look at me," he moaned.

Justice wiped her tears and looked at him.

"I love you."

"Just stop it, Khalidi, okay?" she said. "You don't love me."

"How could you say that?"

"You're just saying that so I can untie you, but it's not gonna work."

"If untying me means losing you, then I don't want you to untie me," he stated.

"What do you mean?" she asked, confused.

"Ramon ordered the hit, right? If I live, he's gonna come after you."

"You're willing to give up your life to save mine?"

"For you, yes. I love you that much, Justice," Khalidi said as he suddenly felt his dick getting hard. He looked down at it and then up at Justice, who had a wicked grin on her face. "What did you do to me?" he asked.

"You didn't think I was gonna let you leave this earth without tasting you again, did you?" she said softly, removing her clothes. "You may be a monster, but you have the best dick in the world," she moaned, strutting over to him.

Khalidi didn't know whether to smile or cry. "Justice...what did you do?" he asked as his penis started throbbing.

"Oh, don't worry. It was just a little Viagra in the water."

"Viagra?" Khalidi repeated.

Lusting, Justice couldn't contain herself, and she started massaging his dick. "It's a shame, all of this going to waste," she said, teasing it with her tongue before starting to suck and jerk him off.

"Ahhh, shit...suck it, baby. Suck this big dick. Untie me so I can return the pleasure. Untie me, baby," Khalidi loudly moaned.

Justice crawled up to him. "This is what you like?" she purred, kissing him.

"Yes, baby. Damn, this is what I wanted. Get on top," Khalidi begged, with his dick throbbing. "Please, I wanna feel your juices on me."

"Mi not wet," she moaned, while touching him all over.

"What do you want me to do? I'll do whatever," he groaned.

"You will do whatever mi want?" she asked, licking and kissing his chest.

"Yes, yes."

Since it would be their last night together, Justice sent him off with a banging fuck. She rode him until the tip of his dick swelled up like an apple. This time, she made sure they used protection, so it was no longer pleasurable for him. He begged her to stop, but Justice wanted him to feel the pain he had inflicted on those children he raped. After her seventh orgasm, Justice had enough. Besides, she was sore. However, Khalidi was still fully erect.

"Shit. How many Viagra pills did you slip me?" he asked, squinching from the painful erection.

"Three."

"Three! Are you trying to kill me?" he snapped, breathing and sweating heavily.

"Not yet. Hopefully, it will wear off," Justice said, getting dressed.

"So you just gonna get your shit off, huh?"

"Isn't that what you do?" she shot back.

"Your cousin, the one in the picture…she was Daniel's bottom bitch. She used to dance at Lavo Nightclub," Khalidi said, changing the subject "That's where Arty remembered you from."

"Arty had a big mouth," Justice grumbled. "He got what he deserved."

"You killed Arty?" he asked.

"No. One of the other girls did. He was a piece of shit."

"You think Arty pimped your cousin out, but it wasn't Arty. It was Ramon. He told Arty to pimp her out so Daniel could see her for the hoe she was."

"Bullshit! I saw the way he treated her, the men he made her bring home."

"She brought men home to support her drug habit. She was a dancer, Justice. Arty ran Lavo. Bringing men home to fuck was her idea."

"So why was she killed?" Justice asked.

Khalidi looked up at her. "She was killed because of you. She died to protect you. You came to visit her in Vegas, right?"

"Yes. So?"

"Word got back to Daniel about how beautiful you were. He figured if he put you on the street, Ramon would leave Patra alone."

"Who told you that?"

"Daniel wanted a piece of you, but Patra wouldn't allow it. When he threatened to harm you, Patra blackmailed him, saying she would go to the police. Word got back to Ramon, who ordered Daniel to kill her."

Justice's eyes filled with tears. "You're lying."

"You know I'm not. They cut off her hands and feet, right?"

★ ★ ★ ★ 198

In a subdued way, Justice nodded her head. "Yeah," she cried.

"You are priceless, Justice. I know you won't believe anything I say, but I love you."

"Khalidi...don't." She raised her hand for him to stop. "Don't do this."

"Justice, if killing me means you get to live, then I'm willing to die. Like your cousin, I will give up my life to save yours. That's how much I love you."

Justice wiped her tears away and looked at Khalidi. "Did you have sex with her?"

Khalidi lowered his head.

"Yeah, just what mi thought."

"So what happens now?" he asked.

Justice closed her eyes. So many things were running through her mind. There she was holding the fate of the man she loved in her hands. She opened her eyes.

"Because of you, so many children will never be the same. Because of you…" She kicked him in his ribs. "…many will need therapy, you bastard." She stomped him.

"I'm sorry," he sobbed.

"So am I," Justice said, walking out.

*****

While Justice had been raping Khalidi, Patience flew back to D.C., while Chance and Seven stalked Rich, who was an easy target. He was coming out one of the brothel houses.

"Guess he's getting acclimated to the job," Seven sarcastically commented.

"Well, in order to sell the product, you gotta taste it to make sure it's good," Chance joked.

"So what's the plan?" Seven asked.

Chance looked around. "Follow them for now."

From a distance, they followed Rich and his entourage for the next couple of hours. As he pulled up to his house, Chance and

Seven jumped out with ski masks on and fired until their guns were empty, killing everyone in the car.

When they returned to the house to check on Justice, she was sitting in the foyer with the lights on.

"Where's Khalidi?" Chance asked.

She tilted her head and replied, "Down there."

"Are you okay?" Seven asked, rubbing her back.

"Now I am," Justice answered.

Killing him would've been too easy, so they left him there with his demons.

CHAPTER 15
WWW.JEREMIAH.COM

Even with all the bullshit surrounding the organization, Ramon still wanted to conduct business as usual. As for Patience, Jeremiah kept her close but away from Ramon and Daniel.

Ramon called an emergency meeting with the lieutenants, which would be held in Michigan at one of his many homes. Seth, Zhang, and Cowell were there by the time Jeremiah arrived.

"Jeremiah," Daniel greeted, glaring at him.

"Daniel," Jeremiah said with a smirk, while thinking, *Clown-ass nigga.*

Ramon was a no-nonsense type of guy. He got right to it. "As of today, there's still no leads on Khalidi. According to my sources, the last time he used his cell phone was in Vegas. Before that, he received two calls from an unknown caller. I need everyone to start closing holes in their shops. You need to start poppin' up, but not be seen. Until we know who we are dealing with, I want y'all to closely monitor everyone."

"What about the transaction?" Jeremiah asked.

"Everything is still a go. Understand something; we are not closing down shop," Daniel told them.

"Daniel is right. Everything moves full speed ahead," Ramon stated.

"What about Khalidi's shop?" Zhang asked.

"We have that covered , if that's alright with you," Ramon responded.

Figures, Jeremiah, Zhang, and Cowell thought.

"While Jeremiah is out on sick leave, Daniel will be handling his operation," Ramon announced.

Daniel looked confused. "What? Sick leave?"

Ramon shot Daniel an evil look. "Like I said, Daniel will be handling Jeremiah's operation. Does anyone have a problem with that?" he said, staring at Daniel.

Pissed, Daniel bumped Jeremiah and snidely said, "Maybe after the surgery you will feel like a man."

Jeremiah got into Daniel's face. "Why are you fucking with me, huh? You wanna suck my small dick, is that it?"

Daniel laughed, infuriating Jeremiah more. "I tell you what. While you're recovering, I'll lay some serious dick on that Patience bitch for you," Daniel said, grabbing his penis. "I'm gonna show her what a real man feels like."

Jeremiah shrugged his shoulders. "Do your thang, player." He smiled at him and then walked away. *Fake ass thug*, he thought.

*****

Knock! Knock!

"Patience," Jeremiah said, entering her office.

"Hi, Jeremiah." She flashed a smile while still typing on the computer.

"Got a sec?" he asked, standing in the doorway.

"Sure. Come on in."

"Check it, I'm gonna be out for a couple of weeks," Jeremiah informed her, taking a seat.

Patience nodded. "Okay…"

"I've decided to have the surgery." Jeremiah grinned.

Surprised, Patience came from behind her desk. "What? When? Where?" she asked, taking a seat in the chair across from him.

"In Cali."

"Hollywood, of course!" she exclaimed with excitement, making Jeremiah laugh. "I'm happy for you. Now tell the doctor you don't want it too big. You don't need an anaconda," she added, making him laugh again.

"That might not be a bad idea," he managed to get out.

Both laughed some more.

Jeremiah stared at Patience for a second. She was the only female he had ever gotten close to. If he didn't have his boys to think about, he would ignore Ramon's orders and run away with her. He felt she would make a great wife and mother.

"Patience, have you ever thought about having kids?" he asked.

"Of course, but I need a man first," she stated, wondering where he was going with the conversation. "What about you? Do you want any?"

Other than Ramon, only Daniel and the people close to him knew Jeremiah had two boys. For their protection, he didn't talk about them.

"I have two beautiful boys."

Of course, Patience already knew that. "Two?" she repeated.

"Yeah, twins."

She smiled. "Wow, that's great."

"Yep, they are my life," Jeremiah stated proudly. "But, I didn't come in here to talk about that. As I stated, I'm gonna have the surgery and will be out recovering for a couple of weeks. So, Daniel will be here handling everything."

"Daniel?" Patience said, pretending not to know who he was talking about.

"Daniel...the fat guy you cursed out at the meeting."

"Oh... him," Patience responded. "That's fine."

Jeremiah stared at Patience. She had no idea how much of an arrogant ass Daniel could be. He knew that as soon as Daniel got the chance, he was going to try to fuck her.

"So today is your last day?"

"Nah," he told her. "I have a few things to take care before I leave."

"You want me to handle it?"

Shaking his head, he replied, "Nah, I got it." Of course Jeremiah didn't want her to handle it; he was expecting a huge shipment of heroin and cocaine.

For a split second, Patience almost felt sorry that she was going to have to kill him. But he was killing other people's kids, so fuck him and his kids.

"Alright. Well, let me know if you need me for anything," Patience said, walking back around her desk.

"You be careful, and I'll see you when I get back."

Patience grinned. "That's a promise I'm gonna make sure you keep."

*****

As Jeremiah arranged the deal, Patience and the girls worked on another plan. They were in the warehouse brainstorming, when Patience thought of a something.

"Hey, you remember years ago when the mob used garbage trunks to transport drugs?"

"Drugs, bodies, money…you name it. What's your point?" Seven asked.

"We steal a couple of trucks to run up on their operation."

Listening, Chance said, "It's a good idea, but there's no way we're gonna be able to hit all those stops."

"It's impossible to do that anyway. Let's do like we did with Khalidi…shut down a few," Seven suggested.

"Not enough time! Besides only half of the drugs are coming to New York City," Patience informed them.

Chance and Seven sighed. It was back to the drawing board. As the ladies threw ideas at each other, Justice entered.

"Hey," she said.

"Hi," they greeted in unison.

"I couldn't stay home," Justice explained, hoping they would let her help.

"It's cool. We could use an extra set of hands with this," Chance said, hugging her.

Unlike Khalidi, Jeremiah's team was ruthless. They killed people for fun. They had also added more security for their meetings, which were scheduled at night in different isolated areas. Jeremiah was supposed to attend, but at the last minute, Daniel ordered him not to go.

Everything was set, but at the twelfth hour, Ramon changed the plan.

"Seven just read an encrypted message Ramon sent to Seth with the new plans. Instead of having everyone meet at one place, Ramon has decided to have the buyers meet at two restaurants in Manhattan and then transport them to two different locations. Four vans will transport the drugs, two for each location. They will be leaving from the Brooklyn Armory," Chance informed them. "This makes it better for us. Justice, you and I will take out the vans before they get to their location. Once that's done, we hit the buyers. Seven and Patience will be in place waiting for our cue."

"Won't Ramon know something's up if the drugs never make it there?" Justice asked.

"We're not gonna blow up the vans until we take the buyers out first," Seven stated.

"Ramon is playing this shit close to the vest. He's not leaving any room for error. All buyers must come alone and be unarmed," Patience illustrated.

Chance nodded. "Yeah, so we can't afford any errors either."

"What about our faces?" Justice asked. "Somebody might recognize us."

"Leave that to me." Patience picked up a huge suitcase and slammed it on the table. "I thought about that. So, I made some prosthetics for our faces and bodies."

"You made these?" Seven asked in amazement, while closely examining them.

"No. The body parts I stole from a research school, and the faces I made."

Impressed, Chance said, "Damn! This shit looks real."

"I want this one," Justice said, picking up one of the faces.

"Pick whatever you want, and I will fit it to your face."

Seven tried hers on. "How do I look?"

Chance laughed. "Now this is scary."

Leaving nothing to chance, the ladies not only had on prosthetic faces, they also had on bulletproof vests underneath their garbage uniforms. As always, they checked their devices and weapons one last time.

"We got everything?" Chance asked, looking around.

"Yes," Seven said, setting the alarm on the warehouse.

They pulled up to the location where they hid the stolen garbage trucks. Before they parted ways, the ladies prayed, wishing each other a safe return.

"See ya in a couple of hours," Patience told them with a wink.

Justice and Chance parked right off the Jackie Robinson Highway and waited.

"We're in position," Chance announced through her microphone.

"Okay," Patience responded.

"Are you sure they're coming this way?" Justice asked.

"Yeah. This is the fastest way to Brooklyn, and there are no police on the highway," Chance informed her, then got out to get into position. "Now, remember, drive slow and steady."

Justice laughed at Chance's instructions. "I know."

"Get ready." Chance tapped on the side of the truck when she saw the vans approaching. "We're up."

As they approached, Justice pulled onto the highway, getting in front of them, with Chance riding on the back of the truck. Ironically there was only one lane open, therefore vans were forced to ride behind the truck.

All of a sudden, the truck came to a halt. Chance jumped down and went to the front, pretending to see what was going on. She then walked back toward the vans, waving to get their attention.

The guy rolled down his window. "What's going on?"

"There's some roadwork ahead. They're backing up a cement truck. It's gonna be about ten minutes."

"A'ight, thanks."

Chance told the same thing to the next seven cars behind them, before running back to the garbage truck. "I'm done," she announced in her earpiece. "We are on our way."

Seconds later, the traffic began moving again. By then, Seven and Patience were in lower Manhattan waiting for the buyers to come out of the restaurant.

"Here they come," Patience said, tapping Seven.

Seven jumped out of the truck to ride on the back.

The buyers engaged in small talk while waiting for the transportation to arrive.

Speeding up the block, Patience mumbled, "Get ready, Seven."

Some of the buyers were laughing, when one of them noticed the truck speeding up the block close to the curb. However, before he could say anything, Seven sprayed them with bullets.

Tat…tat…tat!

Patience stopped the truck and grabbed her Uzi to help Seven finish them off. They heard the sounds of people screaming as they hopped back into the truck and sped away.

Meanwhile, Chance and Justice did things a little differently. They were pretending to be emptying the trash when they attacked their victims.

When Chance had notified the vans of the construction, she placed a small magnet on the side of the door. This magnet was laced with C4, a bomb.

"Seven…" Chance said, "…do your thing."

Seven typed in a code, and the entire factory went up in flames.

Back at the command center, the ladies celebrated.

"WWW.COM!" Chance said, raising her Heineken.

*****

The surgery was a success. The doctor managed to give Jeremiah an eight-inch penis that he could be proud of. Dressed like doctors and nurses, the ladies entered Cedar-Sinai Medical Center and kidnapped him.

When he finally woke up, he was hanging upside down over a barrel with his arms tied behind his back.

"What the..." he looked around in confusion.

"Jeremiah...the surgery was a success," Patience laughed.

Still groggy, Jeremiah asked, "Patience, what's going on?"

"Nothing, just chilling," she responded, sounding like Broman from *Martin*.

He looked down. Not only was his penis enlarged, but so was his stomach. "What the…," he repeated. Squirming, Jeremiah looked around at the other women.

"What's wrong, Jeremiah? You look a little baffled," Justice said.

Feeling nauseous, Jeremiah asked, "What did you put in me?"

"The same thing you put in those children. A little bit of everything, heroin, cocaine, crystal meth," Patience said while walking over to him. "I bet you're wondering what the hell is going on, right?"

"Actually, I'm not," Jeremiah stated after hearing what they did to him.

Patience looked at the other ladies with a puzzled look and then said, "You're not?"

"No. I knew there was a reason why you were working with me. I figured you were working with the FEDS."

"And you still hired her?" Chance asked, confused.

"Yeah. I don't give a fuck about Ramon and them. They would give me up in a second. I was hoping someone would stop them."

"Really?" Patience asked with a surprised tone.

Jeremiah continued. "Yeah. Why you think I kept you away from them and warned you about Daniel? It was only a matter of time before they killed me, just like they killed Khalidi. That's how they get down."

"Killed Khalidi?" Justice repeated.

"Everyone knows Ramon killed Khalidi."

"If you knew all of this, why would you work for them?" Seven asked.

Jeremiah released a laugh. "You know that saying, 'Be careful what you wish for'? Well, that's how I feel. On the outside, shit looks sweet, but it's not. People believe you control shit, but you don't. Ramon will never let that happen. He's about to clean house and hire new lieutenants. So, I hope you have an army, because killing me will not stop the movement."

"So what do you suggest?" Patience asked.

"The only way to stop Ramon is to hit him where it hurts, and that's in his pockets. He loves money more than anything. Or walk up to him and put a bullet in his head, because he's not gonna stop."

Soaking it all up, the ladies remained quiet.

"Jeremiah, I gotta admit it was a pleasure knowing you," Patience said as she turned to leave.

"Wait! Patience, can you do me a favor? Make sure Ramon doesn't hurt my boys."

"I will," she told him.

Although Jeremiah's last words were heartfelt, he had still destroyed too many lives. It was time for him to repent. It would be only a matter of time before the drugs leaked into his bloodstream.

"Let's go. In a couple of hours, he will be dead," Patience said, walking out.

Jeremiah was right; killing the lieutenants wouldn't make a difference. Ramon was not going to stop.

CHAPTER 16
WWW.COWELL.COM

The more Ramon thought about Cowell's story, the angrier he became. Something didn't seem quite right, so he reached out to one of his informants at FBI headquarters.

"Burgos…" Ramon smiled while shaking his hand. "It's always good to see you. How's the family?"

Jittery, Burgos wondered why Ramon had called him. "Good. Everyone is good. Thanks for asking."

Ramon had other things to do, so he wasted no time. He led Burgos over to the table and unbuttoned his suit jacket. "I'm gonna get straight to the point. A few weeks ago, Cowell fucked up a deal. He told me the Russian tried to make a move, but I heard differently."

Still shaking from nervousness, Burgos asked, "What did you hear?"

"There was a woman who accompanied him to dinner and then the meeting."

"A woman?" Burgos repeated. "Where did she come from?"

"That's what I want you to find out. I don't know who she is, but I'm hearing he has brought her to other deals without my approval."

Burgos lowered his head and then looked up at Ramon. He wasn't sure if this was a test. Ramon was known for asking a question when he already knew the answer. It was Burgos who referred Chance to Cowell, but Cowell said he had cleared it with Ramon.

"Cowell did come to me asking for some help, but he said he cleared it with you. He didn't?" Burgos asked in a panicky tone.

"No, he didn't. Do you know her name?" Ramon asked, glaring at Burgos.

"No. I gave him about twenty names. I don't know which one he chose."

"Do you still have the list?" Ramon asked.

"No, but I think I can remember most of the names. Just give me a few days to put it together for you."

Ramon nodded as he got up and walked over to his desk. He picked up an envelope and threw it at Burgos. "This is for your time. I want the list on my desk by next week. And Burgos…" Ramon's voice trailed off.

"You don't have to say anything, Ramon. It will never happen again," Burgos promised while looking around, hoping no one would jump out and shoot him.

On the way to his car, Burgos stopped to catch his breath. He looked down at his hands. They were shaking like a leaf on a windy fall day. He looked around hoping no one was following him. He knew once he gave Ramon the list of names, he and Cowell were dead.

Just as Burgos was about to pull off, someone knocked on the passenger's side window, causing him to damn near jump threw the roof. It was Cowell.

"Hey, what brings you out here?" Burgos asked.

Cowell flashed a wicked grin. "I should be asking you that question. Have a safe trip back to L.A." he snidely said, then walked away.

Burgos confirmed what Ramon had already suspected. Shaking his head, Ramon released a devilish giggle. *When will motherfuckers learn?*

Cowell wasn't like the other lieutenants. He felt their stupidity got them in trouble and maybe even killed. Cowell, on the other hand, thought he was slick. Not only was he skimming the books, he was also recruiting people behind Ramon's back.

Ramon was in deep thought when his secretary buzzed in, letting him know Cowell was there.

"Cowell…" Ramon greeted, flashing a fake smile.

"Ramon…" Cowell smiled back.

Both men monitored each other's movement as they took a seat at the conference table.

"I ran into Burgos in the parking lot. He didn't look too good," Cowell sarcastically stated.

Ramon stared angrily at Cowell. *He has no idea who he's dealing with.*

"I guess something is bothering him. How's the hand?"

This motherfucker is trying to be funny. Cowell released a chuckle. "The hand is great. It's healing just fine."

"That's good to know."

Much tension filled the room as both men sized each other up.

"Are you on target for our next meeting?" Ramon inquired.

"Everything is on target, just as you requested," Cowell said in a condescending tone.

Ramon smirked. He started to say something smart, but chose not to. Cowell wasn't worth his breath. "And the girl?"

"She will be taken care of."

"Good. I want you to take Trey along. Teach him the ropes."

"Trey?" Cowell repeated

"Yeah, is there a problem?"

Cowell grinned. "Not a problem at all," he replied and rose to leave, because as far as he was concerned, their meeting was over.

Normally, Ramon would break someone's neck if they got up and walked out without being dismissed, but this time, he let it slide. Besides, Cowell was a walking dead man anyway.

Once Cowell left, Ramon called Trey into his office. "You're gonna go with Cowell. He's bringing the girl along. After the transaction, he's gonna put a bullet in her. When he's done, I want you to put a bullet in him."

"No problem," Trey said, and then walked out.

*****

Once the ladies received word about the hit, they came up with the perfect plan. Ramon didn't trust Cowell, so he planned to change the location at the last minute.

Meanwhile, Justice went back to Atlanta, and Patience continued working for Daniel. As for Seven, she had Zhang eating out of her hand. Chance flew back to L.A. to check in with Burgos.

"Sir," she said, entering his office.

"Agent Cohen, come in." He removed his glasses. "How's everything? Any update on your family's murder?" he asked.

Chance stared at him and thought, *Why is he asking me about something that is off the record*? Rule number one, when an agent is undercover, you never talk about their case in the office. Burgos knew better. *Something's up.*

Chance cleared her throat. "I'm sorry, sir. I'm not investigating my family's murder."

Burgos looked up at her. "Oh, that's right."

Fuck, Chance thought, remembering she didn't have on her earpiece. Something was definitely up with Burgos, who was sweating and kept looking at his watch.

"Are you okay, sir?" Chance asked.

"Need to stop smoking and lose some weight. Other than that I'm great," he humored.

Chance flashed a weak grin, but she didn't find anything funny. Once Burgos realized she was too smart for his ass, he changed the subject, and they made small talk for the next hour.

As she proceeded to the door, Burgos blurted out, "Remember what I said, Agent Cohen."

That statement was code for, *Someone is listening.*

Chance smiled. "No, you remember what I said," she responded with a wink.

Someone got to Burgos, Chance thought. She wanted to pull out her phone to call Seven, but didn't in case someone was watching her. *Shit!* Just when she thought her day couldn't get any worse, Cowell was leaning on her car when she reached it.

"You're a hard person to find," he commented and smiled.

"Apparently, not hard enough. What can I do for you?" she asked.

"Since I haven't heard from you, I figured I'd stop by to see how you're doing."

Who the fuck is he kidding? Chance smirked and said, "Funny that you would come see me here."

"I came to see an old friend." Cowell flashed a devilish smile.

"The same friend who recommended me?"

Not acknowledging her comment, he asked, "Hungry? Let's go eat."

After going to one of The Secret Society's restaurants to eat, and while waiting for their food to arrive, Cowell said, "I have another assignment for you."

"I'm done with your assignments," Chance declared in a calm tone.

"Done?" Cowell repeated, then sipped his water. "As I stated before, Agent Cohen, leaving isn't an option."

"I guess I just made it one," she stated, getting up to leave.

Cowell looked around before replying, "Little girl, don't you know who I am? I will fucking destroy you. I have done things to people that will give your unborn children nightmares. So, I suggest you sit back in that motherfucking chair and listen, because I'm not going to repeat myself."

Remaining calm, Chance did as she was told. "I'm all ears."

"You know, you should be grateful considering I took a bullet in my hand for you."

"A bullet in the hand? Wow, the person didn't have good aim."

Cowell laughed. "You have a smart fucking mouth. Maybe I made a mistake; I should've let the Russians teach you some respect."

"I guess that makes two of us," Chance shot back. "Cowell, you should know I don't scare easily."

She got up to leave again. This time, Cowell grabbed her by her wrist and held it tightly. "Sit your ass down. I'm not

finished," he grumbled through his teeth, forcing her to sit back down.

She was starting to piss Cowell off. She poked her chest out a little too much. He ordered his team to clear out the dining area. Then he grabbed the steak knife and put it to her throat.

"Do you know what I can do to you, huh?"

Wiggling but still showing no fear, Chance muttered, "Then do what you have to do."

Cowell looked at his hand. He wanted to cut her throat from ear to ear, but Ramon said he wanted her dead *after* the transaction, not before. So, he took the steak knife and plunged it into a basket of bread.

"Next time you might not be so lucky," he warned before sitting back down.

Chance was so heated that her body was burning up. Her eyes filled with tears, and her hands were trembling.

"What's the assignment?" she asked.

Cowell glowered at her. "I've had enough of you," he proclaimed nastily. "I'll be in touch. Just don't leave town or try anything stupid you may regret."

Composing herself, Chance took a deep breath and stood up. As she turned to walk away, Cowell grabbed her hand and kissed it.

Once outside, Chance broke down. She needed to let off some steam, so she hit the shooting range. She thought about Burgos and felt something was up. So, she reached out to Seven, asking her to pull up everything on John Burgos. Chance should've known Burgos was corrupt. He was the one leaking information to Cowell. Chance was just a cover up. Cowell had something up his sleeve, and Chance needed to know what. She jetted back to New Jersey to meet with the girls and instruct them to take different routes in case someone was following them.

However, none of the ladies was there when Chance arrived. Therefore, she took a minute to collect her thoughts. *Burgos looked me in the face, pretended to care about my family, and then threw me to the wolves.*

"You alright?" Seven asked, startling Chance as she entered the room.

"Yeah. Did you pull up everything on John Burgos?" she said, brushing off her thoughts.

"Yes, but am I looking for anything in particular?" Seven asked, heading to the computer area.

In a daze, Chance replied, "No."

While Seven went to get the information, Chance drifted off again, this time thinking about her family who she missed so much.

"Chance...Chance!" Seven called. "Hey, are you okay?" she asked, noticing Chance's behavior.

"Yes, I'm fine. What's the story with Burgos?"

"Lieutenant John Burgos has offshore accounts with three hundred thousand dollars in them. But, that's not the only thing that sticks out. It seems your boy Burgos has a mistress who works at one of Ramon's brothels," Seven said, leading her into the surveillance room.

"So he's on Ramon's payroll?" Chance asked.

"What's going on?" Patience asked as she and Justice entered the room.

"Just schooling Chance on Lieutenant Burgos," Seven replied before continuing. "You think he sold you out?"

Disgusted, Chance wiped her face while staring at the screen. She couldn't believe Burgos was corrupt.

"You okay, Chance?" Seven asked, trying to break the silence.

"Yeah, I'm fine," she mumbled.

"You know this guy?" Justice inquired.

"He's my supervisor. That's how Cowell found me. Burgos gave him my name," Chance explained.

"But why?" Patience asked.

"That's what I'm gonna find out." Chance walked out, pissed.

"Chance...Chance!" they called out, running after her. "Chance, wait!"

Justice grabbed her by the arm. "Chance, you can't just confront him like that, especially if he's on to you."

"She's right," Patience agreed.

"Like you told us, an emotion can get you killed, and you're acting on your emotions," Seven stated. "Chill the fuck out and let's come up with a plan."

Chance looked each of them in the face; they were right. Confronting Burgos would be like putting a bull's-eye on her back. Coming to her senses, Chance went back inside.

"Come on, girl. Let's put our heads together and get these motherfuckers," Patience said, while Seven walked to the computer.

"God may have answered your prayers, Chance," Seven blurted out.

"What?" she asked, confused by Seven's comment.

"Ramon sent Seth an email," Seven said, pulling it up "He wants him to create Trey Hayes a profile"

"Trey Hayes? Who's that?" Patience asked.

"I'm not surprised. Pull up Trey's photo," Chance told Seven. "Ramon must know Cowell is up to something. Cowell told me that he took a bullet in his hand for me," Chance said.

"Damn, he was at the Russian meeting. He must've told Ramon what happened. Which means Ramon wants me dead, too."

"How? Ramon doesn't even know who you are. Your picture or name hasn't come up on the site," Justice pointed out.

"Not yet," Chance stated, raising an eyebrow. "It's only a matter of time. Once they do that, it's only a matter of time before they put all of us together."

"So what should we do?" Seven asked.

"I think Burgos gave me up. We take Burgos, then Trey and Cowell."

The ladies went back in the lab and started brainstorming until they came up with the perfect plan. Cowell wasn't like the others, so luring him to an isolated area would be dangerous. As for Burgos, they needed it to look like a hit.

Chance stood up, walked over to the large computer screen, and stared at Burgos and Cowell's pictures. Some jobs needed to

look like accidents. Others must cast suspicion on someone else. And a select few needed to be sent a clear message.

*****

The ladies arrived in L.A. together, using different names and wearing prosthetic faces in case they were being watched. They went straight to the location Chance had given them the day before so they could change.

According to Seven, every Thursday evening Burgos visited the brothel. Afterwards, he would stop off at McDonald's to get a bite to eat. The ladies thought it would be best for Chance to sit this mission out, especially since it needed to look like a hit. Besides, knowing Cowell, he had someone tailing Chance.

Seven followed Burgos to McDonald's. They thought about running up on him, but Burgos had already arrived at the fast-food restaurant, pulled into the parking lot, and went in. Dressed in black army fatigue outfits with hats to match, the ladies hopped out of the car and followed him inside. The place was packed. Seven walked over to the left side, while Patience went to the right and Justice stayed in the center. Surrounding him, the ladies waited patiently. A customer, who noticed the suspicious nature of the women, was about to say something, when the women pulled out. Burgos turned around, facing the unthinkable. With no hesitation, the women released fired, filling his body with lead. Everyone in the restaurant screamed and ran for cover. Seven and the ladies fled the scene, hopped into the car, and sped away. Two miles down the road they switched cars, burning the first one.

By the time Cowell sent Trey to pick up Chance, the ladies were already in position. As always, they checked her for devices and then blindfolded her. Anyone else would've been shitting their pants from fear, but for some reason, Chance wasn't. Two things were going to happen tonight. Either she was going to be with her family in death or be with her new family in life. Either way, she'd be happy.

On the car ride to the location, the radio disc jockey reported that an FBI lieutenant had been murdered inside a McDonald's restaurant that evening.

Chance smiled. *My girls did their thang.*

"We're here," Trey announced.

After helping her out of the car, they removed the blindfold from her face. Chance looked around. They were at an abandoned airport outside of Los Angeles. Trey and another worker led Chance inside where Cowell was just finishing up the transactions.

Trey looked at the guys and then at Cowell. In his gut, he felt like something was up.

"Ramon said he wanted…"

Before Trey could finish, Cowell quickly drew his gun and put a bullet in his head and the other worker's head. He then looked at the men who he had just performed the transaction with and said, "Sorry, guys," before executing them, as well.

Saving the best for last, he turned towards Chance. He took a deep breath, staring at her.

"When did you know Ramon was gonna kill you?" Chance asked, stalling with her hands up in the air.

"A couple of months ago. Ramon doesn't keep any lieutenant more than three years."

"And me?" she asked.

Cowell cocked his gun. "Collateral damage. But look at it this way. At least you get to be with your family."

Chance smiled. "You're right. I will be with my family."

The room echoed with the sound of guns cocking.

"I love it when a plan comes together." Chance winked at Cowell.

Cowell thought about opening fire, figuring he would shoot at least two of them.

"Don't even think about it," Seven said, walking up and snatching the gun from him.

Cowell laughed. For the first time, someone was smarter than Ramon. "You know Ramon was responsible for killing your family, right?" he told her.

"Yes. Just like I knew about Burgos recommending me, Khalidi and Jeremiah disappearing…oh, and the hit on me." Chance winked.

"Khalidi, Jeremiah? Ramon had them killed."

Chance released a fake high-pitched laugh .

"You killed Jeremiah and Khalidi?" Cowell asked in a surprised tone.

Chance smiled and winked again. "You're not just a handsome face after all."

Cowell looked around. Out of all the people he thought would've set him up, never did he imagine women would outsmart him. "You know killing me isn't gonna change anything. Ramon and Daniel will continue their criminal enterprise."

"I never said it would. Don't worry, though. They'll join you," Chance replied.

"Don't you wanna know—"

"You already told me," Chance said, interrupting him. "It's money."

"No. The money isn't why I did it. I did it to save my country. Agent Cohen, sometimes you have to dance with the devil in order to get out of hell."

"A dance I promise you won't dance alone. They fucked up when they killed my family. Now I'm gonna make sure every one of them rots in hell," Chance grumbled.

"Who else is on Ramon's payroll?" Seven asked.

Cowell smirked. "Names are not important. Knowing them can be dangerous."

"And a bullet in the back of your head can be deadly," Patience said.

Cowell was not shaken by her threat. "Agent Cohen, tell them nothing is approved without the government. You think the government doesn't know what's going on? Shit, wars are a billion-dollar business. You wanna raise taxes? Scare the hell out of people. You know what's called human wickedness? Unfortunately, you can't kill that shit with a fucking gun. I served my country so you bitches could sleep at night, and this is the thanks I get?" Cowell scolded.

Having heard enough, Chance raised her gun. "And for that, we thank you," she said, then let off a single round into Cowell's head. "Let's clean and burn everything, guns and all," she ordered before walking out to get a breath of fresh air.

CHAPTER 17
WWW.ZHANG.COM

Zhang didn't know if it was the death of the lieutenants or the fact that she was seeing a woman, but Ramon had been treating Zhang like shit. Auditing her files, popping up at her apartment unexpected, fucking her in the office and then dismissing her. One would think with all the bullshit going on that Ramon would focus his attention on replacing the lieutenants.

She didn't understand why he was acting like that. It's not like they were in a relationship. Plenty of nights he stood her up to fuck one of his other girls. Even if she wanted to feel sorry for him, she couldn't because he was such a bastard. None of the lieutenants' bodies had been found, and he had already replaced them.

Zhang should've known better, though. Ramon only cared about one thing: money. One day she knew her day was going to come, and when it did, she was going to tell him to kiss her ass.

Three lieutenants killed in four months. Who does Ramon think he's kidding? He had something to do with it. But, Zhang couldn't worry about that now. She was meeting her boo Seven for lunch. Ramon purposely kept her busy so she couldn't have a personal life. Today, though, Zhang had cleared her schedule so she could see Seven.

However, on her way out the door, the receptionist told her that Ramon was on his way up. Zhang threw her head back. *This motherfucker has to have someone watching me.* Before she could respond, Ramon was coming through the door.

"Going somewhere?" he asked.

Tired of his games, Zhang replied, "Yes, I was. I was going to have lunch with a friend."

"Is this the same friend I wanted you to invite to dinner?" he asked, looking Zhang up and down.

She rolled her eyes. "How can I help you?" she said, ignoring his question.

Ramon laughed. Like the others, Zhang had grown a set of balls. "I tell you what. I don't want to hold you up since you made plans, but I want you and your bitch at my townhouse tonight," he ordered, then kissed her and walked out.

Zhang was so pissed she wanted to scream. She was tired of being his slave, but what could she do? She was afraid of him. After glancing at her watch, she got herself together and headed out to meet Seven for lunch at The Olive Garden.

"Hey," Zhang said, kissing Seven on the lips.

"Hi. What's wrong?" Seven asked, noticing the expression on Zhang's face.

While they had only been together a couple of months, Seven knew when something was bothering her.

"It's that obvious?" Zhang said, releasing a giggle.

"I just know when something is bothering my baby."

Zhang looked into Seven's beautiful eyes, and her heart melted. "It's my boss."

"What about him?" Seven asked.

"He's an ass."

"Aren't they all?" Seven said, making Zhang laugh.

Zhang looked around to make sure no one was listening. "No, Seven, I'm serious. Before you came into my life, I had a relationship with him," Zhang told her, then looked away in shame.

"A relationship?"

"I wouldn't even call it a relationship. He just used to fuck me. Anyway, he found out about you, and now he's treating me like shit."

"How?"

Zhang sighed. What she was about to say could get her and Seven killed, but she needed someone to talk to. She'd been holding this in for years, and she felt if she didn't tell anyone, she was going to go crazy. Also, if something should ever happen to her, she wanted someone to know who was responsible.

"Have you ever heard of The Secret Society?"

"The what?' Seven said, pretending not to hear her.

Zhang looked around again. "The Secret Society."

"No. What's that, some gay activist group?" Seven asked, causing Zhang to bust out laughing.

"No, silly. They are people who actually run the world," Zhang whispered.

As a part of her act, Seven gave Zhang a sideways look. "Run the world? What world?"

Zhang exhaled. "Our world."

This time, Seven busted out in laughter. "Are they human?"

Annoyed, Zhang rolled her eyes and snapped, "Just forget it."

Seven reached out, touching Zhang's hand. "Come here, baby. I'm only joking, but come on…The Secret Society?"

"Shhh! Someone might be listening."

"Alright, say I buy what you're saying. What do they do?"

"You're making fun of me, right?" Zhang said, twisting her face.

"No, ma. I heard about the free world. I just thought they were made-up stories."

Over lunch, Zhang told her everything about The Secret Society, leaving Seven speechless.

"And you work for these people?" Seven asked, appalled.

"Yes, but it wasn't like that. If I had known in the beginning what these people were about, I would've never taken this job. Now I'm stuck ," Zhang cried. "I hate them so much…what they do to people. They need to rot in jail."

Seven nodded while thinking, *Oh, they'll rot.*

"You can't go to the police?" Seven asked her.

Zhang wiped away her tears. "Police? Please! Ramon plays golf with the commissioner. I'll be dead before I leave the precinct."

"I wish I could help," Seven said, trying to comfort her.

"Listening helps a lot. For years I've wanted to tell someone, but who could I trust, you know?"

Seven nodded her head. "I can't do nothing, but I'm always here if you need to talk."

"Thanks," Zhang replied, smiling. "I have a favor to ask, though."

"Go ahead."

"Remember I told you about my boss wanting us to have dinner with him."

"Yeah," Seven said in a leery tone.

"Well, he wants that to happen tonight."

"Tonight?"

"Yes. Please," Zhang begged. "Please…"

Seven sighed. "But I don't have anything to wear."

"Let's go shopping," Zhang suggested with a broad smile.

Instead of going back to the office, Zhang took Seven shopping. She was in awe at how Seven looked good in everything. Watching her undress, she wondered why Seven hadn't touched her in a while. They were in a private dressing room, when Zhang walked up behind Seven and started licking on her back.

"We're in a dressing room," Seven whispered with a giggle, despite not being in the mood.

"So?" a bold Zhang replied. She was so open she didn't know what to do with herself.

Seven faced Zhang who was so aroused that she crossed her legs trying to contain her horniness. "Why are you crossing your legs?"

"I'm not—" Zhang tried to reply but was caught off guard by Seven's hand rubbing up her thigh.

"Open them," Seven whispered, then sucked on Zhang's earlobe.

Fiending for Seven, Zhang opened her legs. Seven slid her hand further up her thigh and into her panties. Zhang was wet.

"I missed you," she moaned.

"I know," Seven replied as she fingered Zhang. "But what if someone comes in?" she asked, removing Zhang's clothing.

Zhang paused, exited the dressing room, and said something to the sales rep.

"Now, where were we?" She kissed Seven in the mouth when she returned.

Seven laughed. "I love a women with power," she said, then proceeded to take Zhang to heaven.

*****

After they killed Cowell, Justice flew back to Atlanta. When Daniel wasn't trying to fuck Patience, he had her working like a slave.

"Where the hell have you been?" Chance asked when Seven entered the warehouse.

"With Zhang. We went shopping."

Chance laughed. "You got that girl open."

With a disgusted look on her face, Seven took a deep breath and replied, "Yeah, tell me about it. Over lunch, she told me everything about The Secret Society."

"Get the fuck outta here?" Chance said in surprise.

"Yeah, she told me so much shit."

"Anything we can use?"

"Not really. Don't worry, though. After tonight, I'm gonna know Ramon's blood type."

Chance giggled. "Tonight? What's supposed to happen tonight?

Seven took a seat. "Ramon found out about me and Zhang."

"What!"

"Yeah, and he told her to bring me to dinner tonight."

Chance stood up, pacing back and forth. "Seven, I don't like this. What if Zhang is tryna set you up? What if he knows we are behind the killings?"

"Calm down. I think he just wants to meet me." Seven looked at the clock on the wall. "I have to get ready. Pull out some devices for me while I jump in the shower."

Hearing this made Chance nervous. How long had Ramon known about Seven? Why did he insist on Zhang bringing her to dinner? Ramon wasn't like the others; he was on point. So, Chance made sure the devices Seven would use that night were the ones the Black Ops team used. She wasn't taking any chances.

"Ready!" Seven announced, modeling her outfit. "How do I look?"

"Damn, Seven, you look nice. You know what? You look better than Amber Rose."

"Of course, I do, because I don't have those ghetto-ass tattoos on my arm." Seven winked.

Chance handed her the devices. "Seven, I'll be watching the whole time. Don't go out there tryna be no fucking hero."

"Don't worry. I'm leaving my red boots and cape at home tonight," she joked, causing Chance to laugh.

Zhang had called Seven a thousand times asking her where she was because Ramon had sent a car for them, and he didn't like to be kept waiting. When Seven arrived by cab, Zhang was standing in front of her building. Zhang almost tripped at how gorgeous Seven looked dressed in a body-hugging Stella McCartney's dress and wearing a pair of black Walter Steiger pumps. For a second, Zhang was jealous.

"Wow!" Zhang smiled.

"You like?" Seven asked seductively.

"Yes. Now, come on. We're gonna be late."

When they pulled up to a huge mansion in Connecticut, Seven tried hard not to look impressed. As for Zhang, she was upset because she thought they were having dinner at Ramon's midtown townhouse. She rolled her eyes as one of the workers led them inside to the foyer. Once there, the butler led them into a media room where Ramon greeted them.

"Zhang darling, you look lovely."

"Ramon," she replied, flashing a fake smile and kissing him on the cheek.

"And who is this beautiful woman?" Ramon said in awe.

Motherfucker, you know who this is. Isn't she the reason you invited us? Zhang thought, but replied, "This is Seven. Seven, this is Ramon."

"Charmed," Ramon said, kissing her on the hand.

"Hello." Seven smiled while trying not to glare at him.

"Shall we?" Ramon led them over to the bar.

He couldn't take his eyes off Seven. *She's stunning and sexy, but is she the right person for the job?* He looked over at Zhang. *Yeah, she's pretty, but insecure and needy. And I've grown tired of that.*

"So, Seven..." Ramon handed them each a drink. "...where did you and Zhang meet?"

Seven looked over at Zhang before responding. "I work at the gym she works out at."

"Seven has been helping me tone up," Zhang added.

Ramon looked over at Zhang and then back at Seven. "How long have you been working there?" he asked, totally disregarding Zhang.

"For a while," Seven said.

When the cook informed them that dinner was ready, Ramon held Seven by the waist and guided her into the dining room, ignoring Zhang.

"Seven, are you enjoying the food?" he asked while they ate.

"Yes, it's delicious. Thank you."

"What about you, Zhang?" he asked to be polite, not that he really cared.

"It's good."

For a brief moment, there was complete silence, until Ramon blurted out, "So, Seven, how long have you been fucking Zhang? I didn't know she was into women."

Zhang damn near choked on her food, while Seven, although stunned, played it cool. She glanced over at Zhang, who was drinking water, and then back at Ramon, who had a smirk on his face.

"Well, I don't know who or what she was into before me, but we've been dealing with each other for a couple of months."

"Are y'all serious?" he asked, glaring at them.

Completely humiliated, Zhang cut her eyes in a subdued way. "Why?" she asked in a tone that suggested she was pissed off. "I didn't know my love life was tonight's dinner topic."

Seven looked at Ramon, who had a look that said, *This bitch must be crazy look.*

Feeling the need to intervene, she smiled and said, "It's cool, baby. I don't mind talking about our relationship. While it's too early to tell, right now, we are taking our time enjoying each other."

Yes, baby, you tell him, Zhang thought while looking over at her. That's why she loved Seven. She didn't take shit from anyone, not even Ramon.

"To be her boss, you seem to be very interested in Zhang's love life," Seven added.

"Well..." he said, looking over at Zhang, "...we were close at one time. Does that bother you?"

Seven smirked inside. "Not in the least. Trust me, I've never had a problem satisfying a woman."

"I can testify to that," Zhang snidely whispered, sipping her drink.

As the evening came to an end, it was clear to Zhang that Ramon was very interested in Seven, but for what reason? On the ride home, Zhang was silent. She couldn't believe Ramon. He blatantly flirted with Seven in front of her. She glanced over at Seven and wondered if she was interested in Ramon. She remembered Seven saying she use to mess with men. Could Ramon win Seven's heart? The more Zhang thought about it, her eyes filled up with tears.

Noticing something was wrong, Seven asked, "Why are you so quiet?"

"Nothing," Zhang mumbled, staring out the window.

Seven gently grabbed her face and turned it towards her. "What's wrong?"

Zhang looked into Seven's eyes. She started to say something, but didn't because she feared Ramon might have the car tapped.

★ ★ ★ ★

"Let's talk about it later, okay?" she said, giving Seven the eye to hint that someone might be listening in on their conversation.

Seven nodded to acknowledge she understood.

A block away from Zhang's apartment, Seven asked the driver to let them out. Zhang looked at Seven like she was crazy.

"Come on. It's not that cold outside, so let's walk," Seven said, grabbing her hand.

Seven continued to hold Zhang's hand as they strolled.

"What's up?" Seven asked.

"Nothing."

Seven swung Zhang around. "So now it's nothing?"

"It's Ramon. He was flirting with you all night," Zhang said and started to walk.

"And?"

"And I know he's attracted to you."

"No, he isn't. Ramon's just mad because I'm fucking you and not him," Seven explained, causing Zhang to crack a smile. "For real, men like Ramon are insecure. They hate when someone has bigger balls than them."

By now, Zhang was laughing her ass off. "Yeah, that's him. Are you attracted to him?" she asked, her laughter dying as she held her breath waiting for Seven's answer.

"He's nice looking, but I'm not into men like that. Yeah, I will fuck them if I like them, but men aren't my thing." Seven stopped walking and grabbed Zhang by her waist. "You're my thing. I'm into you," she said, then kissed her.

"You better be, because I'm into you," Zhang replied, kissing her back.

Seven really didn't want to, but she made love to Zhang all night.

*****

The following morning, Seven received a huge bouquet of long-stemmed roses at the job. After last night, she assumed they were from Zhang, but they weren't. They were from Ramon, thanking her for last night. This left Seven puzzled.

A couple of days went by, and Zhang was still smiling. Not only was she in love with Seven, she hadn't heard from Ramon since they had dinner at his place. Hopefully, he was busy recruiting lieutenants to meddle in her personal life. Unfortunately, she spoke too soon. He called requesting her to meet him at his townhouse. Zhang could only wonder what for this time. When she got there, Ramon was on the phone.

"Zhang," he said, kissing her on the cheek after ending his call.

"Ramon."

He grabbed her hand. "Listen, I was thinking. You've been working so hard, and I think it's time for a vacation."

This wasn't the Ramon she worked for. "A vacation?"

"Yes. I know I haven't been the best boss, so I'm taking you on a vacation."

Most employees would have been thrilled at the idea of their boss taking them on vacation, but not Zhang. She felt Ramon had something up his sleeve.

"Just you and I?" she asked.

"Well, I was hoping you could convince Seven to come along."

Zhang sighed. She knew there was a catch. "I don't think so. It's last minute. I'm not sure Seven can get the time off from work."

"Don't be silly. I already called the owner of the gym, and they said they would be more than happy to give her some days off with pay."

"So you have everything covered, huh?" Zhang spitefully said.

"Of course. You should know I always get what I want."

With that being said, Zhang had no choice; she and Seven were going on vacation. Initially, when Zhang told Seven, she declined, lying about how she didn't feel comfortable with Ramon taking them on vacation. However, the real reason was that Seven didn't know what Ramon was up to. The girls didn't like the idea either, but Seven was in too deep to turn back now. If she didn't, Ramon would suspect something and have her killed.

The worst part about it was Ramon didn't let them know where they were going. He just picked them up and headed to the airport where they boarded a private plane. For the first time, Seven was nervous. She was ten thousand feet in the air without her girls.

Ramon took them to an exotic island called Bali in Indonesia, where he owned a home. It was breathtaking. This time, Seven couldn't contain herself; she was amazed. Though pissed off, Zhang had to admit it was beautiful.

Zhang was exhausted from the long flight. Meanwhile, Seven was too excited to sleep. So, she stood on the deck taking in the scenery, when Ramon walked up behind her.

"It's beautiful," he slowly whispered.

Startled, Seven jumped. "Oh, you scared me. Yes, it is."

Too bad Ramon wasn't talking about the ocean view.

"Can I ask you a question?" he said.

"Sure."

"How can someone so beautiful be with a woman?"

Seven blushed. "I don't understand your question," she responded, playing naïve.

"You and Zhang…surely you can't tell me that she's satisfying your needs."

Seven took a step back. "My question to you is, are you jealous because she's with a woman now?"

Ramon let out a fake laugh. "Zhang isn't the one I want. I've seen you in action," he said, undressing Seven with his eyes.

"So you like to watch?" Seven said, flirting back. "Stick around, and you might get a show tonight," she moaned before walking back inside the house.

Ramon looked down at his penis, which was rock hard. *Oh yeah, she's the one,* he thought.

Zhang kept Seven away from Ramon throughout the vacation. She knew Ramon's intentions.

While they were getting a massage, Zhang informed her, "Ramon wants to fuck you."

"Huh?" Seven said, wondering where that came from.

"He does. I can tell by the way he stares at you. The only reason why he invited me on this trip was to get you here so he could fuck you," Zhang angrily stated.

"No, he didn't."

"Yes. Ever since that day he saw us having sex in my apartment, he's wanted you."

"Whoa!" Seven rose up from the massage table. "What are you talking about?"

Shit! Zhang realized she had forgotten to tell her. "The first time we had sex he saw us."

"How?" Seven asked, shouting.

"I don't know, Seven, but he did."

Seven glared at Zhang, wanting to beat the shit out of her. *Was Chance right? Is this a set up?* Seven started to worry, but knew she needed to calm down.

"You should've told me, Zhang," Seven said, walking out.

For the remainder of their trip, Seven gave Zhang the cold shoulder. She couldn't believe Zhang didn't tell her.

Since it was their last night on the island, Ramon thought it would be nice if they had dinner together. Seven was silent throughout the evening. As for Zhang, she looked like she had lost her best friend.

"Seven, you're awfully quite tonight," Ramon said.

"Just thinking about how much I have to do when I get back."

Seven wasn't aware that Zhang had been drinking all day and was feeling a little tipsy.

"I told Seven that you saw us having sex," Zhang blurted out while strutting over to her.

If looks could kill, Zhang would've been dead. However, Zhang felt she needed to clear the air.

"I know you wanna fuck Seven," she moaned, touching Seven's breasts. "Isn't that right, Ramon? You wanna taste this pussy," she said, pushing her hand between Seven's legs.

"Zhang…" Seven removed her hand. "…stop! You're—"

"I'm what? Ramon likes to watch. Don't you?" she asked, looking at him.

Seven looked over at Ramon, who was enjoying the show, and then she whispered to Zhang, "I'm not in the mood. You had too much to drink."

However, Zhang wasn't trying to hear that. She ripped open Seven's shirt, pulled up her bra, and start sucking her breasts. If Seven had been physically attracted to Zhang, she might've enjoyed it, but she didn't. She could tell Ramon was enjoying it, though.

Okay, Zhang, let me show you how it's done, she thought, wanting to get it over with.

Knocking all the dishes on the floor, she can put Zhang on top of the table. Zhang didn't know if it was the liquor or the fact that she was horny as hell, but the idea of Ramon watching them turned her on. Ramon's dick was so hard he could've lifted the table up with it. As she and Zhang kissed and touched each other, Seven started to get into it. She looked over at Ramon, signaling for him to join them.

It had been a long time since she experienced the pleasure of a man and a woman's touch. She sucked Ramon's dick while Zhang ate her out, and then they switched. Taking turns giving each other pleasure, Seven brought out the freak in Ramon. Pushing Zhang aside, she started riding him. Ramon thought he had died and gone to heaven. He wasn't sure if it was the tightness of Seven's pussy when she squeezed her muscles or its wetness. He couldn't remember the last time his dick felt like that. Zhang stood there like a bump on a log; she couldn't believe how much Seven was enjoying herself.

Seven looked over at Zhang, hopped off of Ramon, and made Zhang lick her juices off of Ramon's dick. That night, Zhang and Ramon got a taste of Seven's deadly sins.

Seven was sleeping when Zhang decided to confront Ramon. She knew with him it was just about sex. For her, she truly loved Seven.

"So are you happy now?" she asked an exhausted Ramon as he exited the bathroom after taking a shower.

"What do you mean?"

"You know what I mean. You've been dying to fuck Seven ever since the day you laid eyes on her."

"She is something, isn't she?"

"Well, I'm warning you, Ramon. She's the best thing that ever happened to me, so leave her alone."

Ramon chuckled. "You know what, Zhang? I think she's the fuck of the century."

Furious, Zhang stormed back to her room where Seven was still sleeping. Tears fell down Zhang's face as she stood in the doorway. She knew Ramon would never let the two of them be happy, and the thought of him hurting Seven killed Zhang. So, there was only one thing left to do.

*****

Ever since they returned home from the trip, Zhang had been avoiding Seven. She knew Ramon had special plans for her. Zhang wasn't about to allow the same thing happen to Seven that happened to Janice. Sitting at her desk in the living room, Zhang poured herself a glass of scotch. Then she reached into the drawer and pulled out a .44 Magnum.

As tears rolled down her face and with her hand trembling, Zhang muttered, "Fuck you, Ramon, and The Secret Society."

Putting the gun to her temple, she mumbled her final words, "I love you, Seven," And then blew her brains out.

Seven hadn't heard from Zhang since they came back from Bali. When they got off the plane, Zhang didn't even say goodbye. She just hopped into her awaiting car service. Seven knew she was upset about the threesome, but Zhang started it. Starting to worry, she decided to stop by her apartment. The doorman recognized Seven and stopped her at the front door.

"You're Ms. Lee's friend, right?"

"Yes," Seven replied.

"I was wondering when you were gonna come around. She left this for you," he said, handing her an envelope.

"Where is she?" Seven asked, taking it out of his hand.

"Ms. Lee killed herself a couple of days ago. Shot herself in the head."

Seven felt like she would faint. "Shot herself?"

"Yes. The cleaning lady found her."

After thanking him, Seven left and went back to the warehouse to read the letter. Chance and the girls were there, as well.

"Hey," Patience said. "Are you alright?"

"She killed herself," Seven muttered, still stunned. "Zhang killed herself."

"What! Why?" Chance asked, stunned.

Too distressed to talk, she handed them the note.

Seven,

By the time you read this note, I will be gone. I just wanted to say thank you for showing me what I had been missing. For that, I will always love you.

Love,
Zhang

The ladies went over to console Seven, who stood there in shock.

CHAPTER 18
WWW.SETH.COM

Things had been quiet with The Secret Society for the past couple of weeks. So, the ladies took a break and went back to their daily living. Their lives had been turned upside down, and they needed a moment to digest everything.

This was great for Seth, the only lieutenant whose life they had spared. The ladies needed him since he was the only link to their site. As for Ramon, he was analyzing everything that had happened over the last couple of months.

There's one connection in this, and that's Seth. Is he leaking information? He's the only person that knew the plan. Not even Daniel knew, Ramon thought.

Ramon reflected back to the day he met Seth. They were attending a Google convention. He was in charge of their IT Security Web Design. Ramon had heard through the grapevine that Seth was unhappy with Google and was looking to leave. When Ramon initially approached Seth about the job, he declined. However, like the others, Ramon made Seth an offer he couldn't refuse, promising him more money and his own company. After Seth signed his life away, Ramon reneged. On the outside, it appeared Seth owned his own company, but on paper, Ramon was the owner.

Seth was the only lieutenant who lasted more than three years, running their entire network from his office. Not only was he the best in the game, but it was also his idea to transform the operation to the net, taking The Secret Society organization to the next level. He built their entire infrastructure from websites to search engines.

Seth resided in Lake Washington right outside of Seattle. Unlike the others, he lived a normal life, married with three kids. But, like the others, he was getting tired of working for Ramon and Daniel, too. While Google didn't pay him what he wanted, at least they respected their employees, which was something Ramon and Daniel never did. They would kill you in a second.

He was upstairs, having just gotten his kids ready and off to school, when the housekeeper informed him that some men were there to see him.

"Did they say who they were?" he asked her.

"No," she said.

"I'll be down in a second."

It was Ramon and Daniel.

"Did we interrupt something?" Daniel asked, noticing the surprised look on Seth's face.

Skeptical, Seth smiled. "Of course not," he replied, leading them into his office. "Would you gentlemen like something to eat," he offered.

"No, we won't be staying long," Ramon said, while looking around. "The house looks wonderful."

"Thanks to Jill. She's into decorating." Seth flashed a nervous grin.

"How are Jill and the kids doing?" Ramon asked.

Seth looked at Daniel and then at Ramon, sensing something was up. "They're great. They just left for school."

Ramon took a seat. "Seth, you know I value you."

"I hope so," Seth humored with a nervous giggle.

"Seth, we think someone is hacking into our site," Daniel said.

"Impossible," Seth proclaimed.

"Then you are leaking information," Daniel stated.

Like the others, Seth couldn't stand Daniel. "Leaking information?" Seth repeated. "Nonsense! I would never do anything like that!" he shouted in a stern tone, looking at Ramon.

Daniel glanced at Ramon, who had a zombie-like look on his face.

"Information is being leaked because the lieutenants are running their mouths," Seth added, sweating.

Ramon stood up, something he did when annoyed. "Seth, you think I got here by default?"

"No, but neither did I. Trust me, Ramon, if anyone hacked into our site, I would know. They are getting their information from somewhere else," he explained with a panicked expression.

Daniel smirked; he got a kick out of making people sweat. "Seth...Seth, we all make mistakes. Or maybe you're just not as good as you say you are."

"Or maybe I'm not the one running my mouth," Seth shot back.

This white boy has lost his mind. Daniel jumped up to approach Seth. "What are you saying?" he said, getting in his face.

Trying not to be intimidated, Seth didn't back down. "You come in my house questioning me and my skills."

Without warning, Ramon pulled out a knife and stabbed Seth in the stomach. Seth gasped while falling to the floor. Daniel shot Ramon a crazy look.

Ramon took out a handkerchief and wiped Seth's blood off the knife. "Next time, I'm gonna gut you like a fish."

Although Ramon had stabbed Seth, there was no way he would kill him, unless he found someone else to run his network.

Holding his wound, Seth moaned from the excruciating pain.

"Ramon, I swear on my kids' life I don't know where they're getting the information from. But, it's not from me. I swear to God," he gasped, pulling himself up from off the floor. In pain, Seth blurted out, "I'll check the system again, but I can assure you no one is hacking into the site."

"For your sake, I hope not. Or I swear on your kids' life…" Ramon warned, then reached into his inside pocket, pulled out an envelope, and handed it to Seth. "Here are the names of the new lieutenants."

Seth took it. "I'll set their profiles up immediately."

"No, don't do anything yet. I just want you to monitor the network for now," Ramon said, ending the conversation.

Seth nodded as the two men left. Before he bled to death, he went to his private doctor to get stitched up.

After returning home, Seth went to his office to check the system. Everything was fine. *What the hell was Ramon talking about? We have the best security system in the world. Is someone trying to set me up?*

He pulled up all the emails from Ramon. Again, he mumbled to himself, "What the hell is he talking about?"

Puzzled, Seth picked up the phone to call one of his ex-workers at Google to see if they knew of anyone who had been hacking into sites lately. However, before the call went through, he hung up, fearing word would get back to Ramon.

Seth lifted up his shirt to look at his wound. One thing for sure, he wasn't going down without a fight. If something should happen to him or his family, Einstein wouldn't be able to hack into the network.

*****

Seven decided to check the site to see if anything popped up. Things were still quiet, but as she got up to leave, she noticed someone was downloading files. At first, she thought someone was hacking into their site, but when she checked the IP address, she noticed it was Seth moving files to a private hard drive. By then, Chance had arrived.

"Hey!"

Seven turned around. "Hey, Chance," she said and then turned her attention back to the computer screen.

"What's wrong?" Chance asked, noticing Seven's concerned look.

"Seth is moving files."

"Okay…" Chance responded, waiting for her to continue.

"Something's up. He's transferring them to a private hard drive."

Still not understanding what this meant, she asked, "So does that mean he's on to us?"

Concentrating on the screen, Seven replied. "I don't think so, but look at this."

Chance walked over to her. "Are those account numbers?"

"Yep!"

Chance started to pace back and forth. "It makes sense now."

"What?" Seven asked.

"Why there hasn't been any activity on the site. Ramon thinks Seth is up to something."

Seven turned around, nodding. "You may be right. The only link to all of this is Seth."

"Exactly!" Chance said.

"Damn!" Seven shook her head "You think Ramon is gonna kill him?"

"Not unless he has a replacement. Remember, he only kills them when he's found a replacement. Is there anyone out there better than Seth?"

"There are a few hackers, but none on Seth's level," Seven informed her.

"Then they won't kill him because they still need him."

Seven nodded. "Yeah, so what's next?"

Chance stared into Seven's face. "We wait."

Meanwhile in the car ride back to the airport, Daniel asked Ramon, "So what are your thoughts? You think Seth is tryna play us?"

"It's hard to say, but reach out to our friends over at the FBI. See who is on their most wanted list for hacking. Let's start looking for a replacement."

"In the meantime?" Daniel asked.

Ramon smiled. "Business as usual…business as usual."

As for Seth, he had transferred all the files. "Y'all screwed with the wrong one," he grumbled in pain.

CHAPTER 19
WWW.DANIEL.COM

Daniel Munger was forty-six years old, divorced, and an ex-football agent. He and Ramon had gone to college together. Over thirty years of friendship and Ramon still treated Daniel like shit. Even after Daniel found out Ramon was fucking his wife, he remained friends with him.

Now the motherfucker thought he was all that. Daniel told Ramon years ago to stop recruiting people off the street. Meanwhile, he had Daniel handling all the operations until they acclimated new lieutenants.

But, it was perfectly fine, because Daniel's day was going to come. Like Ramon, Daniel had an image to protect. Therefore, he had others, who he met with once a week, overseeing the daily operation.

It was the end of the day and Daniel was getting ready to leave, when he asked his assistant to call Patience to his office. Surprisingly, he had convinced Ramon to keep her alive.

"You wanted to see me?" Patience asked after knocking on the door.

"Yeah, come inside," Daniel said, reviewing some papers.

Patience took a seat.

"I like you, Ms. Green, and I think you're an asset to this company."

Here comes the bullshit, Patience thought. "But?" she said.

"But, I think you're not reaching your full potential."

Patience took a deep breath, wondering where this conversation was heading. Before she said something stupid, she remained quiet, allowing Daniel to continue. Smirking inside, Daniel got up to pour himself a drink.

"You want one?" he offered.

Annoyed, Patience responded, "No, thank you," while glaring at him.

"Like I said, you're not reaching your full potential."

"And what is that?"

Daniel licked his lips; he'd been dying to stick his dick in her since the first day they met.

"You figure it out," he responded, sipping his drink.

Patience looked at Daniel in disgust. There was no way in hell she would fuck the overconfident, fat bastard.

"So you're telling me fucking you is reaching my potential?"

Undressing her with his eyes, Daniel grabbed his cock. "Who the fuck are you kidding? I know Jeremiah was hitting that, and I know that lil' dick motherfucker wasn't fucking you right. Me..." he said, touching himself again, "...I'll fuck you like you need to be fucked."

Patience had never felt so disrespected in her life. If Daniel were the last man on earth, she still wouldn't fuck him.

"What Jeremiah and I did is none of your business. If you think I'm gonna sit here and be disrespected by you, you are sadly mistaken. You will have my resignation letter on your desk first thing in the morning." She stood up to leave.

Damn! Daniel thought he was going to force Patience to have sex with him, but she was tougher than he imagined. Maybe she did have feelings for Jeremiah, and that's why she had sex with him.

He jumped up and grabbed her hand. "Patience, wait. I'm sorry for disrespecting you. I don't want you to quit."

Truth be told, Daniel needed Patience. She made him look good. She brought in too much revenue for him to let her quit. In addition, Ramon would've hit the roof and probably killed his ass.

Standoffish, Patience looked down at Daniel's hand, causing him to let her go.

"Look," she said, pointing a finger, "like I told Jeremiah, you hired me to do a job. Fucking me is a bonus. Jeremiah, even with his little dick, earned that bonus."

Daniel stared at Patience for a second. She was a firecracker, and it was sexy as hell. Oddly, he respected the fact that she wasn't easy.

"Well, I know if Jeremiah earned it, I'm gonna own it." He winked.

Patience laughed at Daniel, who was such a clown. "I'm glad you're confident," she snidely replied, then walked out of the office.

For the next couple of weeks, Daniel flew into different states checking on operations. Since he'd been working hard, he decided to get some much-needed R&R. So, he went down to Magic City in Atlanta. In the VIP section surrounded by a bunch of strippers, Daniel felt like a king. He was having such a good time that he decided to take two of the strippers back with him to the Marriot in downtown Atlanta.

Ironically, Justice's shift was about to end, when the manager asked her to take some extra towels to the presidential suite.

Knock! Knock!

"Housekeeping," Justice announced.

Smack!

"Shut up, you stupid bitch," a male voice shouted.

"Please!" the girl cried.

Justice paused, swallowing hard. She remembered hearing those cries in Patra's house. Justice tiptoed inside to see where the cries were coming from. Just like Patra, this girl was tied to the shower pole with a rope. With her face bleeding, the girl looked up into Justice's face, their eyes meeting briefly. Scared, Justice placed the towels on the table next to the door and ran out of there.

All night, Justice tossed and turned. When she finally looked at the clock, it was time to get up. She thought about calling out, but had already been warned about her attendance.

Oddly, Justice was suppose to be off, but was called in for overtime. She was just coming off her lunch break, when Daniel spotted her. At first, he didn't know where he remembered her face from, but then it hit him. *Oh shit, that was Khalidi's bitch,* he thought. *So she's a housekeeper.* He immediately told one of his workers to have her come to the room.

Tired, Justice didn't recognize the room at first, but almost shit on herself when Daniel opened the door.

"Did someone request more towels?" she asked, holding her breath.

Gawking at her, Daniel smiled. "Yeah," he said, opening the door wider so she could come in. "You can place them on the bed."

Hesitant, Justice walked inside, while wanting to kick herself for not having her earpiece in. She kept looking over her shoulder as she laid the towels down, praying Daniel didn't attack her.

Daniel bit his bottom lip, admiring Justice's body. "You don't remember me?"

"Excuse me?" she said, playing dumb.

"You use to fuck with Khalidi."

Damn, he remembers me, Justice thought. "Yes, Khalidi and I were friends."

"Friends?" Daniel asked with a leery look.

"Sir, is there anything else I can do for you?" Justice asked, hoping he would let her go, but of course, it wouldn't be that easy.

"Yes. I need you to clean the master bathroom," he said, leading her to the room. "So what happened between you and Khalidi?"

"Nothing. I haven't heard from him in months. How's he doing?" Justice lied.

Daniel nodded. "Don't know. I haven't spoken to him in months either."

"Oh," Justice said, and then looked at the splatters of blood all over the bathroom. Justice faced Daniel, as if waiting for an explanation.

"I cut myself shaving," he told her.

Justice nodded, put her gloves on, and started cleaning. *So the mystery women beater was Daniel,* she thought.

After she finished cleaning, Daniel reached out for her hand as she walked toward the door.

"Hey, can I take you out to dinner?" he asked, trying a different approach.

"I don't think that would be a good idea."

"Why?"

"It just wouldn't be," Justice stated and started to walk out.

Daniel ran after her. "Alright, how about this? We go out to dinner…as friends only."

Justice sighed and put her hand on her hip. "Is this some kinda joke you and Khalidi are playing?"

Confused, Daniel responded, "What joke? From the first day I saw you, I wanted you, but you were with Khalidi. So, I backed off."

Their conversation was interrupted by a knock at the door. One of his workers entered with a girl behind him.

Justice looked at them and then at Daniel. "Looks like you have company."

Daniel shot his boy an evil look, which made them backtrack out of there. He shut the door to stop her from leaving.

"Sorry about that," Daniel said. "So are you gonna let me take you to dinner?"

"I can't. I have to work."

"I'll come on your lunch break."

Justice laughed at Daniel's persistence. "Hmmm…alright," she replied, giving in.

"Great! Tomorrow?"

"Okay. I usually go to dinner around eight. Is that okay?"

Daniel smiled. "That's perfect. I'll leave a note at the front desk with the time and place."

Once she left that floor, Justice immediately called Chance. "Hey!"

"What's up, Justice?"

"Daniel just asked me out."

"Daniel?" Chance repeated. "Daniel Munger?"

"Yes. He's staying at the hotel. He saw me and asked me out."

"Did he say anything about Khalidi?"

"Just that he hasn't seen him."

Chance grew quiet.

"Chance?" Justice called.

"I'm here. Just thinking. Why is he asking you out on a date? Is he fishing? That's what I'm afraid of," Chance explained.

"Yeah, I know. How about this? I go have dinner with him to see what he's talking about."

Still not feeling it, Chance started pacing and back forth. "Alright," she finally said. "Do you still have your earpiece and other devices?"

"Yes."

"Okay. I'll call Seven and Patience to let them know what's going on. Justice, Daniel is a different type of man."

"I know, Chance."

"Be careful, and don't give away any information."

Getting frustrated with the thought of Chance not trusting her to handle things, Justice responded, "I gotta go," and then hung up.

*****

Instead of taking Justice to a fancy restaurant, Daniel decided they would have dinner in his suite so they could have some privacy. It was a little after eight when Justice showed up.

Daniel, dressed in his best, opened the door. "I thought you stood me up." He laughed with a sigh of relief.

"The thought did cross my mind. Are we alone?" she asked while walking inside.

"Yes," Daniel replied, leading her into the dining area. "Since we're pressed for time. I took the liberty of ordering for us. I hope you don't mind," he said, trying to be a gentleman.

"That's fine," she said, looking around.

Daniel dimmed the lights and opened the drapes, allowing the starlight to shine on them. As for Justice, she was a little nervous since she didn't know what to expect. To her surprise, he acted like a perfect gentleman, pulling out her chair and asking if she was comfortable.

"Is your food okay?" he asked.

"It's wonderful. Thanks for asking."

Mesmerized by her beauty, Daniel said, "May I ask you something?"

Justice looked at him sideways. "Sure. What's up?"

"Why are you working as a housekeeper?"

"Why?" She was a little confused by the question.

"I've traveled all over the world, and women like you don't clean toilets."

"Women like me?" Justice repeated.

Not wanting her to be offended, Daniel decided to explain further. "I don't mean it like that. Most women with your looks usually are models, singers…you know."

"I don't know what women you are referring to, but me, I'm working to keep a roof over my head. I don't plan on doing housekeeping forever."

Noticing her accent, Daniel asked, "Where are you from?"

"Barbados."

Daniel stared at her for a second. *Patra was from Barbados*. He wondered if they knew each other. Now looking at Justice, she did remind him of Patra, with her beautiful skin, sexy accents, and a body to die for.

"Are you okay?" Justice asked, noticing Daniel had become real quiet all of a sudden.

"I was just thinking about something." He glanced at his watch. "Your lunch break is almost over."

Justice was surprised by Daniel's consideration for her job.

"So…" he said, standing in front of the door, "…can I see you again?"

Justice looked away. Although he was nice, Daniel wasn't Khalidi.

"Tell him you don't know," Chance said through the earpiece. "Don't make it seem like you're easy."

"I don't know."

"Well, what do I have to do to make you say yes?"

Justice smiled. "Thanks for dinner. Have a good evening."

Daniel loved a challenge, but first, he needed to make sure she wasn't up to something. Normally, he would ask Seth to run a background check, but he didn't want Ramon to find out. So, he ordered someone to follow her around for a couple of days.

Justice wasn't even down the hall before Chance called her. "Give me a sec," Justice mumbled, walking to a secluded area. "So what do you think?"

"He seemed to be interested in you."

"Yeah, so should I mess with him?" Justice asked.

"I still don't know. You already messed with Khalidi. I don't want you to fuck the entire organization," Chance explained.

"Tell me about it, but he was the one in Patra's room. He was the one who beat her just like he beat that girl last night."

"What!"

Justice sighed. "Last night, just before my shift ended, I took some towels to a room and saw a girl getting the crap beat out of her. Daniel had her tied to the shower pole, just like he did to Patra. I know he killed her."

Chance took a deep breath. She could tell this was bothering Justice. "Alright, get some rest, and let's talk about this tomorrow."

*****

Chance didn't like the way Justice sounded, so she asked Seven and Patience to fly down to Atlanta before she did something stupid. Instead of going to the hotel, they parked across from Justice's house and waited for her to come home. Once she pulled up, they waited a couple of seconds to make sure she wasn't being followed. After Justice went inside, a car pulled

up to the house. A guy got out, looked around, then got back in and drove off.

Chance looked over at Seven. "You see that?"

"Yeah," Seven said.

"Who was that?" Patience asked from the backseat.

"Daniel probably sent someone to check her out," Seven told her.

They waited a couple more minutes before getting out.

Justice was upstairs when the doorbell rang. She looked at the time and wondered who it could be. She ran downstairs and peeked through the curtains. It was Chance and the girls.

"Is something wrong?" she asked, surprised to see them.

"No, but we need to talk," Chance said, brushing past Justice with Seven and Patience following her.

Justice closed the door behind them. "What do we need to talk about?"

"Daniel," Chance replied, peeking out the curtains.

"What about Daniel?" Justice snapped.

"We don't think it's a good idea for you to mess with him," Seven said, sitting on the couch.

"We?" Justice repeated with her face screwed up.

"Yes...we," Chance said.

Instead of getting defensive, Justice took a deep breath, sat down, and listened. "Alright, tell me why."

"We're worried about you with Daniel."

"Worried?" Justice responded in a confused tone.

"Yes. He killed your cousin," Seven stated.

"And you think I can't handle it? Chance, weren't you the one who told me good judgment comes from experience and a lot of that comes from bad judgment?"

"Yes, but I also said your emotions can get you killed," Chance shot back.

"I didn't let my emotions get in the way with Khalidi," Justice proclaimed, glaring at them.

"Daniel isn't Khalidi," Seven pointed out. "He's the one who actually killed Patra. Are you still sure you can mess with him knowing all of this?"

Justice sighed and fell back into the loveseat. "Me don't know. All me can think about is the night he was with Patra," Justice explained, her voice cracking. "He treated her like a dog. Me want him to see me face just before he goes to hell."

The girls looked at each other and then at Justice, who was crying. Patience handed her some tissue, while Seven and Chance held their heads down. There was a brief moment of silence before Patience spoke.

"I think Justice should mess with Daniel."

"Messing with him isn't the problem. I don't trust him," Chance pointed out.

"Chance, we're not supposed to. But, it's been weeks and nothing. It's like we did all of that for nothing. The Secret Society is still in business," Patience stated.

Justice and Seven looked at Chance. Patience was right.

"So what do you suggest, Patience?"

"We went after their lieutenants and nothing. It's time to come up with a different plan, and Daniel just gave us one."

"What you think about this, Seven?" Chance asked.

Seven looked at all three ladies. "I agree with Patience and Justice. We killed their entire team, and they're still in business. I've been told you that it's time to take off the gloves. We tried going after the lieutenants. Now it's time to go after Daniel and Ramon."

Chance sighed. "But what if Daniel is on to us? What if it's a set up? Y'all saw that dude pull up to Justice's house."

"Who?" Justice asked.

"Chance, you're making up excuses. We knew after Daniel had dinner with Justice that he was gonna have her followed. It's a precaution they do when they're interested," Patience explained, getting fed up with the bullshit.

"What if—" Chance tried to say, but was cut off by Seven.

"If it was a fifth, we'd all be drunk. Cut the bullshit, Chance, for real. Either we get these motherfuckers or abandon the whole operation," she exclaimed, frustrated.

By the tone of their voices and looks on their faces, Chance could tell they were adamant. Therefore, she had no choice but to go along with them.

"So what's the plan?" she asked, smirking.

Seven, Patience, and Justice burst into laughter while shaking their hands. Since this was Daniel, the ladies stayed up all night coming up with the perfect plan.

*****

Daniel was at his house in Miami when his worker walked in with the report on Justice.

"What's the story?" an anxious Daniel asked.

"Nothing. I watched for a couple of days just like you said. She works and attends school on the weekends. She lives alone."

"You didn't see a man?" Daniel inquired.

"Nope. She's good."

Daniel had a huge grin on his face. "Thanks."

"Anytime," the worker said before he left.

Justice is perfect, he thought. Suddenly, Patra popped into his head. Strangely, Justice reminded Daniel of her. She had that natural beauty like Patra. *Damn, I miss her.*

Daniel decided to use a different approach with Justice. He wanted her to get to know the real Daniel Munger, besides the money and power.

He was in a deep thought when his butler told him some gentlemen were there to see him. They were the new lieutenants who were taking over Khalidi, Jeremiah, and Cowell's places.

"Gentlemen," Daniel said, entering the office. Just as he was about to say something, Ramon walked in. "Ramon's here, so now we can get started."

Daniel and Ramon went over the job functions and expectations with the new lieutenants. After they were done, they went to Lanai to celebrate by having lunch. Ramon asked Daniel to stay behind so they could talk.

"What are your feelings about them?" Ramon asked Daniel.

Daniel stared at Ramon. *Are you serious? Now you want my opinion?* he thought. He shrugged his shoulders. "Time will tell. What about Zhang's position?"

"I think I have someone in mind."

"Who?" Daniel asked.

"Let me do a little research first," Ramon told him.

Daniel glared at Ramon. *Always playing mind games,* he thought, but responded, "Alright. I just need a vacation," he stated jokingly, switching the subject.

Ramon laughed. "You deserve it. Have you decided where you're going?" he asked, standing up and getting ready to join the others.

"Atlanta. I'm thinking about buying Evander Holyfield's mansion."

"Atlanta?" Ramon repeated with a suspicious tone.

"Yeah, I've always wanted to live down there around my people." Daniel laughed and started to walk off.

Ramon twisted up his face. *Who is Daniel kidding?*

"This sudden move wouldn't have anything to do with that housekeeper Khalidi was fucking, would it?"

Daniel froze in his step and turned around. "You were watching me?" he asked, pissed.

"Let's face it, Danny. You have poor choice when it comes to women."

Daniel slammed the door shut and stormed over to Ramon. "This is about Patra, isn't it? Maybe you're upset she wasn't fucking you."

Ramon laughed. "Don't be silly. I don't stick my dick in crackhead whores."

"You don't stick your dick in women period. Everyone knows the only thing you care about is money. When was the last time you had a good time with a lady? Better yet, when's the last time you had your eye on someone? And don't give me that bullshit about Zhang. We both know she was a charity fuck."

This was the first time someone had silenced Ramon. He glared at Daniel and started to walk away, but paused. "You know the number one cause of death among men? Women," he said and then turned to open the door to leave. "Don't let that be your cause," he added before slamming the door behind him.

Daniel was fuming. It was bad enough Ramon treated him like a worker, but now he was watching him, too.

"You're right, Ramon. Women can kill you, especially when you're fucking with mine," Daniel grumbled to himself before picking up the phone to call one of his workers. "Book me a flight to Atlanta," he ordered and then slammed the phone down.

CHAPTER 20
WWW.RAMON.COM

Ramon Ramirez, who was forty-four years old and half African American and Cuban, looked like a younger version of Michael Nader, who was better known *as Dex Dexter* from the well-known television show *Dynasty*. Ramon wasn't your average criminal; he didn't have a wife or kids. Having graduated from Yale University with a PHD in Psychology, he was considered to have one of the greatest minds. While others wanted him to use it for good, Ramon had different intentions. With the support of the most powerful people in the world, Ramon became *Mr. Untouchable.*

After what took place with the last lieutenants, Ramon decided to handle things a little differently. Instead of giving them unlimited access, which eventually went to their heads, he restricted the new lieutenants' access.

Ramon was having breakfast out on his balcony, when he thought of a replacement for Zhang. Seven would make an excellent lieutenant, but was she up for the job? There was only one way to find out. So, he decided to invite her to dinner to broach the subject.

"Sir Ramirez, your parents are here to see you?" his butler announced.

"My parents?" he repeated, shocked.

"Yes. Your mother and father, the ones who gave birth to you," his mother spitefully proclaimed.

"Mother...father." Ramon laughed while getting up to greet them with a kiss. "Please," he said, extending his hand for them to have a seat. "What brings you here?" he asked, sitting back down.

"Your mother. She's worried about you," his father Adolfo said, rolling his eyes.

Camille twisted up her face. "Don't pay your father any attention. He's just mad because his young girl found another sugar daddy."

Before an argument started, Ramon interceded. "Mother, you're looking younger and younger every day."

Camille blushed. "You see, Adolfo, your son knows how to treat a lady. He must've got that from my side of the family," she grumbled.

Adolfo, who was reading something on his BlackBerry, pretended not to hear Camille's slick comment.

"So what's going on, Ma?" Ramon asked.

"Like your father said, we're worried about you."

"I'm great. There's no need for you to worry."

Adolfo and Camille glanced at each other in a subdued way. Who was Ramon kidding? It was only because he was their son why they hadn't turned his ass in. He represented everything they were against. They saw the people Ramon was doing business with. It's because of him they retired early to protect their pension and good name.

"When are you gonna get married and have some children?" Camille asked, changing the subject.

Ramon sighed. It was too early in the morning for this. He looked at his watch and stood up.

"Mother..." he said, kissing her on the forehead, "...did you have breakfast yet? Have some pancakes. They're delicious," he said before attempting to exit the room.

"Ramon!" Camille called, causing him to stop in his tracks and turn around. She walked up to him. "Life isn't about money. It can be very lonely at the top. You better remember that," she warned, then returned to her seat.

*****

Ironically, Seven was going to quit her job after Zhang died, but Chance told her to keep it in case Ramon was watching. It was a good thing she did, because her boss called her into the office. There was a gentleman in the office. The manager looked at the guy and then at Seven before walking out.

"Mr. Ramirez is requesting your company," the gentleman told her.

"Huh?" Seven said.

"Mr. Ramirez wants you to have dinner with him tonight at his midtown apartment."

"Ramon?"

"Yes," he said.

"He's requesting my presence?" she repeated in a confused tone, thinking it was some type of joke.

"Yes. Where shall the car pick you up?"

Caught off guard, Seven remained quiet for a couple of seconds. "Hmmm, have the car pick me up at 1515 Gibbon Street in Brooklyn," she finally responded.

"Very well. The car will be out front at eight o'clock. Please be on time. Mr. Ramirez doesn't like to be kept waiting," he stated, then walked out.

Once he left, Seven called Chance. "Hey, are you at the house?"

"No, but I will be in a couple of hours. Why?"

She looked around, making sure no one was listening. "Okay," Seven said, glancing at her watch. "I get off in a couple of hours. I'll meet you there."

"Is something wrong?" Chance asked.

"Don't know yet. See you in a couple of hours."

Click!

*****

Ramon was in a meeting with one of the senators when he got the word that Seven had agreed to have dinner with him. He glanced at his watch and smiled.

Chance was running a system check on the warehouse, when Seven came barging through the door.

"What's wrong?" Chance asked.

"Ramon..." Seven said, out of breath.

"What about Ramon?"

"He wants me to have dinner with him tonight," Seven said, trying to calm down.

"He asked you out?" Chance repeated in a stunned tone.

Seven walked into the other room to get something to drink. "Well, not exactly. My manager called me into the office. When I got there, this man was in there with him. My manager walked out, leaving me alone with him. That's when he told me that Ramon was requesting my presence tonight for dinner. He's sending a car to pick me up at eight o'clock."

Chance threw her head back. "You're fucking kidding me! What is going on?"

Shaking her head, Seven replied, "I don't know. It's not like them to mess with the lieutenants' women."

"Seven, Ramon isn't stupid."

"Tell me about it, but I don't think he's fishing," Seven said.

Chance raised an eyebrow. "Oh really? Then why did he invite you to dinner?"

Seven flashed her devious smile and winked at Chance. Both women busted out laughing

"You fucked him?" Chance asked.

"I told you on the vacation we had a threesome. That's why I believe Zhang killed herself."

"Damn. So what are you gonna do?"

"Show him just how deadly a woman can be."

Chance shook her head because she knew Seven was about to turn Ramon out. Chance gave her some new devices and went over a quick plan before she left.

Strangely, Ramon was nervous as he got ready for their dinner. This was the first time he found himself anxious to see someone.

Arriving on time, Seven was led to the family room. She was admiring his paintings, while Ramon stood in the doorway admiring her. She was truly beautiful. She had on a grey turtleneck dress with some royal blue pumps.

"Glad you could make it," he said, entering the room.

"According to your messenger, I didn't have a choice." She flashed a wicked grin.

"Well, I always get what I want," he said, kissing her hand.

"I see, but be careful what you ask for."

"I'll make a note of that. May I pour you something to drink?"

"Do you have 1945 Chateau Mouton-Rothschild Jeroboam?" she asked.

Ramon paused for a moment. "You're a wine lover?

"No, why?"

"Because you just named a bottle of wine that sells for over a hundred thousand dollars."

Seven smiled. "Do you have it?"

Ramon gawked at her and bit his bottom lip. *Yeah, she's the one.*

He called one of his servants to go downstairs to his wine collection and get that bottle. A couple minutes later, the servant returned and handed him the bottle.

"A glass of Chateau coming up," Ramon said, opening the wine. He poured her a glass and handed it to her. "So, Seven, tell me about yourself."

"I think we're past that. In fact, I know you didn't invite me here to ask me about myself," Seven stated in a serious, yet sexy tone.

Listening through the earpiece, Chance whispered, "Seven, what are you doing?"

Ramon nodded and walked up to Seven. "You're right. I didn't invite you here to ask about your past," he slowly answered before kissing her.

Seven surrendered to his kisses, pressing her body against his and wrapping her arms around him. Ramon held her tightly, massaging her ass. Before things got out of hand, she pulled

away. As for Ramon, he was harder than Chinese arithmetic. He'd been dying to touch Seven.

"How's Zhang's family?" she asked, switching the subject as she sat on the arm of the chair.

"They're good. I haven't seen them since the funeral," he lied. "Why didn't you attend?"

"I didn't find out until a couple of weeks later."

"Why?"

Seven stared at Ramon for a second, wondering why he was asking all these questions. "You tell me. I didn't hear anything more from her after we came back from vacation. Did something happen?

"Not that I know of," Ramon said, actually telling the truth.

There was a brief moment of silence before the servant came in and announced that dinner was ready. Instead of eating in the formal dining room, they had a candlelight dinner in Ramon's private room.

"Is everything okay?" he asked.

"Yes, thank you."

"Seven, I wanna get straight to the point. I like you. From the first day I laid eyes on you, I wanted you."

His words caused Seven's pussy to tingle. "Really?" She smiled, then got up and strutted over to him.

"Really," Ramon said, feeling a hard-on growing.

Seven pushed the table back and sat on Ramon's lap as if she were riding him. "Tell me what you like," she moaned, kissing him on his neck.

Ramon closed his eyes. *God this feels good.*

Ripping open his shirt, Seven started licking and kissing on his chest.

"I...like—" He tried to speak, but couldn't.

He moaned in ecstasy as Seven shoved her tongue down his throat. She pushed the table back further, got on her knees, and unbuttoned Ramon's pants. Seven teased his head with the tip of her tongue.

"Ahhh, shit," he loudly moaned while rubbing her head.

She looked up at Ramon who was in another world. Then she licked him again, this time sucking it, too. Ramon couldn't take it anymore. He grabbed Seven by the face.

"Stop or you're gonna make me," he moaned, and then kissed her.

It was time to return the favor. He picked her up and put her on the table. He then pulled her dress over her head, exposing her flawless skin. He started kissing her all over. Their eyes met briefly before Ramon sat in the chair, pulled the table closer to him, and brought Seven to a climax.

Afterwards, Seven hopped on Ramon and rode him like a cowgirl. Just as he was about to cum, Seven jumped off him, finishing the act with a Superhead blowjob. As cum dripped from Seven's mouth, Ramon leaned forward and kissed her.

"You're something else," he moaned, trying to catch his breath.

Seven laughed. "So I've been told." She got up and grabbed her glass of wine to help wash down his cum. "Looks like we might have to order out," she stated with a smile.

"Nonsense," he said, fixing his clothes. "I'll have them clean up and reset the table. We can go into my private area and wait."

Staring at him, she smiled. "Just like that you're gonna have them do this all over again?"

Ramon grabbed Seven by the waist. "That's what they get paid to do," he told her, then planted another kiss on her lips.

*****

From that night on, Ramon practically saw Seven every day. She wasn't like any woman he'd ever met. Not only was she sexy and smart, she was also very outspoken. Let's not forget she was a tyrant in the bedroom. Ramon couldn't get enough of her.

At first, Chance was skeptical about Justice and Seven messing with Daniel and Ramon. However, she changed her mind once she saw how the men were treating them like queens.

If the men could have it their way, the ladies would never work another day in their lives. While everyone knew Daniel was a sucker for love, it was Ramon who surprised everyone. He had become so smitten with Seven.

With Ramon and Daniel closely monitoring Seven and Justice, Chance felt it was best that the ladies fall back from talking to each other. But, tonight, Ramon and Daniel were out of town. Therefore, the ladies decided to hook up and fill each other in on their lives. Chance and Patience were already there when Seven and Justice arrived.

"Wow!" Chance and Patience said at their new looks. Seven and Justice looked like runway models.

"Don't start," Seven said, taking off her shoes.

"You guys look like a million bucks," Patience complimented.

"Please," Justice grumbled, rolling her eyes.

She couldn't stand the sight of Daniel. Although loving and caring, all Justice saw him as was a women beater. She couldn't wait for the day to wipe the smirk off his face.

"What's wrong, Justice?" Chance asked, noticing her facial expression.

"Mi don't know how much longer mi can take this, Chance," she blurted out in disgust.

"What? Is he beating on you?" Patience asked.

Justice took a seat on the couch. "Hell naw. Mi would kill him dead. He's just..." her voice trailed over

"He's not Khalidi," Seven teased.

"No, he's not, but it's not that. I just can't stand him. He's arrogant."

"Tell me about it. I have to work for him," Patience teased. "But you knew that already."

"Yes, mi did. Mi just want this to be over with. I'm starting to feel like a slut," she expressed with a shiver, causing the women to laugh.

"What about you, Seven?"

"It's not as bad as Justice, but I'm not into him like that."

"Does he suspect anything?" Chance asked.

"No," Seven said.

"Are you sure?"

"What is that supposed to mean, Chance? Of course, I'm sure," Seven snapped.

"Why are you so defensive? I'm only asking because Ramon is different. He doesn't show any emotion," Chance explained.

"I'm not getting defensive, but how long have we been watching these guys?"

"Okay, can we get back to the topic?" Patience interjected before an argument started.

Seven glared at Chance, then got up and went to check the system. "Anything new on the site?" she asked.

"Of course not. You're too busy sucking Ramon's dick," Chance blurted out sarcastically.

Seven spun around. "You need some dick in your mouth. I'm getting tired of your fucking slick comments, for real."

"Enough already! Damn!" Patience shouted. "Chance, what's your problem?"

"I just asked Seven a fucking question, and she's getting defensive."

Seven ignored them and continued to the room. She didn't have time for Chance's shit.

Wanting to get the hell out of there, Seven scanned the site. "Okay, I gotta go. I'll be in touch." Then she left before she and Chance came to blows.

Patience and Justice looked at Chance, who rolled her eyes and went into the other room. *This isn't good*, they thought.

On the other hand, Ramon received a call from one of his crooked detectives who had some information on the missing lieutenants. So, Ramon asked Daniel and Seth to join him. They were meeting at Ramon's Connecticut home.

"Mr. Ramirez," Detective Price said, entering the office.

"Price," Ramon greeted, shaking his hand. "What can I do for you?"

"Sir, I..."

Just as he was about to share his discovery, Daniel and Seth joined them.

"Mr. Munger," Price said, greeting only Daniel since he didn't know Seth. The detective just smiled and shook his hand. "Hello."

"Detective," Daniel replied, smiling also.

When Seven arrived, the butler informed her that Ramon was in his office. As she walked to the office, she heard voices coming from inside.

The men took a seat on the couch.

"You said you have some information about the other lieutenants?" Ramon asked.

"Yes...yes. They are dead," he said, pulling out some photos.

"We kinda figured that already," Daniel said with a hint of sarcasm.

"We found Khalidi's body in an abandoned house outside of Vegas. Jeremiah's body was in a warehouse in California, and Cowell was in Chicago along with some men," Price said, showing them the pictures of the bodies. "We believe the same person is behind the other incidents." Price stared at the men. "Whoever's behind this covered their tracks very well. However, I recovered some video from traffic cameras around those areas.

"Anything stick out?" Ramon asked.

"A few things, but I'll let you see it for yourself." Price replied, handing Ramon a flash drive.

Ramon nodded. "Thank you, Price. Someone will be in touch with you," he said, which meant money.

"Thank you. Please let me know if there's anything else I can do to help," he said before exiting.

Seven, who was eavesdropping, felt a chill through her body as her mouth dropped. *Oh shit, they found the bodies. Game over*....

Sneak Preview of

SCATTERED LIES 4
"ROMAN'S REVENGE"

"The courtroom was packed. The infamous Anthony Omari Flowers, Jr. was on trial for first-degree rape, sexual assault, and kidnapping. His father was rap legend Tony Flowers, who was killed by his ex-girlfriend Christina Carrington in a murder-suicide. His siblings, London, Justin, and Justine, joined Mr. Flowers in court. Also in the courtroom were his grandfather Felix Marciano and his mother," the newscaster reported.

"It's hard to believe that someone with great looks and with more money than some countries could do this," another reporter stated.

"Well, they say money doesn't fix everything."

"So true," the reporter agreed. "Now we take you inside the courtroom where the key witness will be taking the stand momentarily."

"All rise!" the bailiff announced.

"You may be seated," the judge instructed as he took his seat and adjusted his robe.

The bailiff swore in Clarice Brown. "Clarice Brown, raise your right hand. Do you promise to tell the truth, the whole truth, and nothing but the truth so help you God?"

"I do," she replied.

"You may be seated," the bailiff told her.

"Ms. Brown, how long have you known the defendant, Mr. Flowers?" the prosecutor questioned.

"For about six years," Clarice responded.

"Intimately?" he asked.

"About five years."

"Can you tell us what happened on…" The prosecutor paused to walk back over to the table and pick up a piece of paper. "…October 21st?"

Clarice looked over at the jury. "I bumped into Anthony at a party at Trump Towers."

"And?"

"We had a couple of drinks, and he invited me back to his place. I really liked Anthony, so I said okay."

"What happened when you got there?"

Clarice looked over at the jury again. "He started acting strange. He snorted some coke and ordered me to take off my clothes so he could snort some off my stomach."

'Did you do it?"

"Yes. I mean, I thought it was cool…" she said, her voice trailing off.

"What happened next?" he inquired.

"He snorted a couple of lines off my stomach. Then he put some on his penis and asked to have sex with me."

"Coke?" the prosecutor asked.

"Yes, and again, I said okay."

"Then what happened?"

"I started to feel numb down there and asked him to stop."

"Did he?"

"No. He flew into a rage and started choking me."

"Out of the blue, he just started choking you?"

Clarice began to cry. "Yes. I tried to remove his hands, but he overpowered me. He grabbed me by my neck and tossed me across the room."

Gasps echoed throughout the room. Some of the jury members looked over at Tony.

"Then what happened?" the prosecutor asked.

"He raped me," she said, breaking down on the stand.

"No further questions. Your witness," he told the defense attorney.

Bill Fish, Anthony's high-profile attorney, stood up, buttoned his suit jacket, and walked over to the witness. "Ms. Brown, you stated that out of the blue, my client started choking you and then raped you?"

"Yes."

"So why did it take you three weeks to report the rape?"

"I was confused and scared. Anthony is very powerful."

"Or is it because my client refused to give you any money?" Bill Fish asked spitefully.

"That's not true! He raped me!" she shouted.

"Your Honor, I would like to enter Exhibit L. This tape will show Ms. Brown plotting to extort my client. At first, she told him that she was pregnant. When that didn't work, she accused him of giving her an STD, and now rape."

As the tape started to play, mumbles filled the room. This time, everyone glared at Clarice. Women twisted their faces up, while men shook their heads.

"He did rape me!" Clarice cried. "Anthony is a monster!"

"Sure, he did. I have no further questions," Bill said.

Anthony sat with a smug look on his face, staring at Clarice as she stepped down from the stand.

*****

It was the day when twelve men and women would decide Anthony Omari Flowers' fate. He entered the courtroom accompanied by his family, friends, and legal team. Most people would've been nervous, but not Anthony. At his mother's request, Felix had everything covered. Five members on the jury had been paid off. Even the prosecutor had been paid off to present a weak case. So, either way, Anthony would walk away scot-free

"All rise!" the bailiff said.

"Has the jury reached a verdict?" the judge asked.

"Yes, Your Honor," the foreman replied.

"Will the defendant stand and face the jury."

The courtroom was so silent you could hear a pin drop. Like the O.J. Simpson trial, this case had divided a country. Some believed greedy women were setting up Anthony, while others believed he was a serial rapist, with money, power, and political connections, who would get off.

Anthony looked back at his family. His great grandmother nodded, letting him know everything was going to be fine.

"How do you find the defendant?" the judge asked.

The foreman stared into the defendant's eyes and then at the paper. She knew the world was watching and waiting. As she looked around at the victims in the courtroom, her eyes started to tear up.

"How do you find the defendant?" the judge repeated.

Before she gave the verdict, she said a silent prayer. *God, please forgive us.* Then she replied, "We, the jury, find the defendant not guilty."

The courtroom filled with mixed emotions. Some were crying, while others cheered.

"Order! Order!" the judge yelled, banging his gavel. "Mr. Flowers, the jury has found you not guilty. You are free to go."

Anthony hugged his attorney and then reached over to hug his grandmother.

"I told you only in America can you buy this kind of justice," she whispered in Anthony's ear.

Mobbed by the media, with his family and legal team proudly standing behind him, Anthony spoke with reporters.

"Anthony, how do you feel about the verdict?" one female reporter asked.

"I'm happy, of course. I'm happy to be able to put this behind me."

Bill interceded. "There will be a full press conference tomorrow. Thank you."

Family and friends went back to Anthony's penthouse to celebrate. Felix pulled Anthony aside.

"Got a second?"

"Sure, Grandpa," he said, walking with him to the other room.

"I think you should lay low for awhile. Let things cool down," Felix suggested.

Anthony nodded before smiling.

"I'm serious, Anthony. Next time, you might not be so lucky," he angrily whispered, while staring directly into his face.

"As long as I got money, I will always be lucky," Anthony replied arrogantly.

Felix laughed. "Your father would've said the same thing."

"Well, my father was a wise man."

Felix glared at Anthony. The only reason he didn't put a bullet in his grandson's head was because it would've broken his mother's heart. Anthony was everything Felix despised in a man.

"A.J.," he said, using his nickname, "you're my grandson, so I will always be there for you. But, if you rape any more women, I will not help you."

Anthony, being the self-righteous bastard he was, stepped up to Felix. "Help? My father left me a shitload of money. What makes you think I need your help?"

Felix released a devilish chuckle. "You are your father's child…a punk who raped women."

"My father never had to rape women, just like I don't. They just need help saying yes."

It infuriated Felix to hear Anthony praise his father. Maybe if he knew the truth, he might think differently.

"Your father always felt he had to have the best. That's why he's not here today, because the best cost him his life. Now you listen to me, you punk motherfucker. It's only because my blood runs through you that I tolerate your ass. Because if I had it my way, your sorry ass would be spending the rest of your life in prison where you belong with the rest of the niggers."

Anthony smiled. "Now I know how you've really felt about me all of these years. It killed you that my mother married a black man. I knew you were a racist bitch. You never liked my father because he was black."

"No, I never liked your father because of what he did to my daughter," Felix quickly interrupted.

"Bullshit! My father treated my mother like a queen. You didn't like him because he was black. But, that didn't stop you from taking over his estate."

"Is that what you think?" Felix started to tell him the truth, but changed his mind.

"Well, my mother did love my father, and it's because of her that I don't take you out of your misery," Anthony shot back.

"Watch it, boy. Before I forget—"

Anthony jumped in his grandfather's face. "I already did. Now get the fuck out of my house before we do something we both regret."

Felix smirked. Anthony didn't know who he was dealing with.

"There's my favorite great grandson," Felix's mother cheered, entering the room.

"Hi, Grandma," Anthony said, kissing her on the cheek.

"Be a dear and get your grandma something to drink."

"Sure," he told her, glaring at Felix before exiting.

Once Anthony was out of sight, Felix's mother turned towards him. "What was that all about?"

"That young punk has the nerve to challenge me, when it's because of his fucking father my daughter is dead."

"Felix, he's your grandson."

"Don't remind me."

Still steaming, Anthony went into the other room to cool off and take a hit.

"Anthony?" London said, knocking on the door before opening it.

With white powder on his nose, he replied, "Yeah."

"You never did stop," London snapped.

"What is it, London?" Anthony said, tired of everyone judging him. "What the fuck you want now?"

"You're a son of a bitch, you know that?" London yelled.

By that time, his brother and sister had joined them.

"What the fuck?" Justin said.

"Alright, so I'm caught. Considering the amount of stress I've been under I deserve a little recreational play."

Everyone looked at him in disgust, while thinking the same thing. *What's the point? Anthony was going to be the cause of his own downfall.*

"Fuck you," Anthony screamed under the stares of the judgmental eyes. "Fuck all of you! This is my father's empire, and he left it to me! I am the king of this empire!"

Standing afar and listening, Felix thought, *and sometimes kings need to be overthrown.*

COMING BLACK FRIDAY 2012!!!

5 STAR PUBLICATIONS
WWW.5STARPUBLICATIONS.NET
KAI
PUBLICATIONS PRESENTS...
A Novel by
AMANDA LEE
KAI
GHOSTS OF THE EX
ADONIS
WELCOME TO THE JUNGLE
WHERE LOVE AND LOYALTY
DONT EXIST
Xtasy
AMANDA LEE
PUBLICATIONS PRESENTS
DEATH BY THREE
J. MARIE
PUBLICATIONS PRESENTS
WWW.COM
MADISON
AMANDA LEE
PUBLICATIONS PRESENTS
Internal Affairs
TOYER

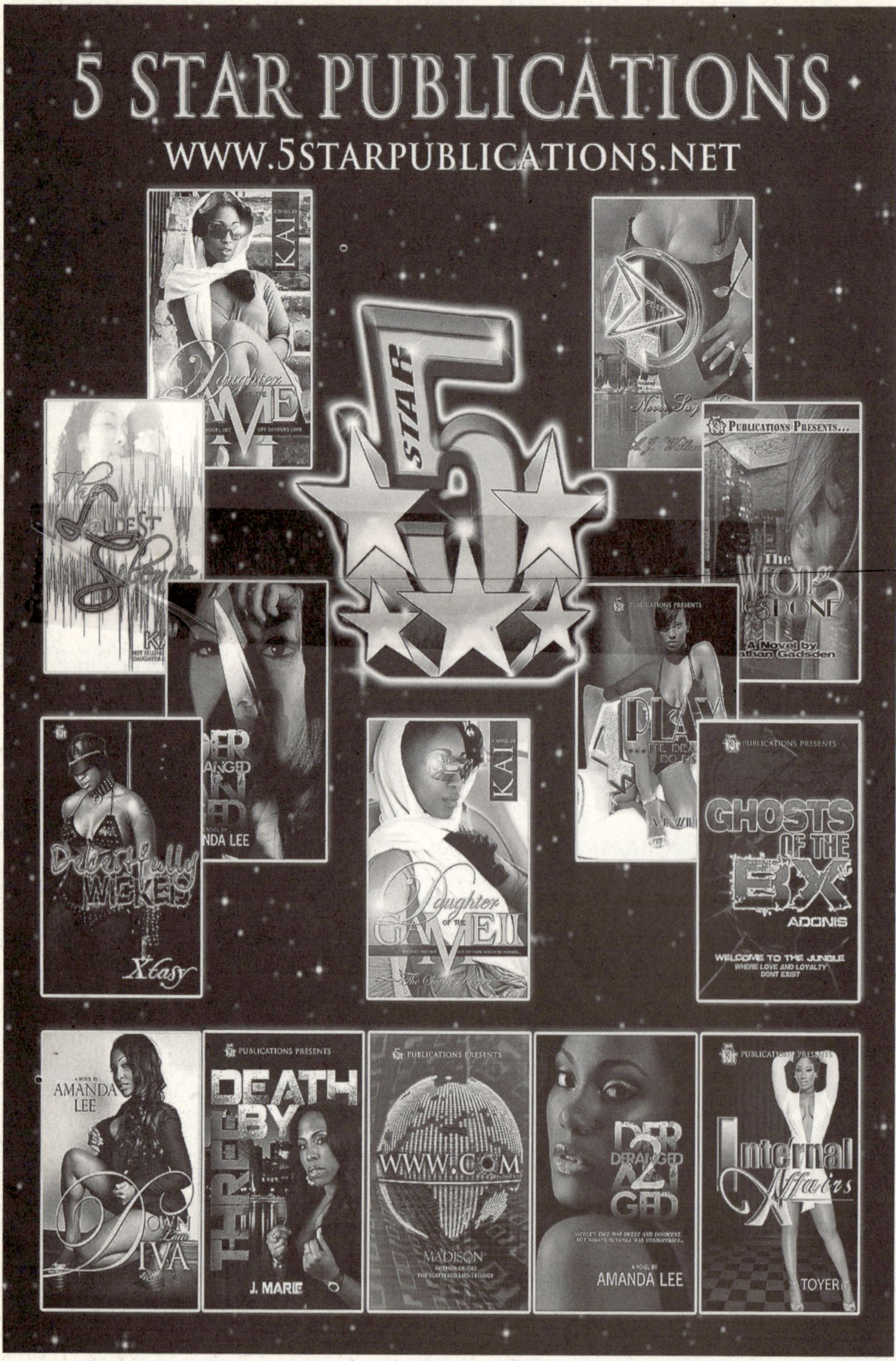

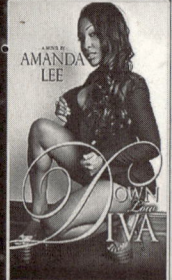

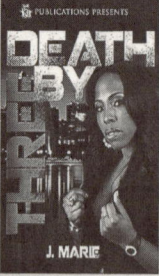

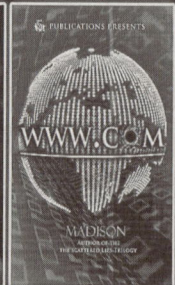

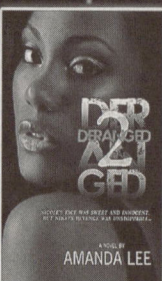

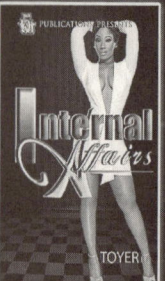

SCATTERED LIES TRILOGY

THE TRUTH CAN GET YOU KILLED...

Madison

Available Now in Stores and on Kindle & Nook

SCATTERED LIES
SCATTERED LIES 2
SCATTERED LIES 3 — FINALLY THE TRUTH
by Madison

 **PUBLICATIONS PRESENTS**

In Deranged, Nikki achieved her goal of capturing Jeremy for Nicole, but fell short as Cowboy spoiled their plans. One year later, Nikki refuses to fail and no longer needs Nicole or her assistance. In Deranged 2, Nicole's face was sweet but Nikki's revenge was unstoppable as she moved heaven & earth to be with her man and live the dream life that they planned together. Once free, AND she sees he's cheating and living their dream life with someone else, Jeremy and his family have nowhere to hide. The question is: Will she finally get what she wants or will she die trying?